MYSTERIES OF

C�OVE

The City of Cove

MYSTERIES OF

C⚙VE

FIRES OF INVENTION

To Enzo —

J. SCOTT SAVAGE

"Change the World!"

SHADOW
MOUNTAIN

Warriors

Words and Music by Alexander Grant, Daniel Reynolds, Daniel Sermon, Benjamin McKee, Daniel Platzman and Joshua Mosser

Copyright (c) 2014 SONGS OF UNIVERSAL, INC., ALEXANDER GRANT, IMAGINE DRAGONS PUBLISHING, SONGS FOR KIDINAKORNER and JOSHUA MOSSER

All Rights for ALEXANDER GRANT Controlled and Administered by SONGS OF UNIVERSAL, INC.

All Rights for IMAGINE DRAGONS PUBLISHING and SONGS FOR KIDINAKORNER Controlled and Administered by SONGS OF UNIVERSAL, INC.

All Rights Reserved Used by Permission

Reprinted by Permission of Hal Leonard Corporation

Library of Congress Cataloging-in-Publication Data

Savage, J. Scott (Jeffrey Scott), 1963– author.

Fires of invention / J. Scott Savage.

pages cm. — (Mysteries of Cove ; book 1)

Summary: Even though technology and inventions have been outlawed in the mountain city of Cove, in order to save the city Trenton and Kallista must follow a set of mysterious blueprints to build a creature to protect them from the dragons outside their door.

ISBN 978-1-62972-092-0 (hardbound : alk. paper)

[1. Dragons—Fiction. 2. Robots—Fiction. 3. Technology—Fiction.] I. Title. II. Series: Savage, J. Scott (Jeffrey Scott), 1963–. Mysteries of Cove ; bk. 1.

PZ7.S25897Fi 2015

[Fic]—dc23   2015010149

Printed in the United States of America

Edwards Brothers Malloy, Ann Arbor, MI

10   9   8   7   6   5   4   3   2   1

To Bill Sheehy,
the high school English teacher who
sparked the creativity inside me.

And to LuAnn Staheli,
who encouraged thousands to
love reading and writing.

And to all the other teachers
sparking creativity throughout the world.

In youth you'd lay
Awake at night and scheme
Of all the things that you would change
But it was just a dream

The time will come
When you'll have to rise
Above the best and prove yourself
Your spirit never dies!

—IMAGINE DRAGONS, "Warriors"

1

This was going to be the best thing Trenton had ever built—assuming he could finish assembling it without getting crushed. The "getting crushed" part was a real possibility. Every sixty seconds exactly, the horizontally spinning gear he clung to carried him beneath a cast-iron beam that would smash his head if he didn't press himself flat against the spinning surface. If the impact didn't kill him, the twenty-five-foot fall to the ground would.

Gripping his wrench in his right hand and clinging to the gear with his left, he counted silently. At fifty-seven, he tightened the bolt with one last twist.

Fifty-eight . . . He pulled the wrench free of the bolt.

Fifty-nine . . . He looked up to see the beam coming toward him.

And . . . sixty. He pressed his cheek against the grease-coated metal and passed so closely under the beam that he felt it brush his curly brown hair.

As soon as he was clear of the beam, he popped up and double-checked each bolt. A rumble came from the small metal building nearby—the power-conversion machinery turning the gear. The wind blowing against his face carried the scent of oil, metal, and burning coal—a smell he could never get enough of.

"Trenton," one of the kids below yelled up at him. "If you get killed, can I have your tool set?"

"What would you want with my tools?" Trenton shouted back. "As clumsy as you are, you'd end up cutting off one of your fingers and getting blood all over my kit."

General laughter sounded from below, and Trenton grinned. With the bolts checked, he swung through one of the holes in the giant gear and wrapped his legs around the second of two chains hanging below it.

"You look like a monkey," a redheaded girl called.

Although none of the kids had actually seen a real monkey, they'd read about them in their history of Earth class that year. Swinging from the chain, Trenton hooted and pantomimed eating a banana. The girl laughed, and he felt a pleasant heat rush to his face. Simoni was the main reason he'd gone to all this trouble.

Two weeks before, he'd overheard her telling a friend that there was nothing fun to do. The idea of using the huge gear attached to the conversion station to power his ride had popped into his head as if it was meant to be. Since then, he'd scavenged spare parts and sketched out the plans for what he hoped would show Simoni that he was more than someone who happened to be good at fixing bicycles and greasing playground equipment and roller-skate bearings. He shimmied up the chain to where he'd rigged a complicated series of pulleys, cables, and a metal lever that engaged the contraption.

Holding a screwdriver between his teeth, he hooked a spring to one end of the lever. He took the screwdriver from his mouth and used it as a pry bar to stretch the spring until his arm began to shake. Then he looped the spring around a metal hoop that had once been part of a water pump, and the whole thing snapped into place.

"Look," said a voice that was all too familiar—Angus. "The

grease monkey made a toy so he won't have to play in the coal pits anymore."

Trenton hadn't invited him to the lot outside the power-conversion station, but the boy with the perfect hair and big biceps followed Simoni everywhere like a puppy. Making coal jokes was one of Angus's favorite taunts, partly because Trenton's last name was Coleman, and partly because Trenton's father worked in the mines.

Trenton tied a rope around the end of the lever, yanked it tight, and slid down to a leather seat hanging between the two chains. From there it was a drop of only six or seven feet to the ground. Still, he had to make the jump carefully because the seat spun at the same rate as the gear it was connected to.

He hit the ground, rolled on one shoulder, and leaped to his feet. He might not have been as big or as strong as most of the other boys his age, but he was nimble. Folding his arms across his chest, he looked up at his finished work with pride. With one chain attached to the inside of the gear and the other to the outside, the seat swung gracefully overhead, powered by the rumbling equipment of the station. The rope hung in easy reach, trailing around and around like the tail of a circling beast.

"What's it supposed to be?" asked a second grader who'd tagged along with his older brother.

Trenton, who was about to graduate from eighth grade and start vocational training, patted the kid on the head. "I'm glad you asked."

He yanked on the rope as the swing passed by, and the pulley on the outside moved toward the center—the two chains drawing together until the seat was only a couple of feet above the ground. "This is going to be the most fun any kid has ever had." He looked at the redheaded girl out of the corner of his eye. "I call it the Simoni Swing."

"You named it after *me?*" Simoni asked, watching wide-eyed as the swing circled around and around.

This was exactly how Trenton had planned it—except for the part about Angus being there. He held out a hand. "Do you want to be the first to try it?"

She looked up at the pulleys and springs. "Is it safe?"

"Safer than riding the trolley to City Center." Trenton had done the calculations over and over, making sure everything would work perfectly. Of course, it might have been better to try the swing for the first time with no one around. But he'd been too excited to show off his work for that.

"You're not really going to get on that *invention*, are you?" Angus asked Simoni.

Trenton couldn't believe what he heard. He spun around to face the bigger boy. "*What* did you call my swing?"

"Exactly what it is." Angus sneered. "An *invention*. And you're an . . . an *inventor*."

Several of the smaller children gasped at the curse word, and part of the group moved away, as if even standing close might associate them with something which could land them in serious trouble.

Trenton balled his fists. "Take it back, or I'll—"

"You'll what?" Angus stepped forward and stared down at Trenton. "You going to hit me? You want to be guilty of violence and *inventing*, all in one day?"

Forcing his hands to unclench, Trenton gripped his tool belt. Violence of any kind was nearly as big a crime as creating anything new, but he couldn't stand there and let someone call him something so dirty—so humiliating.

Simoni stepped between them. "It's not an in—" She licked

her pink lips as though saying the word would dirty them. "A *you-know-what*, is it? Because I don't want anything to do with something like that. Or anyone who would make one."

Trenton felt his face go red again, this time in a bad way. His great plan of impressing Simoni was quickly falling apart. He had to pull things together before people got the wrong idea.

He looked around the group. "How many of you have been to the playground by the air-circulation pumps?"

Everyone except Angus raised their hands.

The central exhaust pipe, which sucked used air out of the enclosed city and pulled filtered air in, ran up the center of each level. No one was allowed near it because the suction was strong enough to knock you off your feet. Each section of the city also had its own park and smaller circulation pumps to move the air around.

All of the kids used to go to that playground after school until they got too old for it. Everyone except Angus. His dad was the marshal, the chancellor's head of security, which gave him access to the executive playground used only by family members of city employees.

"Right," Trenton said, ignoring Angus's snub. "And how many of you have been on the swings?" Of course, the same kids raised their hands.

Simoni pointed to the gear. "But those swings aren't hooked up to, you know . . ."

"Which makes this an invention," Angus said. "When my dad hears about it, he'll put you into retraining."

Trenton swallowed. He didn't know exactly what retraining was, except that it involved both physical and mental punishment. He'd seen a few people come back from it, and they all looked like they'd been through a war.

This was part of the reason he hadn't wanted Angus around.

Technically, the swing could be viewed as building something not on Cove's list of approved devices—*inventing*—but only if you looked at it the wrong way.

He pointed to the swing. "Swings are already on the approved list. They've been around since long before we were born." The kids nodded. He pointed to the spinning gear. "The power station equipment is the same thing they've used since level two was dug out of the mountain."

Angus opened his mouth, but Trenton hurried on before he could be interrupted. "All I did was take one approved device and hook it to *another* approved device using approved screws, bolts, springs, and levers. There is absolutely nothing new here. Which means this is not an *invention*. If anyone is an *inventor* here, it's Angus, for *inventing* stories."

It was a good thing his mother wasn't there. She'd stick soap in his mouth for an hour for using that kind of language.

Simoni looked from Trenton to Angus and then at the swing. What she said next would determine whether Trenton would be taken in for retraining. Angus would never tell his father about something Simoni approved.

But if she decided Trenton's swing was something new . . .

She took the end of Trenton's shirt and wiped grease from his face. "I don't think it's an . . . *invention*." Trenton released a pent-up breath. "But maybe you should try it first. To make sure it's safe."

Trenton jumped into action. "Absolutely. I'll show you. It's so safe a baby could use it." He grinned over his shoulder at Angus, who scowled. "Which makes it perfect for you."

He slid the wrench back into his belt and trotted to the circling swing. Because the chains currently hung near the inside of the gear, they weren't moving very fast. The next time the seat came around, he stepped in front of it and sat down.

A girl shrugged. "Not very exciting."

"Not yet." Trenton said, circling around. "But watch this." He grabbed the rope hanging above his head. "Everybody stand back."

Once the rest of the kids were clear of the radius of the gear, he pulled the rope, unlocking the spring. Attached to the pulleys, the chains and seat began to slide outward. The closer to the edge it moved, the faster the swing went. By the time he reached the outside of the gear, the chains were nearly horizontal. High over his friend's heads, Trenton flew so fast that the force pushed him down into the seat.

He grasped the chains with both hands, amazed at how well his swing worked. From this height, he could see a trolley chugging along its metal tracks with little puffs of steam coming from its polished smokestack. Near the city offices, the clock struck four, and the mechanical figures of a baker, a miner, a teacher, and—Trenton's favorite—a mechanic, emerged from a set of brass doors set into the clock face. If he craned his neck, he could just make out the apartment building where he lived. His hair blew back from his forehead, and he grinned down at the faces staring up at him as he circled high above them.

"Look at him go!" one kid shouted.

"I want a turn," another one yelled.

Simoni waved at Trenton, her eyes alight. "It's wonderful."

Trenton waved back. Things were working out better than his wildest expectations. Everyone pushed forward excitedly. Even annoying Angus stared up, eyes wide.

"My turn, my turn!" all the kids shouted.

"Stay back," Trenton yelled as he passed over them. "You don't want to get hit."

"Can I try it next?" Simoni called, shaking back her long

red hair. Trenton could imagine it streaming out behind her on his swing.

"Simoni gets the first ride," he called. If Angus told his father now, every kid in the school would hate him. He pulled the rope again, and the springs began winding up.

He was halfway back to the inside of the gear when a loud clang sounded from inside the power station. Then a crunch. The gear slowed, and the kids moved away—delight turning to fear.

As the swing slowed to a stop, warning bells clanged throughout the city. What had he done? The swing couldn't have caused this, could it?

One by one, the lights in that section of the city went out.

2

Trenton paced the small room, staring at the locked door. The electric bulbs in little brass cages on the wall were still dark, and the flickering gas lamp in the corner made his shadow waver like a frightened ghost. Even inside the security building he could feel the vibration of the emergency air exchangers, which had kicked on to keep the atmosphere breathable ever since the power went out.

How could this have happened? He'd gone over and over the numbers in his head, but the calculations made no sense. He sat behind the metal table in the center of the room and sketched the figures with his finger again. The weight of the swing combined with his own. The speed and balance of the gear multiplied by the momentum and vibration. It didn't add up. Even if he weighed ten times as much as he did, the pull of his swing should not have affected the gear enough to throw it out of alignment. And if it had, it was only a conversion station. There was no way his swing could have shut down the lights and fans.

Yet clearly it had.

Despite the stuffiness of the small room, he shivered. Right now people all over this side of the city were asking each other where the power went. Was there another accident? Who was responsible? And the answer to the last question was Trenton

Coleman. Word of what he'd done would spread quicker than a gas fire. Soon he'd be as notorious as Leo Babbage, who'd exploded himself and part of an apartment building while illegally trying to improve a water heater.

Neighbors would gossip with neighbors. The story would spread until even his own mother—

He clenched his hands in his hair. His *mother*. This would kill her. How many times had she warned him that tinkering would get him into trouble? How many times had she made him sit at the table, writing line after line: *We are all gears and cogs in a magnificent machine. When we do our part as it has been prescribed, the machine runs smoothly. When we do things differently, society suffers.*

They wouldn't make her come here, would they? Injured in a mine accident years before, her crippled legs weren't strong enough to walk more than a few feet at a time, and she had no one to push her wheeled chair. Her heart couldn't stand the stress of hearing about this. His father worked in the mine, so *he* wouldn't hear what had happened until tonight. But Trenton could imagine his mother darning clothes on the couch, a knock sounding, and old Mrs. Patsy down the hall asking, "Did you hear what your boy has done now?"

The lock rattled, and Trenton sprang to his feet. When the door swung open, he was relieved to see it was only Angus's father, Marshal Darrow. Maybe he could still talk his way out of this, and his parents would never know. But behind Marshal Darrow came Chancellor Lusk himself, dressed in a long, velvet jacket, wearing a monocle, and carrying a silver walking stick.

His heart plummeted. This was serious.

As the two grim-faced men entered the room, Trenton noticed a third figure behind them. He recognized the stooped shoulders and slightly bent right arm before the man stepped into the light, which revealed his coal-stained face.

His father. *No.* Trenton's throat tightened, and he started forward, but his father shook his head ever so slightly.

"Sit," Marshal Darrow said. He waited for the chancellor to take a seat before plopping his heavy frame onto the only other chair in the room, leaving Trenton's father to stand inside the doorway.

Marshal Darrow slapped a folder on the metal table, making it ring. He opened the folder and thumbed through the pages inside. "You have been formally charged with creation of an unapproved device, modification of approved equipment—"

"I didn't *create* a device," Trenton said, sweat beading on his forehead. "It was a standard swing. I just connected it to the gear so my friends could have a ride. I swear, I didn't make anything that hasn't been approved for use."

"Vandalism of city-owned property, loss of power," the marshal continued, ignoring Trenton's explanation.

He tried again. "I know how it looks. I don't understand what made the power plant shut down. But I promise, it wasn't because of anything *I* did." He ran his fingers through his hair. "I've done the calculations a dozen times, and they don't add up. I'd never have connected the swing if . . ." He looked from the security marshal to the chancellor. "Give me a piece of chalk and a slate, and I'll show you."

"He's a good boy," Mr. Coleman said, speaking for the first time. "Perhaps a little impetuous, but he means no harm." His pale blue eyes and the white skin where his mask had been were the only parts of his face not covered in coal dust. They must have brought Trenton's father straight here from the mine.

"We let you listen in as a favor, Ray," Marshal Darrow said to Trenton's father. "I haven't gotten to the theft charges." The marshal stared at Trenton. "Would you like to explain where you got the parts to make your—pardon my language—*invention?*"

Trenton saw his father's head drop and realized how much his actions had humiliated his family. This whole time, he'd imagined what people would say about *him*. But they'd be saying the same things about his parents—and questioning what kind of people could raise an inventor for a son. "I was only trying to let the kids have a little fun."

Chancellor Lusk crossed his legs and adjusted his pants with a quick pinch and a tug. He steepled his fingers in front of his chest, and, without looking at Trenton, asked, "You've taken city history in school this year?"

Trenton nodded. Of course he had. The history of Cove was a required subject every year from first grade on.

"Would you be so kind as to recount why our city was founded?" the chancellor asked, staring at a spot somewhere up and to the left. Trenton had to resist the urge to turn to see what the man was looking at.

Grudgingly he repeated the facts he'd spent far too many boring hours in school memorizing. "In Outside Year 1939, the city of Cove was built as a safe haven for honest citizens fleeing the disease, destruction, and mayhem of a world spoiled by rampant technological advancements," Trenton said, giving the textbook answer he and everyone in his class had memorized.

"*Technological advancements*," the chancellor repeated, savoring the words as though it was the first time he'd heard them. "Have you ever wondered why scientists, architects, and engineers continued to make bigger buildings, faster engines, and machines that spewed out toxins so thick the very air became unbreathable, when it was clear they were killing each other?"

Trenton looked down at the table, where a few smudges

remained from the calculations he'd made with his finger. "No, sir."

"I believe it was because they wanted to have a *little fun.*" He adjusted his monocle and looked at Trenton for the first time. "They convinced themselves that getting from one place to another a few minutes quicker, making a few more dollars, having more thrills, more laughs—more *fun*—was worth destroying their very world. Does that sound like a fair tradeoff to you?"

Trenton shook his head, wondering what he could have been thinking. He'd tried to impress Simoni, and now, on top of everything else, she wouldn't want anything to do with him.

"Those who destroyed our world put the good of the one above of the good of the many," the chancellor said. "They lined their own pockets at the expense of millions of lives."

Trenton felt sick to his stomach. The back of his shirt was damp with cold sweat. What kind of people would behave that way? They must have been monsters.

The chancellor slid his chair forward and recrossed his legs. "What you did today was the same thing; you endangered our entire city. You took equipment that didn't belong to you. Then you not only damaged one of the power distribution plants that makes it so everyone in Cove can eat and breathe—can *live*—you did it by creating a device that was untested, unapproved, and unsafe. Did you consider the fact that your device could have killed one of your classmates?"

"I'm s-s-sorry," Trenton moaned. Tears slid down his face. He *was* an inventor. He was every bit as bad as the people who had ruined the outside world so completely that the only safe place was the mountain into which Cove had been dug.

The chancellor looked at Marshal Darrow and nodded. The head of security slammed the folder closed. "Your actions are some of the most serious crimes I've ever come across. Frankly, under the original City Charter, they would have been grounds for expulsion."

Trenton's head snapped up. His mouth went dry. No one was forced to leave the city anymore. Being sent outside was a death sentence.

"No," his father cried, stepping forward.

Chancellor Lusk polished the head of his walking stick—the image of a fierce-looking beast with a long snout and sharp teeth—and grinned. "Obviously, exile is not a possibility now that the city is sealed."

Trenton's father visibly relaxed.

Marshal Darrow held out an arm. "Despite the fact that you endangered my own son, who tried to stop you, I explained to the city council that you are young. That this was probably all a foolish stunt."

"It was." Trenton nodded vigorously. "I didn't think it through."

"True." The marshal nodded. "Unfortunately, several members of the council brought up your past history of modifying devices. They reminded us that this isn't the first time charges have been brought against you. You have a record of being—I'm afraid there's no other way of saying it—*creative*."

His words hung in the air. Trenton couldn't deny that in the past he'd tweaked things a bit to make what he'd viewed as improvements. Now he could see that those little mistakes had brought him to the point of committing a crime against the city. What price would he have to pay for it?

Marshal Darrow waited a moment before saying, "Fortunately for your sake, the chancellor spoke up for you. He thinks there still might be a chance, however small, that, with the proper motivation and education, you could become a useful member of society."

Trenton felt a spark of hope.

"Thank you," his father whispered, clasping his chapped hands. "Thank you, Chancellor Lusk."

The chancellor's narrow lips curled as he glanced toward his head of security.

"Therefore," Marshal Darrow continued, "you have been sentenced to six months of retraining."

Trenton's throat seized like a fuel line that had been pinched closed. His father gasped aloud. *Six months* of imprisonment, hard labor, and forced memorization? He'd never heard of a child receiving such a harsh punishment.

"But his schooling . . ." Mr. Coleman said. "He'll have to retake the entire year."

Chancellor Lusk turned sharply. "He's lucky to have any schooling to return to at all."

A sharp rapping came from the hallway and the door flew open. A man in a work helmet and goggles stood in the doorway, breathing heavily.

"What are you doing here?" the chancellor snapped. "I told you I wasn't to be interrupted."

"I'm sorry, Mr. Chancellor," the man chuffed, trying to catch his breath. "I wanted to tell you that . . ." He put his hands on his knees and panted as though he'd been running. "We discovered what caused plant eleven to shut down."

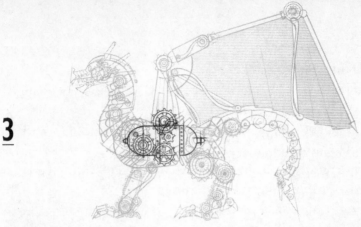

3

What are you talking about?" the marshal demanded, pushing himself up from his chair. "We know what caused the outage."

"No, sir." The man shoved his goggles up onto his head, shooting an anxious look between Marshall Darrow and the chancellor. "That is, we think we may have discovered another—"

"Outside," Chancellor Lusk shouted, pointing to the door. "Let's take this discussion somewhere private."

The three men walked out into the hall, locking the door behind them. Trenton met his father's eyes for a second but couldn't bear to see the look of disappointment there. "Has Mother heard?"

Mr. Coleman shoved his hands into the pockets of his faded gray workpants. "I don't know. But you can count on the fact that if she hasn't yet, she will soon. Mrs. Patsy hates to let anyone beat her to delivering bad news." He clucked his tongue. "What were you thinking?"

"I *wasn't* thinking," Trenton said. He wanted to stand up and hug his father's worries away, to see his bent shoulders rise a little. But he was afraid his dad would turn away.

Trenton's father rubbed a hand across one cheek and examined his palm. "The problem is not that you weren't thinking.

It's that you were thinking too much. That brain of yours has no brake on it."

It was true. Trenton had tried to stop thinking—to focus on his homework and memorizing passages from his school texts. But his brain couldn't stop asking, "What if . . . ?"

His father sighed. "What was it this time?"

"I was showing off for Simoni."

"A girl."

For a brief second, Trenton thought his father's lips twitched in what could possibly have been the beginning of a smile, but it disappeared too quickly for him to be sure.

He rubbed away the marks on the table. "What I did couldn't have caused the plant to shut down."

"I know," his father said.

Trenton looked up. "You *do?*"

"Knew as soon as they told me. That swing was foolish and dangerous. Someone could have been seriously hurt. But it couldn't have shut down the plant. I did the math on the way from the mines, and the numbers don't add up."

Trenton stared. His father was a miner, what did he know about *math?*

Before he could find out, Chancellor Lusk and Marshal Darrow came back through the door. The man in the helmet stayed in the hallway.

The marshal turned to Trenton's father. "We have sort of a situation."

"What kind of a situation?" Mr. Coleman asked.

Something seemed different about the two men. They looked less confident—almost nervous. What could have happened in the hallway to change their expressions so completely?

Marshal Darrow shot a look at the man in the hallway and

frowned. "There's been an accident in the mines with one of the coal feeders."

Trenton's heart leaped. "The power outage *wasn't* my fault. I knew it."

The marshal glared at him. "Maybe it was, and maybe it wasn't. You've still committed dozens of crimes."

Chancellor Lusk clasped his hands behind his back. "It appears that something has jammed the feeder belt to a power plant on level three. It is *possible* that this feeder belt incident— in *conjunction* with the device your son illegally attached to one of the conversion plant's gears—caused the shutdown."

Mr. Coleman scuffed his boot across the floor, creating a black spot. "No offense, Mr. Chancellor, but the minute the feeder jammed, the power plant would have shut down. My son's poorly thought-out ride couldn't have had anything to do with it."

Trenton couldn't believe what he was hearing. His father was a miner; he didn't know anything about power-plant mechanics.

If the chancellor was surprised, he covered it well. "Be that as it may, we find ourselves in an uncomfortable situation. Your son still faces serious criminal charges, not to mention damage to his—and your family's—reputations. As much as I would hate to see your name dragged through the muck, he brought this upon himself."

Mr. Coleman stood silent, his jaw set.

The chancellor smiled. "I, too, have a problem. Until the obstruction in the feeder belt can be located and cleared, a good portion of the city will be without power."

"It'll take weeks to disassemble the feed belt and pull it out of the shaft," Trenton's father agreed. "The tunnel was made too small for a man to climb inside." He stared at the chancellor. "But of course you know that."

What was his father talking about? What did feed belts have to do with the chancellor?

Chancellor Lusk's face hardened. "Indeed. The tunnel—*dug according to approved specifications*—is too small for a man to enter." His eyes flicked toward Trenton. "But it's not too small for a *boy*."

Trenton leaned forward. They were talking about him. About having him climb from the mining level on one of the belts that fed coal into the furnaces to figure out why it had broken. He could do it. He knew he could.

"No," Mr. Coleman said. "Absolutely not. It's too dangerous."

Chancellor Lusk nodded. "I understand your concern. It's admirable how much you care about your son. I'll deal with my problem on my own, then. I'm sure I can find another way to resolve the situation. You may tell your wife that she won't see her son for the next six months. Hopefully no one will get the impression that your boy was at fault for them being without power for weeks."

Trenton jumped to his feet. "I'll do it."

• • •

Standing between his father and Mr. Sheets, the head of city maintenance, Trenton clutched the bars of the elevator car. He stared out of the cage as it clanked and rattled its way down the fifty-foot shaft drilled through the solid rock between levels two and three. Although he'd passed these cars hundreds of times, this was his first chance to ride in one. His eyes traced the grillwork of the door as it slid open and closed at each level, the lever the security guard pulled to engage the gears and pulleys that controlled their movement, and the cable disappearing high overhead. He imagined the cable winding around a metal drum. He almost thought he could make out the steady chugging of the engine that wound the drum—although it was too far overhead for that.

Mr. Sheets noticed him studying the elevator's mechanics. "It's quite something, isn't it?"

Trenton nodded. "Does it use some kind of counterbalance to help offset the weight of the car and the people inside?"

Mr. Sheets straightened his leather vest and whistled. "Learn that in school, did you?"

"No, but it makes sense. The elevator would use less energy that way. Only . . ." He studied the cables and gears, analyzing the mechanics the way a cook might break down a recipe. "I don't see any kind of backup break system in case the cable—"

"Trenton," his father scolded, interrupting his thoughts.

He looked up, realizing he'd been imagining ways to improve the system—to *change* it. Why did his brain insist on doing that? Why couldn't he leave things the way they were?

Fortunately, at that moment, level three, where steam and coal were turned into power, came into view. Trenton gawked at the rows of buildings filled with pumps, smokestacks, and all sorts of moving equipment—grinding, growling, and squealing in a symphony of gears and pistons. He'd never seen so much machinery in his life. "This is where I want to work once I get out of school."

"We can always use a good mechanic," Mr. Sheets said.

Trenton wiped the sweat from his forehead. "It's so hot down here. Is level four like this too?"

"Level six," Mr. Sheets said. When Trenton looked confused, he added, "Most folks think of the food-production level as one, the city proper as two, power generation as three, and mining as four. What they forget is—"

But Mr. Sheets cut off when Trenton's father shook his head and continued instead with, "What they're forgetting is that this level feels hot because of all the steam and burning coal. Even with the exhaust fans, the temperature hovers around ninety degrees all of the time. Enough heat is fed to the city to keep it comfortable. Down below . . . well, see for yourself."

Trenton thought he must have missed something, but he didn't have time to dwell on it. He studied the factories, stretching on tiptoe until the last plant disappeared from sight. As the elevator rumbled down to the lowest level of the city, the air quickly took on a chill.

"There's a reason miners are called ice rats," Mr. Sheets said. "It must be sixty degrees down here."

"Closer to fifty," Mr. Coleman said. "But after a few minutes of work, you warm right up."

At the bottom of the shaft, the car clanged to a halt. Chains rattled overhead, and a puff of steam shot up from beneath them. The security officer running the elevator slammed the lever to STOP and pulled open the gate. Unlike the city, which was hundreds of feet high and brightly lit during the day, or the power generation level, which was dim and not quite as tall, the roof of the mining level was so low it felt claustrophobic.

Lamps near the elevator illuminated the area outside it, but the tunnels branching in different directions quickly disappeared into an inky darkness. Trenton couldn't imagine working here every day like his dad did.

"Put this on," his father said, handing him a leather jacket from a rack on the wall. "It will keep you warm without being too bulky." All three of them put on coats, filtration masks to keep them from inhaling coal dust, and helmets equipped with carbide lamps, which burned with a steady hiss.

Trenton knew from school that the mining level provided

ore, coal, and steam—all vital to the city's stability. Their abundance was one of the main reasons the founders of Cove had chosen to build the city inside this mountain when the atmosphere outside had turned too foul to breathe.

Trenton eyed the heavy mining vehicles nearby. Cars ran on metal wraparound tracks instead of wheels like the city trollies did. Several cars had one or more trailers hooked behind them, while others were equipped with digging claws at the front.

"Are we going to take one of those?" Trenton asked.

"No, it's not that far," his father said, his voice muted by his mask. He led them down a tunnel to the right.

"Is this the coal mine?" Trenton asked as they passed a network of empty black rooms and pillars.

Mr. Coleman nodded.

Trenton studied the men and women operating the mining tools. Somewhere down here, a long time ago, a piece of equipment designed to hold up the walls and ceiling had failed. A section of rock and coal had collapsed, trapping his mother beneath it. Other miners had dug her out quickly, but her legs had been permanently damaged. Even now she could barely walk and had to wear bulky metal braces. His parents didn't talk about it, and he'd learned not to ask.

The deeper into the tunnel they went, the quieter his father became. Was he thinking about what had happened here too? Or was he immune to those thoughts after so many years in the mines?

"There it is," Mr. Sheets said, pointing to a spot where several vehicles loaded with chunks of coal stood idle in front of a belt that rose up through the ceiling.

Trenton started toward the chute, but his father turned and

gripped his shoulder so tightly it hurt. "You don't have to do this."

"I'm not afraid," Trenton said.

In the light of Trenton's headlamp, his father's eyes narrowed. "That's because you don't know any better." He pointed at the chute. "That thing can take a man's arm right off—and it has more than once. Do you know what would happen if the feeder started up while you were inside it? The belt would pull you straight into the furnaces."

"Mr. Coleman," Mr. Sheets began. "We've taken every—"

"Bob, you're a fine man," Trenton's father said, cutting him off. "But don't try to tell me that this is a good idea." He wiped his hand across his mouth and looked at Trenton again. "I don't know why I let the chancellor talk you into this."

Trenton lifted his father's hands from his shoulders. "I'll be all right."

Before his father could say another word, Trenton adjusted his helmet and climbed up the chute.

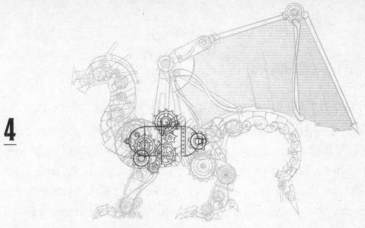

4

If the coal mine had felt claustrophobic, climbing up the feed chute felt like entering his own grave. The chain mesh conveyor belt was covered with sharp metal ridges to keep the coal from falling back down the chute. Loose black chunks of coal slipped out from under his hands and feet as he tried to climb, making him fall against the ridges.

The top of the tunnel was low enough that at times he had to half crawl, half slide to get through. No wonder they needed a kid to do this. The walls were so narrow and the ceiling so low that he kept banging his head and elbows against rocks that stuck out. It if hadn't been for the helmet, his head would have been a mass of bumps and bruises. An adult would have gotten stuck a dozen times over.

Every few feet, he stopped to examine the belt, looking for breaks or rocks jammed in the chain. After fifteen minutes of searching, his back ached, and even with his leather jacket and thick pants, his arms and legs were covered with cuts and nicks. He paused, resting his head against the wall.

"Are you all riiiiight?" his father's voice echoed up to him.

Trenton pulled down his mask and shouted, "I'm fine. Just taking a break."

"Don't be too loooooong," his father called. "You don't want your light to run out of fuel."

That could happen? Why hadn't anyone mentioned it before? The thought of trying to crawl back down with no light was terrifying. He crawled up the belt again, pushing himself to move quicker and check more thoroughly.

His father had said he didn't need to do this, but Trenton knew that he did. Partly to make up for the swing, because it was true that he didn't know how to put a brake on his brain. When he got an idea, he felt like he could only focus on that one thing. Never on what the consequences of his actions might be.

More than that, though, he needed to do this for his mother. Their relationship had always felt strained. His father said things had been different before the accident, but Trenton had a hard time remembering that far back. He had a vague recollection of her singing as she cooked and dancing around the kitchen with his father. That could have been his imagination, though. She didn't sing anymore, and clearly she couldn't dance.

He'd been only six when she'd been crushed from the thighs down. He remembered seeing her legs for the first time after the accident and thinking that he would come up with a device to make them work again. Later he'd sworn to find a way to make the mining equipment better so no one else would have an accident like hers. That was before he understood why creating anything new was wrong.

If *he'd* been injured because of faulty equipment, he would have wanted to find better technology. But his mother went in the opposite direction. When he told her he was going to find a way to fix her legs, she insisted that he mustn't. She said the reason she'd been injured wasn't because the technology wasn't good enough; it was because there was *too much* technology in the first place. That if it weren't for all the machines already in the city, they wouldn't need so much coal. A simpler way of life was the key to happiness.

He didn't understand how she could think that way. To him, machines were fascinating things that made life easier. He couldn't wait to find out how they all worked. But there was no use in arguing. Every time she saw him working on something with his tools, she shook her head. Hearing that he'd been charged with inventing would destroy her.

He was so caught up in his thoughts that he nearly missed a shiny piece of metal reflecting his helmet's light back at him. It fit so perfectly between the mesh links in the belt that, for a moment, Trenton thought it was another ridge. But none of the other ridges were shaped like this, and none were so shiny.

He brushed away the coal to get a better look. It was a cylinder of some kind—twice as big around as his thumb and three times as long, like a very fat metal pencil, but slightly curved. The reddish-gold color looked a little like brass and a little like copper, but not exactly like either one.

What was it, and how did it get here? He'd been expecting to find a broken chain or a chunk of rock blocking the belt. This was definitely something else.

Adjusting his helmet so the light shined directly on the cylinder, he reached down and touched it. It felt solid. It would have to be for it to shut down a feeder strong enough to take off a man's arm. But it didn't seem to have a scratch on it. He tried wiggling the piece of metal loose. It didn't budge. Tilting his head at an angle, he could see the cylinder better now. It was exactly the right size to slip through the belt and catch in the chain below.

"Have you found anyyythiiing?" His father's voice sounded farther away than before, floating up like a disembodied spirit.

Trenton cupped his hands to his mouth. "Found the problem! I'm trying to fix it."

"Okaaay."

Using a hammer and chisel from his belt, Trenton tried knocking the cylinder loose, but it was caught too tightly in the chain below. The easiest way to get it would be to take apart the chain. Unfortunately, he didn't have the time or tools for that. Even if he did, there wasn't enough slack to do it without sending the whole works sliding down the chute. Then they really would need to dig the belt out.

He studied the situation from one side and then the other, calculating the pros and cons of each approach. "You got yourself really stuck," he told the cylinder. "Trust me, I know. I've been there myself. But I think I might see a way to get you loose."

The key would be to twist the cylinder from the top while banging on the chain from below. Easy to do if he had a second set of hands, a bigger wrench, and a sledgehammer. Since he had none of those things, he'd have to make do with two hands, a pair of pliers, and a little ingenuity.

He needed something heavy to pound with, too. His hammer wouldn't do the trick, but it might *get* him what he needed. He eyed the walls of the tunnel until he spotted a good-sized rock he thought he could break off.

He worked at the wall, using the claw side of his hammer to dig and then the head of the hammer to pound the chisel.

"What's taking so loooong?" Mr. Sheets called.

Trenton felt like yelling that if they wanted him to hurry, they should leave him alone and let him work. Instead he shouted that he was almost done.

For a minute, he thought the rock might never come free

and he'd have to think of another plan. Then, without warning, the rock broke away—and smashed his leg.

He yelped in pain, but quickly called down, "I'm fine!" before the men could ask.

Getting the rock around the feeder to the chain below was a trick, but he managed to move it into the right position to bang on the chain. At the same time, he clamped the pliers around the cylinder from the top.

He tried to imagine how he must look lying facedown on a conveyor belt of coal, covered in dust from head to foot, with his arms and legs stretched so far that he probably looked ready to tear himself in half. Not quite the way he'd expected to impress Simoni. The thought of her seeing him like this made him chuckle, and he had to stop before his father called up again.

He raised the rock, pulled on the pliers, and slammed the chain. The clang echoed all through the tunnel. But nothing moved. He tried again. The cylinder was still stuck. One more time. He lifted the rock until his arm shook, yanked on the pliers, and plunged the rock down.

As if it had been toying with him the whole time, the cylinder shot free. The rock bounced off the chain and smashed his thumb. The belt jerked beneath him, and, for a terrifying second, he thought it was coming to life. He held his breath, bracing his hands against the walls, but nothing happened. It must have been the feed chain settling.

After placing the rock on the belt, where it would get harmlessly carried up to the furnace instead of causing a new jam, he examined his thumb. Blood seeped from the nail, which was probably going to fall off; the skin around it was already turning purple. But at least nothing appeared broken.

The belt jerked again.

"Get out of there!" his father screamed.

The belt rumbled forward for a second, carrying him upward with the coal—toward the furnace—then stopped. Trenton shoved his tools into his belt and began scrambling down the chute. The belt moved again, the metal ridges banging his shins and carrying him up a few more feet.

"What's happening?" he yelled, scrambling and tumbling downward.

"Emergency shutoff's not working," Mr. Sheets called, sounding panicked. "You have to get out of the chute now."

He was trying to do just that. But as hard as it had been to climb up, getting down was even harder. It wasn't like he could just slide.

The belt started again, and his helmet slammed against the wall. The light went out, plunging him into darkness.

"I can't see!" he screamed.

The belt moved him upward.

"Hurry," his father shouted. "Get out!"

"I can't turn it off," Mr. Sheets yelled. "I can't stop it."

The feeder jolted to life. This time it didn't stop. Trenton couldn't see, but he could feel himself moving upward. With no thought for metal ridges, broken bones, rocks, or anything but getting out, Trenton launched himself downward with a strength brought on by terror. He jumped, rolled, and leaped through the chute.

Lights flashed in his eyes. His head bashed against something hard, and he lost all sense of direction. Was he moving up or down?

Hands grabbed his arms and pulled him out. He looked up to see his father's terrified face on one side and Mr. Sheets's on the other. They were squeezing his arms so tight he could feel the circulation getting cut off. But he didn't care. He was out.

"You're safe," his father said. "You're safe."

5

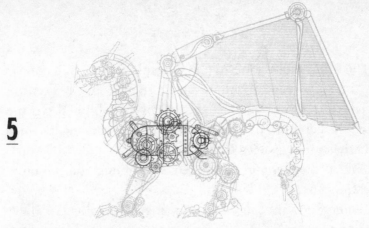

Trenton paused outside the apartment door. "Do you think Mom heard about what happened?"

His father took off his mining helmet and rubbed the back of his neck. "I'll talk to her if she has."

Trenton's mother was cooking when he and his father walked in the door.

She turned from the stove. "Where have you—" Her mouth dropped open, and her metal braces clanked as she stumbled toward them. Trenton leaped forward and wrapped his arms around her as her legs gave way.

"Let me," his father said, lifting her frail body and helping her to the table.

"What happened to you?" she asked Trenton as her husband eased her into a chair. "Did you have an accident when the power went out?"

"I, um . . ." Trenton looked to his father, unsure of what to say.

"Go into the bathroom and wash up," his father said. "Put something on that bump."

Inside the bathroom, Trenton looked in the mirror and could barely recognize himself. The reflection showed a boy with coal-black skin, wild hair sticking out in all directions, and a lump on the right side of his head, which had swollen so much that it nearly forced his eye closed.

In the kitchen, he heard his mother's voice rise. "The *mine*? What was he doing in the mine?"

His father said something too soft to hear, but her response was impossible to miss. "I don't care what the chancellor said. I will not have my son working on mining equipment. I won't have him working on any filthy machinery at all."

Trenton filled the sink with water, using the sound of the faucet to drown out the arguing in the kitchen, which grew louder and louder. She hadn't always been like this, but lately, on more nights than not, his mother found something to go off about.

He peeled off his shirt and carefully scrubbed his chest and arms. It was hard to find a patch of skin that wasn't cut or bruised.

He was finishing up when his father knocked on the door. "Put on a clean shirt and come to the table."

Trenton did the best he could to tame his hair and then changed clothes. He was tucking in his shirt as his father carried food from the stove.

"Mom?" Trenton asked.

His father glanced toward the hall. "Your mother will be eating in her room tonight. She's not feeling well."

Trenton nodded silently and dished himself a piece of fish and as few peas as he could get away with. He hated peas and fish. But like almost everything else, the city controlled which foods were eaten on which days. It was all part of keeping the machine running smoothly.

"Is she mad?" he asked, cutting off a piece of fish.

His father chewed a mouthful of peas and swallowed. "She's worried about you. She wants you to be safe. Her accident . . . It makes her much more aware of the dangers around us."

Trenton gulped his food quickly so he didn't have to taste it any longer than he had to. "What did you mean when you said that the chancellor knew the tunnels for the feed belt were too small?"

His father toyed with his fork. "What I said was out of line. Cove is a difficult city to manage—too many people crowded in too small a space. It's up to us to do the jobs we're assigned the way they've been assigned, while those in authority make decisions that benefit us all."

"Like what we eat?" Trenton asked. "And who is allowed to have children?"

"And what jobs we have, where we live, and . . . how big the belt tunnels are."

It made some sense. If everyone picked their own jobs and decided where to live and what to eat, it would be chaos. Food would run out, and everyone would fight over living in the best parts of town, and vital work might not get done. "I don't care what job I get as long as I can work on things—buildings, mining, power plants. They all sound great."

His father reached across the table and ruffled his hair. "You did a great job today. Because of you, hundreds of people are breathing clean air and cooking fresh food again."

"So . . . what happened while I was up there?" Trenton asked, thinking about how close he'd come to ending up in the furnace. "Why did the belt start?"

"Mr. Sheets is looking into it," his father said. "A lot of the equipment in the mines is old, and we don't have enough good mechanics to keep up with the repairs." He seemed on the verge of saying something more but instead finished his food and began making a plate for Trenton's mother. "In all the excitement, I forgot to ask you, what caused the jam? Did something fall into the chain?"

For the first time since he'd nearly been killed, Trenton

thought about the metal cylinder. What had happened to it? Did it end up in the furnace? He glanced down at his belt and noticed a glint of gold. He must have stuck it in with his tools right before the feeder started.

He looked up and realized his father was watching him curiously. "Oh, uh, it was a big rock. It got jammed between the chain and the side of the chute. I thought I was going to have to take apart the chain, but I managed to knock it free."

"Good job," his father said, patting him on the shoulder. "You'll make a fine mechanic."

After his father left to bring his mother her dinner, Trenton did the dishes, wiped down the table, and went to his room. He closed the door behind him, sat at his desk, and turned on the bright light he used when fixing things.

He checked the clock. Twenty minutes until the city mandated lights-out. Carefully, he removed the cylinder and placed it in the center of his desk. The first two things he noticed about the strange piece of metal were how light it was for its size and the fact that it still didn't have a single scratch. Iron and cast iron were the two most commonly used metals in the city, but this was too light to be either of those. The color looked like a mix between copper and bronze, but either of those metals would have been crushed in the feeder.

Steel was rarely used, and even that should have gotten scratched when jammed into the chain the way it had been. He ran his fingers over the metal surface, which was as smooth as if it had just been milled.

The third thing he noticed was that while he'd been assuming the cylinder was solid—a section cut from a ring of some kind, perhaps—that wasn't the case. It was actually a curved tube. Inside one end, he counted at least ten smaller rings going all the way down to a tiny core in the center.

Using a pair of needle-nose pliers, he tried to grab one of the rings to see if he could pull them out, but they were all so perfectly formed that there was nothing to grab. He turned the tube around to look at the other end. It had a groove cut all the way around the outside, and the end was hollowed out with a fitting of some sort at the center—the kind of thing you'd turn with a screwdriver.

Only he'd never seen a fitting like this. In the middle, about two inches down, was a star-shaped opening with a square in the center. He slipped a screwdriver through the star to the square below and tried to turn it. Nothing happened. He pushed on it. It wouldn't move.

He had no way to tell for sure, but maybe twisting the star and square at the same time would unlock something inside. He imagined sliding a tool with a star-shaped shank and a square tip into the opening. But he'd never seen a tool like that. Or heard of one. Why would anyone make something like this when a simple screw or bolt would do the job?

A chime sounded, and he looked at the clock—almost ten.

"Lights out," his father called from the hallway.

Trenton turned the tube slowly in his fingers. He should take it to his father. It was probably only a piece of mining equipment. His dad would take one look at it and say, "Oh, sure. I've seen a million of these. They're all over level four."

But what if his dad didn't say that? What if he looked at the device, frowned, and said, "I've never seen anything like this. It must be turned in to the authorities at once."

Trenton would never know what the device was or what it was for. Of course, if it was something illegal, he didn't want to keep it. If he'd learned anything from what happened today, it was to never again do something that could put him or his family in a situation where they could be accused of breaking the law.

The city *was* a machine when you looked at it from the standpoint of keeping everything running smoothly. And what would happen to a machine if you started swapping out parts with ones that didn't fit together? The machine would break, damaging all the pieces in it and eventually destroying the whole machine.

He started to put the tube in his desk but decided it might be safer under his mattress. Turning off the lights, he made himself a promise. He'd check around a little bit tomorrow. Ask a few questions. As soon as he discovered what the thing was, he'd decide what to do with it.

But if he found that it was something not on the approved list, he'd give it to his father immediately. Better yet, he'd throw it in the trash where no one could be affected by its noncompliance.

Lying in bed, he felt better about the whole thing. One question nagged at him, though, as he tried to get to sleep. How had the tube gotten inside the feed belt in the first place? Had it come off a piece of equipment? Tumbled down the belt from above, somehow? Either was likely.

But if it hadn't gotten there those ways—and if the tube was something not on the approved list—then someone working in the mines with his father was an . . . *inventor*.

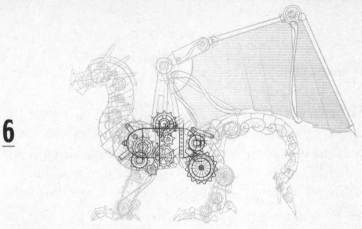

6

W hat did you do, use your face to break rocks?" asked a boy who sat at the next desk over.

"Very funny," Trenton said, trying not to smile. Smiling made his face hurt, and laughing made it hurt even worse.

Angus slammed a hand on his back, making every cut scream in agony. "Does your face hurt? Because it's killing me."

"Good one," Trenton said. "Must have taken you a couple of months to come up with a zinger like that."

Angus sneered. "Maybe next time you'll think before coming up with another *invention*."

Simoni got one look at Trenton and put a hand to her mouth. "Did they do that to you in . . . ? Was it because of . . . ?"

Trenton shook his head, trying not to wince at the pain. "The chancellor agreed to drop all charges. *Especially when they realized my swing had nothing to do with the power outage!*" he added loud enough for his whole class to hear.

"So you didn't get in trouble?" Simoni asked. "What happened to your head?"

"No trouble at all." Trenton grinned at how jealous Angus looked over Simoni's attention. "In fact, you might say I'm a hero. It turns out that the power outage was caused by a jam in one of the coal-plant feeder belts. The tunnel was too small for an adult to climb inside, and they needed someone with excellent mechanical skills, lots of brains, and plenty of muscle. Of course, I was the perfect person for the job."

He went on to tell them about how he'd climbed the belt, fixed the jam, and nearly been pulled into the furnace. When he got to the part where his light went out and he hit his head, the entire class was sucked into the story.

"Just when it seemed like I was a goner, I dove forward, jumped off the belt, and landed in the mine. Mr. Sheets said it was the most heroic thing he'd ever seen."

"Oh, my gosh," Simoni said, shaking back her hair. "It must have been terrifying."

"I'll admit I was a little scared," Trenton said. "But if you're planning on working with machines as a career, you have to be prepared for a little danger now and then."

Angus snorted. "They probably figured it didn't matter if you got sucked into the furnace. There's always another monkey willing to get his hands greasy. I'm going into security like my dad."

Simoni shook her head. "No one knows what their job will be." When Angus only smirked, she said, "I want to go into food production. Working with plants and animals all day sounds wonderful."

It sounded like the most boring thing Trenton could imagine, but he didn't say that.

"None of you will be doing anything if you don't take your seats and turn in your homework," their teacher, Mrs. Staheli, said. "Because if you don't, you won't graduate."

Homework. Trenton clapped a hand to his head, forgetting the bump, and gave a yelp of pain. With everything that had happened, he'd forgotten about his homework. As everyone took out their slates and handed them to the front, he did as many of the equations as he could, then hurried it up to the teacher's desk.

Even though he'd guessed at a few of the problems, math was his strongest subject, and he felt pretty sure he'd squeak by. He couldn't forget another assignment again, though. With less than two weeks to go until graduation, he was first in his class in math and science. As long as his scores stayed at the top, he was almost guaranteed to get a job working with machines of some kind.

The rest of the school day went by quickly. Word of his near-fatal experience spread around the school. With each telling, the story grew bigger, but he didn't mind. It was fun to be the hero for once instead of the kid who got in trouble. A few of the younger kids asked if he'd be hooking up his swing again so they could try it.

Each time someone asked, he shook his head and said, "It may sound like fun to try something new, but do you know why our city was built?" Pretty soon the kids stopped asking, which was the way he wanted it. He was done getting into trouble. Doing things to help the city run smoothly was much better than taking risks that could put people in danger.

He'd completely forgotten his plan to learn more about the metal tube until the last class was nearly over. As the other kids began putting away their work, he reconsidered his decision of the night before. The best thing to do would be to throw the tube away and focus on his studies. In another two weeks, he'd be learning mechanics on a scale he could only imagine, with a whole new set of bigger and better tools.

Still, he couldn't stop thinking about the fitting on one end of the tube and the rings on the other. What would happen if he found the right tool to fit it? And why go to all the trouble of making such an elaborate fitting in the first place? Unless the whole point was to limit who could use it?

He wiped his slate clean and drew the tube from memory, focusing on getting the curve just right. As he sketched the odd fitting, a small hammer clanged against a brass bell in the corner of the room, signaling the end of class.

Simoni stopped by his desk and leaned over to see what he was doing.

"What are you drawing? Planning your next adventure?" she asked, brow furrowing.

Trenton froze. Drawing schematics of approved items was legal; that was a necessary part of being a mechanic. But drawing anything new was a crime—just like modifying an existing device or writing a new story or idea. They were all considered to be creativity. He wasn't quite sure where his sketch fit in legally. If the tube was an approved piece of mining equipment, then his drawing was fine. If not . . .

"Oh, um, it's something I saw in the mines," he said, quickly erasing the picture with the sleeve of his shirt.

"Hmm." Simoni sniffed and looked around, clearly not interested. "Going home, or are you going to stay here drawing . . . mining stuff?"

Trenton got up from his desk, and a new thought came to him. If it turned out that the item he'd found *wasn't* approved, then someone was inventing. If he could prove it, he'd be a bigger hero than ever. Even the chancellor would be impressed. The city might give him a better mechanic job. His parents might get a better apartment. It would more than make up for the mistakes he'd made.

"I don't think I'll go home just yet," Trenton said. "I need to stop by a repair shop."

• • •

The first level of Cove was where plants were grown and animals raised. Trenton had no desire to see that. He'd heard that it all smelled like animal dung, and besides, they used only the most basic of machines on level one.

The third level had the machines that ran everything from power generation to sewage, and the fourth level was mining. Yesterday was the first time he'd seen either of them, since they were typically considered too dangerous for children. But hopefully he'd start his vocational schooling on one of them soon.

The second level—what everyone meant when they said "the city"—was made up of shops, apartments, parks, schools, city offices, and all of the other businesses people visited on a day-to-day basis. The city was divided into four quadrants, split by Main Street running north to south and Center going east to west. A map of the level looked like a pie cut into four pieces.

The sections were simply referred to as North East, North West, South East, and South West. Each quadrant had its own schools, shops, and apartment buildings. Trenton's family lived in South East, which was where he decided to start his search, first, because he knew the businesses there best, and second, because it was the section fed by the power plant that had shut down.

He stopped at a repair shop, where Trudy Finster, the owner, recognized him the moment he stepped through the door.

"If it isn't my good friend Trenton," the elderly woman said. She wore a leather apron and a pair of goggles that had rotating lenses attached to the side. Depending on the size of whatever she was repairing, she flipped from one set of lenses to another. At the moment, the medium lenses were flipped to the front, and she appeared to be studying the parts of an adding machine spread out on the worktable.

"Hi, Mrs. Finster." Trenton watched over her shoulder as she tweezed a gear the size of his pinky fingernail from a narrow spindle. Even without magnification, Trenton could tell that it was bent.

"Not adding sums correctly?" Trenton asked.

"Oh, it adds like a jewel," Ms. Finster said. "It should. I built it myself." She typed 12 + 13 on the black metal keys, pulled the handle on the side, and white plates with the numbers 2 and 5 popped from the top. "The problem is with resetting it." She pushed the CLEAR key, and the entire machine rattled with an ugly *clang*. "The fools at City Hall hit the keys too hard. Lazy accountant there has all the grace of a fish on a floorboard." She set the gear on a felt mat and looked for another one.

Trenton studied the broken part. "Maybe you could use heavier gears," he suggested.

"And maybe I could get my shop closed for making un-approved changes." The shopkeeper eyed him with a cranky frown. "What do you need today? Ball bearings? Springs? Oil?"

Trenton wandered over to the tools located on a rack along one wall. He tried to think of a way to explain what he needed without giving out too much information. "Actually, I'm look-ing for a kind of screwdriver."

Ms. Finster flipped her lenses up. "You didn't use yours as a chisel again, did you? I told you that would ruin the blade."

"No." Trenton laughed. "I already learned my lesson. What I'm looking for is a more specialized tool. It has a square tip and a star-shaped shank."

The woman rubbed her wrinkled chin. "Never seen any-thing like that. Specialized, you say?"

Trenton shifted his feet uncomfortably and tried to make

his words sound casual. "I think it may be used in the power plants."

"Try Fez Popper down the block. He works on the larger stuff." She flipped her lenses down again, then gave Trenton a curious glance. "This is an *approved* tool we're talking about, correct?"

"Absolutely," Trenton said, already on his way out the door. "It's for a project I'm doing at school. To prepare for vocational training." Before the shop owner could respond, he was on the street.

The rest of the businesses he checked went the same way. No one had heard of such a tool, and all of them asked if it was on the approved list. By the end of the day, he'd checked with almost every shop in South East. If there *was* such a tool, no one in this quadrant had heard of it. He was becoming more and more sure that no one on any other level had heard of it either—at least no one working on approved equipment.

He'd nearly decided to throw the device away when he remembered one South East place he hadn't tried—a shop that specialized in the sale and repair of mining equipment. He'd seen his father visit it once or twice to fix a lamp or a drill. When Trenton entered, the shop was dark, and, for a moment, he thought it might be closed. Tools and parts were spread haphazardly around the room like toys tossed aside by a careless child.

As his eyes adjusted to the dim light, he noticed a tall, thin boy at the back of the shop. He had a leather cap pulled low over his eyes and was running a steam-powered grinder. The boy noticed Trenton standing inside the door and took off his goggles.

"Need something?" he asked in a high-pitched voice.

"Get back to work," came a gravelly snarl from the rear of

the shop, and a flabby mountain of a man who looked like he'd just climbed out of bed came waddling into view. He pushed his belly up against the counter, eyed Trenton, and said, "You're the kid what climbed a feeder belt in mine two yesterday."

"I am," Trenton said, pleased that someone had recognized him. Maybe his reputation was spreading.

The tall boy returned to his grinding, but Trenton thought he caught a scowl thrown in his direction.

"Darn fool idea," the man groused. "Could'a got yourself killed. So what do you want?"

That wasn't the response Trenton had expected. "I, um, w-was wondering," he stuttered, "if you might ever have heard of a certain tool—a driver with a square tip and a star-shaped shank."

The man rooted his finger around in his ear and flicked something onto the floor. "Never heard of it. Never want to hear of it. Now get out of here before you mess the place up."

Trenton hurried out the door, wondering why his father did business with such a brute. But not before he noticed the boy staring intently after him.

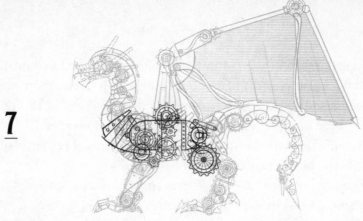

7

Whatever the tube was, Trenton was definitely getting rid of it. Maybe it was an approved device, and maybe it wasn't. But the last thing he needed was a black mark on his record, especially when he was about to start vocational schooling.

He couldn't exactly take it to the chancellor, either. The man would probably ask where he'd gotten it and why he hadn't turned it in immediately. Or worse, blame him for making the device. It would be easy for the chancellor to claim that the tube was Trenton's, even though there wasn't a shred of proof.

He'd have to find a place to get rid of the tube where no one could tie it back to him or his family. Better yet, a place where no one would find it at all—where a bad gear couldn't cause the machine of society to break down.

An incinerator? If the tube melted, there would be no evidence left behind and no way for the owner to retrieve it.

Halfway back to his apartment building, Trenton paused to watch the trolley steam past. Although he'd seen it hundreds of times, he never stopped being fascinated by the gleaming pistons, spoked wheels, and most of all, the huffing and puffing engine that provided the power to pull riders and freight around the city. What he wouldn't give to dig into that engine and poke around.

When the last car chugged by, he crossed the tracks and

turned into an alley between two buildings. A few seconds later, a man followed him into the alley. A coincidence, probably. Lots of people lived in the city, and this was a popular short-cut for reaching apartment buildings down the block. Still, as jumpy as he was, having someone behind Trenton made him uncomfortable.

What if word had gotten out that he was asking questions about a tool no one had heard of? What if a shopkeeper had warned authorities that a potential inventor was on the loose? He picked up his pace while watching the man out of the corner of his eye. He was tall—made even taller by a shabby top hat with a brass-studded leather band. His black coat was buttoned all the way up to his chin and was so long that it dragged on the ground.

Trenton sped up, and behind him, the man walked faster, heavy boots crunching the gravel with each authoritative step. What if it was someone from the security force? Had they recognized him? He broke into a jog, rounded the corner to the right, and ducked into an apartment building. Hiding behind the door, he watched the end of the alley. If the man turned this direction, he'd run up the stairs and wait until they quit looking for him.

What if he came inside the building? What if there was more than one person following him? Sweat dripped down the back of Trenton's neck as he imagined a group of security officers led by Marshal Darrow searching his room. It wouldn't be long before they discovered the tube under his mattress. What then? What would his mother say? This time there wouldn't be an offer of retraining. They'd lock him up permanently, or worse.

The man in the top hat reached the end of the alley and turned left without a pause. His heart pounding, Trenton waited for the man to turn around. But he didn't. Whoever he was, the man in the long coat didn't seem to be looking for him at all. No one had called the authorities. His relief made him so giddy he had to put his hands to his mouth to cover the laughter that forced its way out of him.

A door banged on the floor above him, and a man yelled, "Someone down there?"

Trenton threw the front door open and ran into the street, laughing so hard that the bump on the front of his head throbbed. He ran to the end of the block, cut across the park, and turned into the narrow lane between his apartment building and the next one over.

The man in the top hat stepped out of the shadows.

Before Trenton could react, the man was on him—grabbing him by the shoulders, spinning him around, and shoving him against the wall.

The man began searching Trenton's pockets.

"What do you want?" Trenton gasped, trying to pull away. "I didn't do anything, I swear. Whatever you heard is a lie."

"Where is it?" the man asked. Except it wasn't a man at all. Trenton recognized the high-pitched voice.

"I know you." He spun around, twisting out of the boy's grip. "You're the kid from the shop."

The boy seemed to hesitate for a moment, then shoved him again, knocking Trenton's head on the bricks. "What did you do with it?"

Trenton pushed him away. "Do with what? I don't know what you're talking about." He glared at the boy's pale face and dark, nearly black, eyes. This was no security officer. Trenton regained his confidence. "Does your boss know you treat customers this way? I'll bet he'd can you if he knew what you were up to."

He expected the boy to back down after a threat; no one wanted to lose a job, especially a kid who couldn't be more than a year or two older than Trenton. The boy pulled back a fist and punched him in the mouth.

For a second, Trenton could only stare in shock. Violence against another citizen meant guaranteed retraining. The boy raised his fist again, and Trenton rammed him in the stomach with his head.

The two of them wrestled on the ground in clear sight of anyone who might walk by. What kind of person would attack someone in broad daylight? Talk about a twisted cog. Trenton had never fought in his life, but it was either that or get beaten. Though the tall boy was lightweight—little more than skin and bones—he was full of tricks—biting, kicking, throwing dirt in Trenton's eyes.

He was wiry, too. Every time Trenton managed to get on top of him, the boy twisted away. It was like he'd been fighting all his life. Trenton thought he had the boy caught in a head-lock, but the kid slithered out of it, and suddenly Trenton was on the ground, on his back, with his arms pinned beneath the boy's legs and an arm across his throat.

"Are you going to talk?" the boy said, pressing his elbow against Trenton's Adam's apple. "Or do I have to break your neck?"

"Can't . . . breathe," Trenton croaked.

"And you won't breathe again unless you tell me what you did with what you found."

He *knew* about the tube. Trenton felt his chest grow cold. "What are you talking about?"

"The thing with the star-driver connection."

"Don't . . . know . . . what . . ."

The boy pressed harder with his bony elbow, and everything

began to go gray. Trenton clawed at the boy's coat sleeves, but his strength was rapidly fading. Right before he passed out, the pressure against his throat eased, and he sucked in cold fresh air.

The boy picked up his top hat and shoved it over his spiky black hair. "I'm going to try this one more time. If you don't give me the answers I want, I'll let you suffocate."

"Okay." Trenton's neck ached, and his throat was on fire. He had no doubt that this kid was insane.

"I know you have something. Where did you get it?"

Trenton tried to roll away, but he couldn't move. "The mine," he finally grunted. "In the coal feeder."

The boy gritted his teeth so hard that Trenton heard them rubbing together. "Of course. *I'm* the one they should have sent down there. *He* would have known that."

"*Who* would have known?" Trenton asked, curious in spite of the fact that he was pinned to the ground by a lunatic. "And why should *you* have gone?"

The boy pushed down with his elbow again. "I'm the one asking questions."

Trenton nodded.

"Where is it now?"

"I threw it away," Trenton said. "In an incinerator."

The boy's eyes went wild. He put both hands around Trenton's neck. "I told you—no more lies. If you had destroyed it, you wouldn't have asked about the star driver."

"Okay," Trenton gasped. "I didn't get rid of it. But I'm going to. Trust me, you don't want it. Do you have any idea what they do to people who make unapproved devices?"

"You mean to *inventors?*" The boy chuckled. "Yes. I know what they do to inventors."

Above them, a window slid open, and a woman yelled down. "You there, in the street. What are you doing?"

The boy looked up, and Trenton took the chance to roll out from under him. He jumped to his feet and raised his fists. The boy stepped forward, and Trenton backed away, balled hands held high. He noticed a piece of broken concrete in the street and picked it up.

"Don't come near me, or I'll . . . I'll *hurt* you."

"Fighting!" the woman shouted. "Those boys are fighting. Someone alert security."

The boy glanced around the alley, then backed away. "I know who you are. Next time you'd better have the . . . the thing you found."

"I won't give it to you," Trenton said.

"You will, or you'll be sorry." The boy straightened his coat and hat. "Don't even think about getting rid of it between now and then. If you do, I *will* kill you."

Running footsteps sounded from down the street, and someone shouted, "This way!"

Trenton turned and raced in the other direction. When he looked back, the boy was gone. Trenton ran to his apartment building, pounded down the hallway, through his front door, and into his bedroom. He slammed the door behind him and reached under the mattress. For a second he thought the tube was gone, then his fingers closed around the cool metal.

He stared at the gold tube. What he had found? And what was he going to do about it?

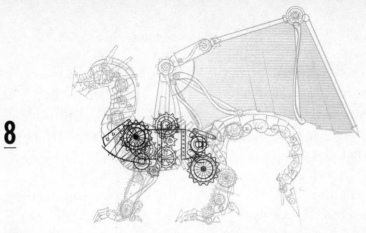

8

The next day at school, Trenton kept glancing toward the door, waiting for either the boy or security to show up. Why hadn't he thrown away the device when he'd had the chance? Or shown it to his father? Right after deciding he'd never do anything to get in trouble, he'd gone straight out and asked every mechanic, tinker, and repair shop about an unapproved tool. He might as well have painted a sign on the back of his shirt saying "Arrest me."

He missed half of the answers on a math test and spent twenty minutes reading the wrong chapter of his English textbook.

"Are you feeling all right?" Mrs. Staheli asked after she'd called on him twice for the same answer. "We studied that two weeks ago."

"What? Oh, yeah, I'm . . . fine," he said to the laughter of the other kids in his class.

But he *wasn't* fine. He ate his lunch inside the classroom and spent every minute of the day watching for the boy in the long coat and top hat. When the final bell sounded, he didn't know whether to be relieved that no one had come for him, or terrified that now he had to face the walk home.

Staying in the middle of the pack of students filing out of the building, he scanned the playground and nearby streets for anyone out of the ordinary. Other than parents waiting for their children, the only person he didn't recognize was a girl with blousy black-and-red-striped pants tucked into knee-high boots, a leather vest laced up the front over a white tank top, and slicked-down black hair. He didn't remember having seen her before, but since she was neither a security officer nor a boy, he didn't worry about her.

He kept with the other kids as much as possible and managed to make it almost to his apartment before someone stepped up beside him.

"You looking for a boy in a top hat and a long coat?" a voice whispered.

Trenton jumped. It was the girl he'd seen outside the school. He looked quickly around, but except for a couple of little kids skipping toward the playground, the two of them were alone.

"Have you seen him?" Trenton asked the girl. "I think he might be crazy."

"Oh, he is," the girl whispered. And then, in a high-pitched voice that Trenton recognized at once, she added, "*I* should know."

Trenton stared at her, shocked nearly beyond words. It was *him*. Or *her*. She looked so different now. But he recognized the eyes. "*You're* the boy."

She held out her hands. "Technically the *boy* is a *girl*. I was a little offended you didn't recognize it at the time. But the coat did hide my shapely figure."

"You hit me," Trenton said, still unable to believe that the girl in front of him was the boy who'd attacked him the day before. She was tall and skinny as a flagpole, and her hair was as short as a boy's. But . . .

"I kind of surprised myself at that. But it was a good punch."

She cracked her knuckles. "*Bam.* I'm kind of disappointed it didn't drop you."

Trenton suddenly realized that the boy—the *girl*—he was talking with was the lunatic who'd tried to choke him to death. He turned to run, but she grabbed him by the shoulder. "I figured that hitting you wouldn't do the trick this time. So I brought this." She held out her right forearm, which was encased in a gold band. The band was covered with wires and gauges and had a small attached lever.

She squeezed a lever, and one of the gauges moved with a click. "Every time I pull this," she said, squeezing the lever twice—*click, click*—"it increases the electricity. By now, I figure it's got enough voltage to throw you clean across the street."

"That's not approved," Trenton said, trying to edge away from her.

Her lips quirked ever so slightly. "Oops. Guess I'm in trouble."

Trenton looked from her to the device. She was insane enough to use it.

She nodded as though she'd heard his thoughts. "If you don't want to get fried, you're going to take me to my—I mean, to *the* thing you found. Hand it over, and I'll be on my way."

Trenton took a deep breath. "I won't do it."

She stared at him as if she hadn't heard right. "Didn't you hear what I said? If you don't give it to me, I'll—"

"You'll shock me," he said, stiffening his shoulders. "I get it. You're crazy." He shut his eyes. "If you're going to do it, get it over with."

He waited for several seconds. When nothing happened, he opened his eyes. "Well," he said. "What are you waiting for?"

Now it was the girl's turn to look surprised. She clicked the lever a couple more times. "You *want* me to electrocute you?"

"No," he said. "But I'd rather go through that than give you the tube. I've been thinking about this all day. If I give you what you want, you'll get caught with it sooner or later. And then it's only a matter of time until security figures out who gave it to you. They'll ask around, find out that I was looking for a tool that fits it, and I'm done. So go ahead and fry me. It's better than being sent to retraining."

"The *tube*," she repeated softly, rubbing a hand over her slicked-back hair. "What if I go to the authorities right now and tell them that you have an unapproved . . . *tube* in your house?"

"It isn't there," he said. She moved the armband toward him, but he refused to back down. "I didn't get rid of it. But I couldn't leave it in my house, either. So I hid it."

"You *hid* it?" She shook her head. "I can't believe this. How old are you?"

"Fourteen—almost," he said. "How old are *you?*"

She glared at him. "Fifteen—almost."

"That's only a year older than I am. What school did you go to, and what are you training for?"

"I didn't go to school, and I'm not training to be anything. I'm a repair technician, grade three." She clicked the lever over and over, seemingly unaware of what she was doing. "Okay, so it's not in your house. I can still tell the nearest security officer that you have it. Like you said, every repair shop in the district will remember that you asked around about the star driver. Cleaver's shop can't be the first one you tried."

Trenton bit the inside of his cheek. He'd feared that things might reach this point. But he was all in now. "I don't think you'll report me."

She folded her arms across her chest. "Didn't you just say that I'm crazy?"

"Oh, you are," he said. "Only a crazy person would fight in

the street and threaten another citizen with death to get their hands on an unapproved device. But you also don't want to lose it. If you tell anyone about me, security will seize the tube, and you'll never see it again."

They stared at each other, and he could see her trying and rejecting one angle after another. They both had a lot to lose.

At last she sighed. "The tube. What does it look like?"

He blinked. "You don't know?" As determined as she was to get it, he'd assumed she knew what the device was and how it worked.

She shook her head, and all the toughness went out of her face. She didn't look nearly as scary when she wasn't trying to be threatening. "I've never seen it. I just—I know it was left for me."

"What do you mean? Who left it for you?"

"I can't tell you," she said. "You wouldn't understand." She looked so sad, he might have felt sorry for her if she hadn't been brandishing a deadly weapon on her arm.

"There's not a lot to tell," he said. "It's about this long and this big around." He demonstrated the size of the tube with his thumb and forefinger. "It's curved and has a—what did you call it?—star-driver slot on one side and a whole bunch of rings in the other side."

"Rings." She crinkled her nose in a way that reminded him of himself when he was focused on a tough problem.

"What does it do?"

She shrugged her skinny shoulders. "I have no idea."

"How can you not know?" he asked, sure she must be lying to him. "You've been following me all over town for this thing. You tried to beat me up."

"I didn't *try*." Her upper lip curled. "I totally beat you up. By the time that old lady looked out her window, you were crying like a baby."

"I was not," he said, his face heating up. "And the only reason you pinned me was because you were biting and scratching."

"And punching you in the mouth and pinning you down—"

"And throwing dirt in my eyes."

They glared at each other.

"All right," she said. "I'm sorry for hitting you." She scuffed her boots on the street. "It belonged to my father, and I was afraid you would lose it. Or turn it over to security."

"Your *father?*" Trenton asked. "Where is he? And how did it end up in the mine?"

She clicked the lever on her armband so fast it made a steady whir like the blades on a fan. "If I show you something, do you promise you won't tell?"

"Show me what?"

She glanced in both directions before whispering, "You were asking about a tool. I can tell you what it is."

Trenton's heart skipped a beat. He couldn't believe he was considering anything to do with this lunatic, but he was curious about the tool. And the idea that the tube had come from her father hit home with him. If his mom or dad ever left him something, he'd do anything to get it back. "Okay," he said. "Let's see it."

"This way," she said, still clicking her armband.

"Are you sure you should do that so much?" he asked. "Aren't you afraid it will explode or something?"

"Explode?" She looked confused for a minute, then glanced at her armband. "Oh, this doesn't really do anything. I just wear it because I like the way it looks."

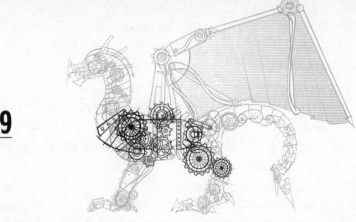

9

renton followed the girl through streets, around buildings, across parks, and behind shops. He thought he knew the city well, but she moved as if she was looking at a detailed map inside her head.

"Are we walking in circles?" he asked, seeing the same shop for the second time.

"Avoiding security patrols," she said. When he paused, she looked back at him. "Or did you want to be seen wandering around the city with me?"

"No, I guess not," he said, hurrying to catch up with her.

They stopped in front of a closed shop—the sign was gone, and the windows soaped over. Empty storefronts were unusual—they meant wasted space, which was a bad use of the city's resources—but this one looked like it had been closed for a while.

The girl stopped and scanned the area.

"What do I call you?" Trenton asked. "The Boy Who Is Really a Girl Who Keeps Trying to Kill Me seems a little long."

She glanced over her shoulder. "You really don't know who I am?"

"Should I?"

She raised an eyebrow—a trick he wished he could do. "Kallista. My father said it means *most beautiful*." She snickered. "But Kallisto is the name of a woman from a story."

"A *story?*" Trenton backed away from her. Not only did she fight and invent unapproved devices, but she also was named after a character in a made-up story. What kind of family did she come from?

Kallista shook her head. "It isn't a *new* story. It's from mythology, long before Cove was even thought of. My dad was into mythology."

Trenton relaxed. That was better. Stories from before the city was founded were fine.

"Anyway," Kallista said quickly, "the woman in the story got turned into a bear. I think my parents picked the name because I was a cranky baby."

"Can't imagine that," Trenton said under his breath.

Kallista checked one more time to make sure no one was in sight, then ducked around the side. The store backed up to an apartment building, which looked like it had seen better days. Several areas of the wall were smoke stained, and an entire section appeared to have been poorly rebuilt.

She knelt in the shade of the two buildings, brushed away the gravel, and pried open a basement window at the back of the store.

"What are we doing?" Trenton asked. She hadn't said anything about trespassing. "Who does this place belong to?"

"It doesn't belong to anyone," Kallista said. "Didn't you see the front? It's been closed for almost a year. Trust me, no one wants to do business here." She stuck her feet through the open window and slid through backward on her stomach.

"What if someone sees us?"

"They won't if you hurry." Her hand darted out of the window and caught him by the ankle. "Now get down here."

Trenton's heart pounded as he squirmed through the opening. How did he get into these situations? He should be home studying for his science final, and instead he was breaking into a shop. He wasn't known for having the best judgment, but even *he* thought this was a bad idea.

Inside the building—with the only illumination coming from the dirty window they'd climbed through—Trenton could barely see. He reached to turn on a light, and Kallista slapped his hand away from the switch.

"Ow!" he yelped, sucking his fingers. "Are you always this violent? How do you manage to keep any friends?"

"I don't." She raised her head as if that should have been obvious. "Really, though, you want to turn on a light? You'd make a terrible thief."

He froze. "Is that what you brought me here for? To steal something? I'm leaving."

She chuckled. "Aren't you the little blast furnace? Always ready to overheat. No, we're not here to steal anything. In fact, if you'll recall, we're here because you stole something of mine."

"I didn't steal anything. I found it. And how do I even know it's yours?"

She tapped her nose. "That's why we're here."

Holding his hands out to keep from running into anything, he followed her across the dim room. Even if they'd wanted to steal something, there didn't appear to be anything worth taking—just a few bits of wire here, a rusty screw there. Even the mice seemed to have left the building alone.

"How is this old place supposed to prove anything?" he asked.

She stopped in front of a metal door. To the right was a raised rectangle with what looked like three rows of brass buttons. Kallista pressed one of them, and there was an odd clicking noise. She pressed three more buttons, each followed by a click. After the last button, something inside the wall gave a thunk, and the door swung slightly open. She pushed it the rest of the way, revealing a room that was completely black, and held out her arm. "After you."

Trenton hesitated. What if this was a trap? Suddenly it seemed all too likely that she'd brought him to this abandoned building to torture him into telling her where the tube was. And he'd been dumb enough to fall for it. He stepped away.

"Don't trust me?" She laughed. "You might not be as dumb as you look." She went through the doorway and switched on the light in the room beyond.

Trenton had seen a lot of repair shops, but what he saw in the room on the other side of the door put them all to shame. He walked inside and couldn't stop staring. Unlike the chaotic shop where he'd first seen Kallista, this room was immaculate. Every spring, screw, gear, and bolt was organized by size and type, with every drawer and box labeled clearly.

And the *tools*. He had never seen so many in his life. A dozen different sizes of wrenches, screwdrivers so big you'd need two hands to hold them, all the way down to ones that would require a magnifying glass to use. It wasn't only hand tools, either. A metal shaft ran most of the length of the ceiling and was connected to pulleys of all sizes. Belts ran from the pulleys to grinders, saws, clamps, compressors, and other equipment he didn't recognize.

All of the tools were clean and shiny, without a spot of grease or rust—they might have come straight from the factory the day before. The glass-covered gauges and dials gleamed. The collection made his little tool set look like something you'd give a first grader to bang on the kitchen pipes with.

Walking down the room, he admired dozens of schematics attached to the walls—detailed plans for everything from iron-smelting equipment to air-purification systems. He reached toward one, then pulled back his hand. "That's"—he swallowed—"*real* paper."

Kallista grinned. "My father said it was easier to get the details right with paper and ink than slates and chalk."

"But how?" Wood and paper were precious commodities in Cove. Other than books and the city's original founding documents, which were kept under glass in the City Museum, he'd never seen a real piece of paper. Yet here were dozens—some as big as two feet square.

"He pressed it himself. From hay."

Trenton glanced at a tall shelf to the right, and his heart nearly stopped. "Are those . . . ?"

"Books?" Kallista nodded. "He was a big reader."

Trenton stared at what must have been at least two hundred volumes. He read the spines, afraid to actually touch them. He found repair manuals, as expected, but also history books, biographies, dozens of volumes about Greek and Roman mythology, and an entire shelf of what appeared to be made-up stories. He stared at Kallista. "All of this belongs to your *father?*"

"It did." Kallista's grin disappeared. "Until . . ."

All at once, Trenton understood. She'd said he *was* a big reader. "He's dead, isn't he? And this building was . . ."

"His shop." Kallista ran a hand across one of the spotless work benches. "I come down once a week or so to keep things clean."

"Your mom?"

"I was too little to remember her, but my father talked about her a lot."

Trenton's father worked long hours, and his mother was . . . well, she wasn't easy to be around at times. But to have both of your parents dead before you turned fifteen . . . He couldn't imagine it. "I'm so sorry," he whispered. "How long . . . ?"

"Since my father died?" She glanced away, clearly uncomfortable discussing the subject. "It's been a while."

Trenton was confused. "Why keep all this locked away? You could sell the tools alone for . . . I don't even know how much."

She immediately bristled. "I'll never sell my father's things. *Never*."

He held up his hands. "Okay, sure. I can see that. But why would you keep a shop like this closed? Why would you work in that mining equipment pigsty?"

"It's all right." She ran her finger through a box of wire connectors. "My boss, Cleaver, was a friend of my father's. He sleeps most of the day, so I can do pretty much whatever I want. And he hired me when no one else would."

"But you could run your own shop," he said. "With a setup like this . . ." He shook his head. "You *do* know how to use this stuff, don't you?"

Her face hardened. "I'm the best mechanic in Cove." Without another word, she bent under the workbench on the right wall and opened a cabinet Trenton hadn't noticed. She took out a metal case and raised the lid to reveal a rotating handle and a series of different-sized fittings.

And the *star driver*.

He reached forward, then paused. "Can I?"

"*May* I," she said. "Doesn't that school teach you anything? Yes, you *can*, and you *may*. But be careful with it."

Trenton gently picked up the handle and fitted one of the tips into place. When he rotated the handle, the star-shaped shank turned, and the square tip pushed down. "It tightens and compresses at the same time."

She took the tool back, put it in the case, and closed the lid. "He was working on something before he died. He wouldn't tell me what it was, but I know it was important to him. I've looked

61

all over the shop, but there's no mention of it anywhere. Until you came along, I thought I'd never find out what it was. Now that you've discovered whatever he left for me, I know I'll be able to figure it out."

Trenton felt sick. He couldn't imagine how much it would hurt to lose your parents. But she was fooling herself if she thought the tube he'd found in the mines was meant for her. "He didn't leave anything anywhere for you. It must have fallen off a mining cart or been picked up by accident. It could as easily have ended up in the furnace."

She fiddled with the laces on the front of her vest. "You didn't know my father. He never did anything by accident. He knew the feed shaft was too small for an adult to climb into. Somehow he figured out a way for the piece to jam it at the right time. He probably planted it long before he died with some sort of timer."

It made no sense, yet hadn't he thought that the tube almost looked like it had been made to slide through the belt and jam the chain?

"He knew I'd be sent to fix it," she went on. "I know mining equipment better than anyone, and an adult couldn't fit in the tunnel. The only thing he didn't count on was you and your stupid swing."

Trenton looked away. "You know about that?"

"Of course," she said. "It sounds like a lot of fun. Too bad they caught you."

He shook his head violently. "It was a terrible idea. People could have been hurt. And even though they didn't, I had no right to use city property to build unapproved things. We are all gears and cogs in—"

"A *magnificent machine*," she finished. "Whatever you say. Can I have the tube now?"

Trenton was about to agree when he noticed something that seemed out of place—a sign shoved in the corner behind one of the workbenches. It looked like the sign missing from the front of the store. He could only see the last two thirds of it.

bage Repairs

He walked across the room, grabbed the sign, and pulled it out.

Babbage Repairs

Babbage. *Leo* Babbage. The man who'd blown up an apartment building while trying to make unauthorized changes to a water heater. The man who had killed himself and dozens of innocent people. *The Inventor.*

It all made sense now. The closed shop no one wanted to fill. The apartment building with the burn marks and recent repairs.

He turned around slowly. "This is *his* shop. These are the tools he used to . . ." He stared at the star-driver case. "Was he using that when he blew up the apartment?"

Kallista stepped toward him. "It's not what you think. They don't tell the real story."

Trenton threw the sign down. He felt filthy for even coming here. "You're his daughter. The daughter of a murderer."

"He was *not* a murderer!" She pushed him in the chest, and he fell, banging his head against the wall. "I'm sorry," she said, reaching to help him. "If you'll only listen—"

"No." He got up, shoved past her, and ran out of the room. "Don't talk to me ever again! And don't ask me for the tube. I'll never let you have it."

He pulled himself back through the window, leaned against the apartment wall, and threw up.

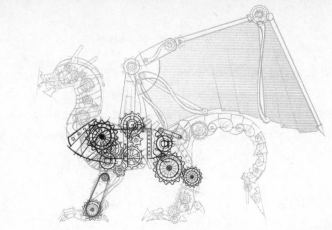

10

Days passed, then a week, and Kallista never showed up. Trenton went from being afraid that she'd try to contact him, to being relieved she hadn't, to being a little disappointed that she hadn't even tried.

Not that he wanted anything more to do with her—the daughter of Leo Babbage was the last person in the world he should be associating with.

Only he couldn't stop thinking about what it would feel like to have both of your parents dead. She'd said she had no friends, and he could understand why. Who'd want anything to do with the daughter of the city's most infamous inventor? After being raised by a man like that, no wonder she was so strange.

He wished she'd been the one to find the tube on the belt. If she came to ask for it again, would he tell her where he'd hidden it? He'd meant to get rid of it a dozen times but always found a reason not to. Too much homework. Someone might see him throwing it into the incinerator. His mother wasn't feeling well.

The night before graduation, all of the eighth graders had a party at the public playground. It was strange being outside when all of the city's lights were dimmed. Usually he was in his apartment at this hour. He sat on a swing, watching as other kids toasted meat and treats over hot coals, sang, and joked.

"Excited for tomorrow?" a female voice asked.

Trenton turned, thinking for a moment that it was Kallista. But the hair of the girl settling into the swing next to him was long and red, not short and black.

"This swing's not quite as exciting as the one you made," Simoni said, smiling in the darkness.

"But safer," he said. "And approved."

Simoni nodded. "Approved is definitely better." She pushed herself back and forth with her feet. "You'll be a great mechanic. The city will be safer with people like you making sure all of the approved machines run smoothly."

He smiled at the thought of working on one of the huge plants or something else equally complex. He'd finished first in math and second in science—second only because he'd been distracted during the final exam. "And you'll be great at food production," he told her. "I'll bet our meals will start tasting better the day you go to work."

"They couldn't taste any worse." Simoni wrinkled her nose. "The carrots last night were as hard as rocks."

Trenton laughed.

Simoni got up from the swing. "Come on. Let's go over to the fire. Some of the kids were talking about starting a dance."

"You go on. I'll be right there." Trenton watched her walk away, then glanced at a small, square-shaped bush at the edge of the park by the slides. He'd buried the tube at the base of the flowering shrub. With vocation school starting the following week, he'd be busier than ever. This might be his best chance to get rid of the tube and stop thinking about it once and for all.

Where should he put it? A trash can? An incinerator? A sewer pipe?

Kallista's face appeared in his mind, telling him that the tube was the only thing her father had left her. What if she came up to him one day asking for it, and he had to tell her it was really gone for good?

A sudden thought occurred to him, and he got off the swing. He needed to get rid of the device. He didn't want anything more to do with it.

But couldn't he leave it wherever he wanted to? Even inside the basement of an abandoned shop? He glanced toward the fire. The dancing hadn't started yet. He could dig up the tube, drop it through the window of the repair shop, and be back before anyone missed him. With a quick glance around to make sure no one was watching, he ran to the bush and began digging.

• • •

Finding the shop again took longer than he expected. For one thing, it was across the border of North East—an area he wasn't familiar with. For another, it was night, and he wasn't used to being out with the streets so dimly lit. Mostly, though, he was terrified someone would discover him and ask what he was up to.

With every step, the tube seemed to grow heavier and bulkier in his pocket. Each time he saw someone, he stepped into the shadows and went a different direction. He could easily imagine a suspicious security officer forcing him to empty his pockets. Trenton didn't want to be caught the night before graduation with an unapproved device.

The dance would have started by now, and Simoni was probably wondering where he was. No doubt Angus would hog every dance. Trenton had just about decided to toss the tube in the nearest trash can and run back to the park when he spotted the soaped-over windows. He paused, wondering what it might have been like having an inventor for a father.

Had Kallista known what her father was doing? If so, had she ever considered turning him in? Trenton couldn't imagine reporting his own father and seeing him sent off for retraining. Of course, he also couldn't imagine the guilt of knowing his father had killed innocent citizens and that he could have prevented it.

Anxious to get rid of the device, he started to cross the street, then froze. Was there someone down the block standing against one of the buildings? He squinted into the darkness. No, it was just a shadow cast by the streetlight. Still, the sooner he could get rid of the tube, the sooner he could stop worrying.

He ran across the street, turned into the space between the shop and the damaged apartment building, and squatted by the wall. The basement window looked as dirty and unused as he remembered. Had Kallista returned since the day he'd called her the daughter of a murderer?

He wished he could take it back. He felt like a coward sneaking here in the middle of the night. It was probably better that he didn't see her. What more could they say to each other?

He pulled up on the window. As dirty as it was, it opened silently—another testament to the fact that Kallista kept up her father's shop. Or maybe she just didn't want people to hear her sneaking in and out. He took the tube from his pocket, stuck his hand through the window, and paused.

He wasn't afraid of damaging the tube by dropping it. If the feeder belt hadn't done that, nothing would. But unlike the work-shop, the basement was dark and filled with debris. What if she didn't notice it on the floor? What if she climbed through the window and slipped on it? She could break an ankle. He should go inside and place it by the door—it would only take a minute.

His heart slamming in his chest, Trenton put the tube in his pocket, turned around, and slid backward through the window. His shirt pulled up, and his stomach scraped against the ledge before his feet touched the floor. Great. Like he needed to get blood on his clothes. His mother would only ask more questions.

As he turned toward the door, something moved. A rat? Was someone there? A small flame lit up the darkness, and a voice said, "Look who's come back."

"Kallista?" Trenton asked. "What are you doing here?"

Kallista touched the lighter to the wick of a candle, and the room was bathed in a soft glow. "It seems like that's what I should be asking you." The wavering flame illuminated her pale face and reflected in her eyes. "What *are* you doing here? I hope you didn't come to steal my father's tools. It would be a shame to kill you right before you graduate."

"No, I . . ." Trenton backed up a step before realizing that she was joking. At least he *thought* she was joking. His hand closed around the cool metal in his pocket and pulled it out. "Here," he said, holding it up.

He expected her to jump up and take it, but she didn't move. Her dark eyes went from the tube to his face. "Why?"

He shifted his feet. Why did she have to make everything so awkward? "Because it's yours. I knew that as soon as you showed me your father's tools."

She rolled her eyes. "Of course it's mine. But why give it to me now? Why go out of your way to help a *murderer's* daughter?"

Trenton felt himself blush and was glad for the darkness. "I'm sorry I said that." He kicked a rusty bolt across the room. "Do you want it or not?"

She got up and took the tube from him. By the light of the candle, he watched her turn it, first in one direction, then another. "It's definitely his work. I'd recognize it anywhere."

"Well . . ." He took a deep breath. "I'm glad you have it back. And I hope it helps you remember him."

He turned to climb out of the window when she asked, "Don't you want to see what happens when we open it?"

He looked back at her. "*We?*"

"Me," she quickly corrected. "When *I* open it. You don't have anything to do with this. If anyone ever asks, I'll swear to it." She turned the tube in her fingers. "I only thought that since you were the one who found it . . . But if it makes you uncomfortable . . ."

He *did* want to see. And then never have anything to do with her again. And he definitely wouldn't have anything to do with the device. But after all this time, a part of him would always wonder what happened when the star driver opened it.

Kallista nodded. "Come on."

She led the way into her father's shop, pulled out the case, and found the right-sized tip. She picked up the tube, started to slide the driver into it, but then paused. "You may want to back up, in case it explodes." Trenton sucked in a breath, and she laughed. "Sorry. That was probably in poor taste."

Trenton shook his head and moved to her side.

She placed the square tip into the slot in the tube and turned the driver. There was an audible click, and a smaller tube extended outward. The more she turned, the more the tube extended, each a smaller one formed by a segment that expanded from the device. The whole thing curved like a slightly bent finger until the sharp point clicked into place.

"What is it?" Trenton asked.

"I have no idea." She removed the driver and turned the device, which was now nearly three times as long. It curved into a sharp tip and looked like a digging or scraping tool.

Trenton noticed markings on the last segment. "What's that?"

Kallista carried the device to a magnifying glass mounted on the workbench. Together, the two of them peered at the markings: two squares, two circles, two more squares, and a rectangle. All of the shapes were outlines except for the second circle, which was filled in.

She looked over at him. "I think it's a code."

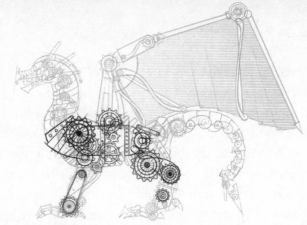

11

Graduation was held at the City Museum. Chairs had been set up, glasses of fruit juice lined a table in the back, and a buzz of excitement filled the air.

"I'm so happy for you," his mother said as he wheeled her chair to a spot near the back. She reached up and hugged him. This was the happiest he'd seen her in months. "You've worked hard for this."

"Thanks, Mom." Trenton looked around, hoping none of his friends were watching. He'd be starting training for a real job the next week. He was too old to be coddled.

No sooner had he managed to wriggle out of the hug than she grabbed his hand. "When I was your age, I had my heart set on administrative training. I was always good with numbers."

He never knew. She almost never talked about her childhood. But why was she telling him that now?

"When I learned I was being sent to the mines," she went on, "I was devastated. I couldn't imagine a worse job. Two months after I started training, I met your father. Four years later, we were married."

All at once, he understood. She didn't want him to go into mechanic training. She was trying to convince him that having some other vocation would be a good thing. She didn't understand that with his high math and science scores, there was virtually no chance of them sending him anywhere else. Even Mrs. Staheli agreed.

"Without machines, life wouldn't be possible," he said.

His mother's smile disappeared.

His father stepped forward and clapped him on the shoulder. "I'm sure you'll be great wherever you're assigned. Why don't you go find your friends? The ceremony will be starting soon."

Trenton gratefully escaped. He tried not to think about how upset his mother would be when the principal announced his training.

He wove his way through the displays of early Cove life— paintings of people sick from outside air or disease, accounts of the many who had starved until the first farms were created, and, of course, the Articles of Incorporation and the City Charter drawn up by the founding citizens. On a pedestal at the top of a small set of stairs lay a large, leather-bound volume called the *Book of Chancellors*. It was a journal documenting events from the founding of the city to now. At the end of each year the current chancellor added a few paragraphs detailing what had happened over the last twelve months.

Trenton tried to imagine what it must have been like before the founders of Cove dug the city out of the mountain and sealed the entrance behind them. The first citizens must have been so grateful to know that unapproved technology would never again endanger them or their families.

Thinking of unapproved things made him remember his trip from the night before. In the light of day, it seemed like a foolish decision. What if the tube was something that could hurt more people? He should turn Kallista in—for *her* good as well as the sake of the city. Maybe a couple of weeks of retraining would help undo the damage her father had caused.

But he couldn't bring himself to do it. Not yet. After everything she'd been through, he didn't want to cause her more pain. As a mechanic in training, he'd have a chance to keep an eye on her. If anything strange showed up, he'd turn her in to security without hesitation.

As he looked for Simoni, Angus's father edged over to him. The marshal was dressed in full uniform. "How was the graduation party?"

"Good," Trenton said, trying to move past. The head of security made him nervous, even when making small talk.

"Didn't stay out too late, did you?"

Trenton felt a trickle of sweat run inside his collar. By the time he'd made it back to the park, the dance was over and most of the kids were heading home. "No," he lied, sliding along the wall. "I was kind of tired, so I headed home early."

Marshal Darrow studied him with an intensity that made Trenton sweat even more. There was no way the man could know that Trenton had seen Kallista. So why the sudden interest in his activities?

"Well, enjoy your graduation," the marshal said. "Your life will take a big turn starting today."

"Right. I, um . . . Thanks for the advice," Trenton said, hurrying away.

He found Simoni talking with a couple of friends. "What happened to you last night?' she asked. "One minute you were sitting on the swing, and the next you were gone. I had to dance by myself."

"I got a, um, a headache and decided to go home early." He wished he'd come up with a better excuse. A headache made him sound like a little old lady, but he'd never been a good liar. "I'm sure Angus didn't let you dance alone."

Simoni sniffed. "He disappeared right after you did. I wondered if I'd suddenly developed a contagious disease."

An icy finger traced a line down Trenton's spine. Angus wouldn't have followed him, would he? Even if he had, Angus couldn't have remained unnoticed. He was strong, but subtlety wasn't one of his talents. Still, what were the odds that he and Trenton would have left the party at the same time?

"Everyone, please take your seats," the principal said from the front of the room.

Simoni took his hand. "Wish me luck in getting a job in food production."

"Good luck," he said. "Wish me luck in going into mechanic training."

She laughed. "You don't need luck. They'd be crazy to put you anywhere else."

True. But if they found out about his involvement with an unapproved device, he'd lose his mechanic job as quickly as he got it.

Simoni's last name was Bertram, so she moved to the front row with the As and Bs while Trenton found his seat in the second row with the Cs and Ds.

As the ceremony began, Trenton glanced across the room at Marshal Darrow, remembering the figure he thought he'd seen before going into the alley behind the repair shop. It had to be a coincidence. Even if Angus had followed him to the shop, he obviously didn't know what Trenton had been doing there or the authorities would have done something about it by now.

He tried to tell himself that he was overreacting. And since he'd never be going back, last night didn't matter.

Instead of worrying about something he couldn't change, he focused on the speeches. Jennifer Johansson, who graduated first in the class, gave a speech about the rewards of hard work. Kasie

West, who graduated second, spoke about why they should all be grateful for the men and women who had founded the city as a place of peace and stability.

The students were followed by the principal and several members of the faculty. They all gave speeches that seemed to spend as much time patting themselves on the back for the fine work they'd done as they did on congratulating the students. Throughout the ceremony, Trenton continued to have the feeling that someone was watching him, but each time he turned around, all eyes were focused on the podium.

As Chancellor Lusk, the final speaker, got up, Trenton finally allowed himself to relax. He would experience graduation only once in his life. No point in spoiling it with worrying. The chancellor gave an excellent speech about the pride the graduates could take in knowing that they would be giving back to the city that had given them so much. He talked about the importance of sacrificing for the good of others and of the great things that could be accomplished when a large group of people worked together for common goals.

He finished by telling the students that he had full confidence that under their direction, the city would flourish even more than it already had, and he promised them that one day their children's children would remember them with the same gratitude they personally had for the founders of Cove. Pointing toward the *Book of Chancellors*, he said, "This year it will be my privilege to record that I have never felt better about the young men and women into whose hands the future of Cove will be placed."

As the chancellor finished, every man, woman, and child in the room burst into spontaneous applause. Trenton was surprised to find a lump in his throat and tears in his eyes.

He wasn't the only one. Many of the people in the audience

wiped their cheeks with embarrassed smiles as they all stood and pledged to be gears and cogs in a magnificent machine. After they sat down, the principal walked to the podium and began calling up students to receive their diplomas and assignments.

Trenton watched with rapt attention as the first ten students received their assignments—two medical assistants, three for mining, two for cleaning, a builder, an apprentice shopkeeper, and an accountant. He had no idea there were so many different jobs.

Simoni was the last student in the first row, and Trenton couldn't help but beam when the principal called out, "School of Food Production," and the chancellor shook her hand. She grinned down at Trenton, and he pumped his fist.

Then it was the second row's turn, and he was on his feet. Waiting in line, he glanced back. His mother and father waved, both looking proud enough to burst. This was worth every bit of hard work he'd put in over the last seven years. Scanning the audience, his eyes froze on a figure at the very back of the room, just inside the door.

A girl wearing a top hat, dark glasses, and gloves. No one else in the room had her cynical expression. *Kallista.* What was *she* doing here? He hadn't invited her, and he was almost positive she didn't know anyone else graduating since she was from North East.

She caught him watching her and made a clearly sarcastic clapping motion.

He hoped the marshal or the chancellor hadn't seen Kallista. He looked quickly away. If he ended up being questioned because of her, he wouldn't hesitate to tell everything. He wouldn't lose his job over her, no matter how hard her life had been.

The girl in front of him took her diploma and was assigned to park maintenance. Trenton stepped forward.

"Congratulations," the principal said. "Your grades were exemplary this year."

Trenton's throat felt like he'd swallowed a handful of gravel. "Thank you," he croaked. "I learned a lot."

The principal handed him his diploma, and, as Trenton moved forward to shake the chancellor's hand, called, "Trenton Coleman. School of Food Production."

Trenton spun around. He must have misheard. "You mean School of Mechanics."

But the principal was already handing the next student his diploma, and Trenton was forced to move forward.

"Congratulations," the chancellor said. "I'm sure your *ingenuity* will serve you well in growing plants and caring for our precious food stock."

"But . . ." This couldn't be right. Trenton had the grades and talent to be a mechanic. How could they send him to the farms? He looked down at his parents. His father was scowling, but his mother wore a wide grin.

There had to be some mistake.

"Move along," the chancellor said. "You're holding up the line."

As Trenton stumbled down the steps, he looked toward the door. Kallista was gone.

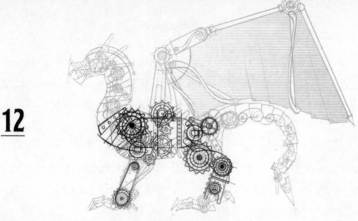

12

I'm not going," Trenton said when his father came to his room to check on him. In the past week, he'd done everything he could to get moved into mechanic training. All he'd been able to accomplish was to put in an official request for transfer. Why wasn't it obvious to everyone else that he'd been placed at the wrong school?

His father stood in the doorway of Trenton's room, face grim. "Do you think that not showing up for your first day of training will increase the chances of your transfer getting approved?"

Trenton grimaced. "I'm not a farmer. I don't know anything about plants or cattle or—or *fish*."

"You're a smart boy," his father said. "You can learn whatever you set your mind to."

"But I don't *want* to set my mind to food production. I'm a mechanic. It's all I've ever dreamed of." Why couldn't anyone understand that?

"We don't always get to do what we want," his father said. "What if everyone wanted to be a medic or work in a shop? What would happen if everyone in the city decided to be chancellor?"

Trenton sighed. His father didn't understand. He didn't want to be a medic, or a shopkeeper, or even chancellor. All he wanted to do was fix and build things. He wasn't going to win the argument, though, and if he didn't leave now, he'd miss the elevator. "Do you think there's a chance my transfer will be approved?"

His father shrugged. "I honestly don't know."

In the living room, Trenton's mother looked up from her wheeled chair and took in his overalls and short, gray apron. "You look so handsome," she said with a smile.

"I look stupid," Trenton muttered.

She ignored his obvious unhappiness. "Bring back some fresh onions."

Trenton knew nothing about food production, but even *he* knew he wouldn't be allowed to bring city resources home from his job.

His father walked him to the door. "My father gave me some advice on my first day of job training that I'm going to share with you now: It doesn't matter whether you sweep streets or become the chancellor himself. Do your job to the best of your ability and take pride in your work."

Trenton reluctantly nodded. "When you were assigned, did you want to be a miner?"

"We'll talk about that some other time. Right now you have to get to work." He noticed Trenton's tool belt beneath his apron. "You don't need that."

"Wherever I go, my tools go."

He expected an argument, but his father simply nodded. "Go on, or you'll be late."

Trenton ran all the way to the South East elevator. By the time he got there, he was out of breath, and all of the other trainees were waiting. The security officer outside the gate checked his identification and waved him inside. The officer closed the gate, pulled a lever, and the elevator car began rattling upward.

"I wondered if you were going to come," Simoni said, squeezing past a couple of other trainees inside the car.

"I didn't want to," Trenton said.

She smiled and punched him softly on the shoulder. "It won't be so bad."

He tried to convince himself of that, but all he could think about was the fact that somewhere else in the city, boys and girls were gathering to begin their training as mechanics. As the metal cage clanked to a halt at the first level, he remembered the last time he'd been on an elevator and how Mr. Sheets, head of maintenance, had said something about other levels. But when Trenton looked through the top of the elevator cage, all he saw above him was solid rock.

The door slid open, and all the students stepped out into more open space than Trenton had ever seen, everything illuminated by banks of lights so bright they made him squint. Even in the middle of the day, the city wasn't half this bright.

Thousands of racks were filled with shelf after shelf of plants. In the distance, he could make out rows of trees and what looked like a barn.

"Doesn't it smell wonderful?" Simoni said, taking a deep breath.

Trenton winkled his nose. "It smells like dirt."

"That is the one thing it *doesn't* smell like," said an extremely tall man with brown, wrinkled skin. "You may find soil in the city parks, but you won't find it here." He held out a hand. "Sid Blanchard."

Trenton didn't have any choice but to shake his hand. "I'm Trenton Coleman."

The tall man gave him a knowing grin. "The boy who doesn't want to be here."

Trenton scowled, his face growing hot.

Mr. Blanchard looked over the group of kids gathered in front of him. "I'm sure a few of you wanted to go into something more interesting than food production—something more exciting. Maybe you've heard that here at the farms you have to work hard. Maybe you've heard you get messy. Maybe you've heard you'll get blisters." He displayed his heavily calloused palms and fingers for all to see. "If so, you heard right."

Moans and groans came from the students.

Mr. Blanchard nodded as though he'd heard it before. "What you might not have heard is that you'll never find a more fulfilling job. You will watch seeds grow into plants because of your care. You'll experience the wonders of life and death every day." He stomped a boot on the ground. "Every person living in the city below is alive because of what we do. Not to mention," he added with a wink, "that nobody eats better than the people who grow the food."

Trenton tried to feel some enthusiasm. The man clearly cared about his job, and he seemed likeable enough. But the thought of a lifetime spent without working on machines made him sick.

Simoni raised her hand. "If there isn't any soil here, how do you grow plants?"

"Excellent question," Mr. Blanchard said. "Come with me, and I'll show you." He reached into his apron and took out a pair of worn gloves. "The first rule of food production: when you step off the elevator, you put on your gloves. We come here to work."

Although he still didn't want to be there, Trenton found himself intrigued by how the farms operated. Mr. Blanchard was serious about there not being any dirt. All of the plants, from alfalfa to fruit trees, grew in solutions of nutrient-rich water. Some of the grasses grew on mats, other plants sprouted in gravel, and some were suspended in nothing but liquid.

Mr. Blanchard led them through an orchard of apple, pear, and cherry trees. "Unfortunately, our founders weren't able to keep bees. They don't do well underground. And because many of the things we grow here require pollination that bees do naturally, part of your job will be transferring pollen from the stamens of one blossom to the stigmas of other blossoms. Think of yourselves as the city's worker bees."

Simoni laughed delightedly. "Isn't this beautiful?"

"Huh?" Trenton looked at her. "Oh, sure." He'd been studying the iron water pipes that ran across the entire building. Pipes meant pumps, filters, and regulators. Maybe he could find a way to work on machines after all.

They left the orchard and moved to rows of round metal tanks that were four or five feet high and twenty to thirty feet across.

"These are where we raise fish and shrimp," Mr. Blanchard said. "Have a look."

Everyone leaned over the tops to gaze at the fish swimming in the pools. "The drain in the center automatically filters out the waste, which we then use to fertilize many of our plants. In turn, the plants remove the nitrogen from the water, so we can send it back to the fish."

"What's that disgusting green stuff in the square tanks?" a girl asked.

"That is plankton," Mr. Blanchard said. "We feed it to the fish, and it's also used in some of the processed food products. The rectangular tanks at the end are called raceways. They give us more useable space and faster water flow for the fish that need it."

Trenton looked at the big metal boxes on the side of each pool, then raised his hand. "Who keeps the equipment running?"

Mr. Blanchard smiled. "Still hoping to be a mechanic, I see. The machinery is serviced by city maintenance crews. But don't you worry. In no time at all, you'll come to realize that our farms are the most complex and efficient machines of all."

Trenton sighed. He had to find a way to get out of here. He *had* to.

After a lunch of fresh vegetables, cheese, and fruit—even Trenton had to admit the food was pretty delicious—they toured the side of the level where cows, sheep, pigs, chickens, birds, and other animals were raised.

At the end of the day, Mr. Blanchard gathered the students in the headquarters building to talk about what they would be learning in the coming weeks and what they'd be expected to study at night. It turned out that even working on the farm they would have homework.

Using a large wall map showing orchards, tanks, and pens, he assigned each student to specific farming areas and gave them the names of the teachers they'd be working with.

As each student was told where to report, he released them for the day, but he held Trenton for last. When the other kids were out of hearing distance, he said, "I notice you brought your tools."

Trenton tensed, his hand going to his belt. "I take them with me everywhere."

"That's fine. I'm sure there are times when they could come in handy here, too, fixing a loose shovel blade or a fish net handle. But I must remind you that you are not a mechanic here. The machinery is off-limits."

"I'm trying to get transferred out," Trenton said.

The teacher nodded. "I know that, too. And if you do, that's fine. But as long as you work for me, you obey my rules. Maintenance crews handle the heavy equipment, and we take care of the plants and animals. Everyone does their job. It works best that way. We're all—"

"Gears and cogs," Trenton said, glaring at the map on the wall. How could he bear to spend the rest of his life feeding tilapia or pollinating cherry trees? He might be a gear. But he had no doubt that he'd been put into the wrong machine.

Mr. Blanchard tapped a finger on the map by a row of fish tanks. "You'll be working here tomorrow, on the plankton tanks, fish pools, and raceway."

"Fine." Trenton started to turn away, then looked back at his assigned area. Two plankton tanks, two fish pools, two more plankton tanks, and a raceway.

Two squares, two circles, two squares, and a rectangle.

It was the pattern on Kallista's device.

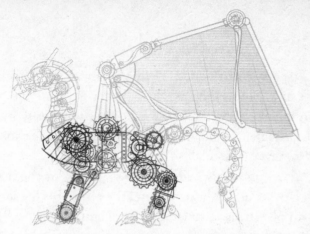

13

When Trenton came back from work, his mother was waiting for him. "You look more like a farmer already," she said, touching a green alfalfa stain on his apron.

He poured himself a glass of water and sat at the table, where she peeled potatoes.

"You know that I've requested a transfer to mechanic training," he said.

She pressed her lips together and peeled harder.

"It's not that I don't like farming. It's actually pretty impressive up there. You should have seen the orchards. There must have been two hundred apple trees alone."

Her lips relaxed a little, and her peeling slowed, so he quickly went on. "They have shelves and shelves of broccoli, tomatoes, and peas. And the fish tanks. There must have been five hundred catfish wriggling their whiskers." He jiggled his fingers in front of his face, which made his mother laugh. He almost never saw her this happy.

"Plants and animals are a good place for a boy," she said. "Sometimes I wonder if this mountain is turning us all into . . . something not quite human." Setting aside the peeler, she leaned forward. "Down in the mines, I started to feel like I was becoming a bug or a . . . a machine. Humans weren't built to spend their lives in the dark. We need fresh air, open space."

She put the potatoes into a pot of water and placed her

damp hands over Trenton's. "I know you think that technology is exciting. Young boys love powerful, noisy things. But machines are what forced us to burrow here in the first place. I won't have you digging like a bug or spending all your time with cold metal."

"Machines are what make it so we can live here at all," Trenton said. "You talk about fresh air. Where do you think we get that from? Exchangers suck it in from outside, filters clean it, and pumps send the used air back out."

"Don't talk to your mother that way," she said, pulling her hands back. "It's because of machines that I can barely walk."

"No," he said, wishing he could make her understand. "You were injured because the machines weren't good enough. Because they weren't maintained. If I'd been in charge of the mining equipment, the accident never would have happened." He tried to take her hands, but she yanked them back. Why was she being so stubborn about this? "Don't you see that I have a talent? I can look at things and see how they work. I may not be the smartest or the fastest, but I know I can make the machines in this city safer. I can protect people like you."

She turned away, her face set.

"I'm sorry," he said. "I didn't mean to upset you."

She shook her head. "Go to your room."

• • •

Trenton fell asleep without eating and spent the night dreaming that he was being chased through the city streets by giant mechanical bugs. One by one, the lights went out, and the air exchangers shut down. Soon he couldn't see anything and was gasping for breath. The only sound was the steady *clink-clank* of the bugs closing in on him.

He woke up the next morning tired and cranky. He ate a

quick breakfast—refusing to talk to either of his parents—and left as fast as he could. He was the first one into the elevator and had to wait for the other kids.

Simoni stopped halfway into the cage when she saw him. "Shooting for teacher's pet now?"

Trenton curled his lip. "Not likely." He looked up through the grate to the fifty feet of solid rock and light shining above them. "Do you think it's wrong that I want to work on machines?"

Simoni fiddled with her gloves. "I remember looking at your swing—at the gears and pulleys—and thinking I could never put something like that together in a hundred years."

"I wasn't trying to create something new," Trenton said.

"I know. And I wouldn't want you to do it again. But I realized then that your mind works differently from the way mine does. I look at a lamp, and I'm grateful for the light. But *you* look at it, and you know what makes it work, where the power comes from, and how to fix it if it breaks."

Trenton nodded. "Machines are easier to understand than people most of the time."

Simoni brushed her hair over one shoulder. "You're saying you'd rather spend your time with a machine than with me? Is that why you left the graduation party early? So you could secretly hang out with a power plant?"

"I—no. I mean—" Trenton stammered, and she laughed.

"Angus is jealous that we work together."

Trenton straightened his shoulders. "He is?" He didn't think Angus had ever been jealous of anything about him.

Simoni giggled. "You should have seen his face when I told him that you fed me melon at lunch yesterday."

Trenton put a hand to his chest. "But I didn't."

Simoni grinned. "Maybe you will today."

• • •

Trenton's job that morning was cleaning dead tilapia out of the pools and netting the fully grown fish to be cleaned and processed. He worked with another trainee named Clyde, who had all the grace of the dead fish they were pulling from the tank and the intelligence of a shrimp. Half the time, he missed the fish he was reaching for, and when he did capture one, he ended up dripping water on himself and Trenton. Soon both of them were soaked and smelled like fish. Trenton didn't think Simoni would want him feeding her anything today.

Their teacher, Mr. Lu, seemed nice enough, though. "You're lucky to start your training here," he told the boys. "These fish tanks are special."

Trenton didn't see anything special about a tank full of smelly fish.

"It looks old," Clyde said.

Mr. Lu grinned and tapped his nose. "Right on the nose." He pointed to the numbers 02 stamped on the side of the tank. "This is where our city's founders first began raising food for our people. The number two tells you that this fish tank was manufactured the second year after the city was built. The next tank down is numbered 01."

Trenton had to admit to being impressed. It was kind of cool to think that he was standing where the city founders had been a hundred and fifty years earlier. He studied the series of pipes and pumps sending water jetting into the pool. "Is this the same equipment they used too?"

"Some of it," Mr. Lu said. "Some has been changed out over time." He pointed to several pipes inside the tank. "See how the input pipes shoot water along the edge of the pool in one direction? That's to keep the water circling in the pool. The current carries food to the fish while also sweeping the debris to the center of the pool."

Trenton could see how it worked. Instead of the bottom of the tank getting covered with muck, it was all carried to a drain in the center. "It looks like the flow can be reversed."

"Good eye. By changing the direction of the flow now and then, you make it so the lead fish aren't always getting to the food first."

As he worked, Trenton studied the second of the two pools. If he was right about the markings from the tube, then this was the spot Kallista's father had indicated in the code. Working his way from one side of the pool to the other, he looked for any shapes or writing her father might have left. There was nothing that he could see.

He stared through the water. It was difficult to tell if there was anything written on the inside of the tank, and he wasn't about to go for a swim with the tilapia to find out.

"Lose something?" Mr. Lu asked.

"No." Trenton quickly went back to netting. "I was just admiring how healthy the fish look."

Mr. Lu beamed. "It's their food. Sometimes I think they eat better than we do."

Making sure to be a little more cautious, Trenton continued to search. The ground was solid rock, so nothing could be buried there. He looked at the pipes overhead. There was no way to reach them without a ladder. And anything placed inside them would have been washed away immediately anyway.

He wasn't planning on getting involved with Kallista or her father again. That part of his life was over. But he couldn't help being curious. Figuring out the code was like learning the way the parts of a machine worked together. All through the morning, as he caught fish, his mind continued to gnaw at the problem.

"Are you going to work straight through lunch?" Mr. Lu asked.

Trenton looked up to see his instructor and Clyde watching him from the other side of the tank.

"*I'm* not missing lunch," Clyde said.

"Sorry." Trenton walked around the tank, past the metal box attached to the side, and joined them. "Guess I was daydreaming."

"I'm dreaming about hunks of fresh cheese," Clyde said, holding out his hands like he was clutching fresh gouda wheels.

Trenton started to walk with them but paused and turned back to look at the box on the side of the tank. The box. Why hadn't he thought of that?

"I'll be right there," he said. "I just want to net a couple more fish."

Mr. Lu tilted his head. "I was told you might be a problem, but you're the hardest worker I've ever trained."

"Guess I like to see a job done right," Trenton said. He waited until Clyde and the teacher were out of sight, then hurried to the box and knelt beside it. Four screws held the cover in place, and he had them out in no time.

He lifted the cover off the box, glancing around to make sure he was alone. Then he looked inside the box. As he'd suspected, it held brass fittings, gauges, and the gears and pistons that ran the tank's pump. Interesting, sure, and under other circumstances he might have spent a little time tinkering with them. But now, he was searching for another clue. And nothing in the box seemed like one.

He stuck his head in the box, looking for more markings or a note of some kind. Nothing. Sighing, he screwed the cover back into place. Of course the box didn't make any more sense than the overhead pipes would have. The filters obviously had to be cleaned and replaced. The first person to open the box after Kallista's father left his clue would have found whatever was inside.

Maybe that's what had happened. Maybe a worker had opened the box, found what was there, and turned it in to the authorities. Trenton put away his screwdriver and checked the box to make sure he'd left it the way he found it. It was probably better that he hadn't found anything. That way he'd didn't have to decide what to do about it.

On his way past the first pool, he glanced at its box and stopped. Were his eyes tricking him, or was the box on *that* pool slightly smaller than the one he'd opened? He went back to the second tank and looked from one to the other. They were definitely different. The second box stuck out a good six inches farther than the first.

Pulling out his screwdriver, he removed the cover again. Carefully, he put his hand into the box and felt the back of it. At the seam where the back of the box met the bottom, his fingers touched the slightest bump. He pressed his hand against it and heard a click. The back of the box popped out ever so slightly. The back panel was a fake.

Sliding his finger under the edge, he pulled the metal out and up. There, hidden in a secret compartment, were two more gold tubes like the one he'd found in the mines. Behind the tubes was a crescent-shaped piece of metal that looked like a bracket roughly twelve-inches wide and eight-inches deep. Spaced evenly across the outside of the bracket were three holes with star-shaped fittings inside. He instantly saw how the tubes could slide into the holes.

He reached for the items, then paused. He'd promised

himself that he'd stay out of this. Did he really want to get involved with unauthorized equipment while waiting for a transfer to mechanics school?

No. He didn't.

Quickly he shoved the false panel back into place again and made sure it wouldn't come lose. He put the cover onto the box and screwed it into place. He'd just returned his screwdriver to his belt when a shadow dropped over him.

"Coming to lunch?" Mr. Blanchard asked.

Trenton stood up and forced a smile. "Yeah. I was just netting a few more fish."

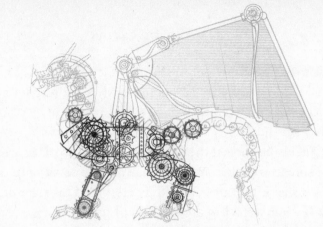

14

Near the end of his third day of training, Trenton fell into a plankton tank. Although *fell* might not have been the right word. *Got pushed into* was more accurate.

It all started when Clyde had hit him in the face with a dead catfish. Trenton wasn't sure whether it was intentional or not. They'd been arguing all morning. First Trenton thought that Clyde wasn't working fast enough, that he was taking too many breaks, daydreaming, and writing on his slate. Clyde said that Trenton worked too hard and needed to relax and enjoy himself.

Clyde brought the dead catfish—which he'd spent twice as long netting as it should have taken—out of the tank at the same time that Trenton was lifting a sack of fish food to dump into the feeder.

The slimy fish, which was already beginning to smell of decay, slapped Trenton's face, smearing slime and stink on his right cheek. As Trenton pulled away, the bag tilted, spilling catfish food all over the ground.

"Look what you did," Trenton yelled, wiping the side of his face with his sleeve. Why was he stuck mucking out fish tanks with a clumsy oaf while other kids picked apples or cross-pollinated blossoms?

"Look where you're going next time," Clyde said with a hint of a grin.

"Give me the net," Trenton said. "I'll scoop fish while you clean up the mess you made." He grabbed for the pole, but Clyde yanked it out of his reach.

"I'm not the one who spilled the food," Clyde said, holding the net over his head. "And I'm not cleaning it up."

Trenton jumped up and caught the end of the pole. Clyde tried to shove him away, and the two of them stumbled backward. Clyde tripped over the bag of fish food, and they fell against the thirty-inch-high wall of the plankton tank.

Losing his balance, Clyde let go of the net. Trenton reached for it, lunging over the water at the same time Clyde seized his arm to keep from falling. For a second, the two of them teetered on the edge of the wall, and then they went tumbling into the murky green water.

Trenton put out a hand to keep his head above the surface, but the floor of the tank was so slick his palm slipped and his whole body went under. He came up dripping with algae and coughing out nasty green water.

Clyde popped up next to him, spitting and cursing.

The two of them glared at each other. But the sight of Clyde with his ears and nose dripping green gunk was so funny that Trenton couldn't help laughing.

Clyde got the pole out of the water and dumped a net full of plankton on Trenton's head.

Soon the two of them were shoving each other under the disgusting green water, slipping, splashing, and laughing.

"What's this?"

The two boys stopped fighting, and Trenton looked up to find Mr. Lu, who had gone for supplies, watching them with his arms folded across his chest. Trenton glanced at Clyde. "We sort of had an accident."

"We kind of fell in," Clyde added unnecessarily.

Mr. Lu's lips rose into a smile. "If you wanted to clean the plankton tank, all you had to do was ask. I could have shown you the boots and special uniforms we have for that purpose."

Trenton ran a hand across his face, not sure if it did any good, and helped Clyde out of the tank.

"Go clean yourselves up," Mr. Lu said. "It's almost the end of your shift. I'll take care of this mess."

They started back to the headquarters building, still chuckling, when Mr. Lu called, "Trenton, I almost forgot. There's someone from the city offices waiting to speak with you. I think it's about your transfer request."

• • •

Standing in the bathroom, Trenton sniffed himself to see if he still smelled as disgusting as he felt. He'd washed off and cleaned his clothes as best he could, but his shoes still squelched with every step, and he could almost feel microscopic plants and animals squiggling in his ears and hair. Not exactly the impression he wanted to make on a city administrator.

He walked into the office, and a woman in a feathered hat and long gloves looked up from her slate. She waved to a chair across from the desk. "I'm Miss Rushton from the department of vocational training. Take a seat."

"I'd better not," Trenton said.

Miss Rushton eyed his dripping clothes and wet hair.

"I was cleaning fish tanks," Trenton said. "Actually, *plankton* tanks. It's a messy job, but I did it the way I was asked. If I were in mechanical school, I'd work even harder."

"I see." She sniffed in his direction and frowned. "It says here that you have been assigned to food production—one of the more desirable schools. May I ask why you are requesting a move? Is your training inadequate? Do you have a problem with the other trainees?"

"No," Trenton said at once. "The teachers are great. The other students are great. It's just that I've always wanted to be a mechanic. I'm good at fixing things. I got top grades in math and science. I'd be a much better mechanic than a farmer."

The woman set the slate on the desk and tapped her gloved fingers on the desk. "Students don't always know what is best for themselves. Many times what one citizen desires personally is not good for the community as a whole."

Trenton felt his heart sink. "How can my being a mechanic not be good for everyone if it means I can make the city's machines better?"

She raised her eyebrows. "*Better?*"

"I mean better *running*," Trenton quickly corrected himself. "I'm great at keeping authorized equipment working the way it's supposed to. I don't even care about what kind of equipment I work on. That has to be good for the city."

The woman tucked a fluff of blonde hair back under her hat. "I'm afraid there are extenuating circumstances."

"Is it because of the swing?" Trenton asked, squeezing his hands together. "The chancellor told me that was cleared up."

"Your unapproved creation was an unfortunate situation," Miss Rushton said. "But it was not the deciding factor. We recently received some *other* information leading us to believe that the mechanical field would not be the best place for you— or for the city."

Angus. Trenton's heart began to thud. Angus had followed him from the park, tracked him to his meeting with Kallista, and told his father. All to get Trenton into trouble. He balled his fists.

"I don't know what Angus told you, but I wasn't doing

anything wrong that night. I was returning something to a person I barely know. If you have a problem with what I did, you should talk to her. I have no idea what it is."

"Angus Darrow?" the woman asked. "You think the marshal's son had something to do with this decision?"

Trenton's scratched his chin. "Didn't he?" What else could she be talking about?

"The information came directly from the chancellor himself. A week before your graduation, Mrs. Coleman spoke with him in person."

"My *mother?*" Trenton didn't understand. "What would she want to talk to the chancellor about?"

"Mrs. Coleman worried that having you involved with machinery on a daily basis would be dangerous to you and the city. She felt it was her duty as your mother and as a citizen of Cove to see that you were placed in a school not involving tools or machines."

Trenton opened and closed his hands as though searching for a tool to fix the problem. "How could I be *dangerous?* She knows I've never injured myself or broken anything I've worked on. She . . ."

Slowly the woman's words sank in. Trenton's assignment *wasn't* Angus's fault. It wasn't because he'd hadn't done well enough in school or because he'd built the swing. He'd been put into farming because his own mother had requested it from the chancellor.

The woman from the chancellor's office picked up her slate and stood. "Your mother feels that you have an unhealthy fixation with machines. She was concerned that if you were given greater access to them, along with more advanced tools, it would be only a matter of time before you started trying to *change* them. She believed that eventually your . . . creativity

. . . would injure yourself and others. She didn't want you to become another Leo Babbage."

Hot tears burned Trenton's cheeks. "My mother called me an *inventor?*" he spat. "My own mother?"

The woman walked out from behind the desk and headed for the door, but he tugged at her arm. "You can't listen to her. What happened to her in the mine, it messed up her head. She thinks machines are evil. That's why she doesn't want me working on them. Ask my father. He'll tell you."

"I'm sorry," the woman said. "Your request for a transfer has been denied. Your position in food production is officially permanent. No other change requests will be considered."

"Please," Trenton cried, following her to the door. "I'd never make unapproved changes to anything. Ever. Let me talk to the chancellor. I'll tell him. Just give me a chance to prove myself. I'll go to retraining first if that's what you want."

The woman walked out the door with Trenton close behind.

"Is everything all right?" Mr. Blanchard asked, walking toward them.

"Trenton Coleman will complete his training with you and be assigned a permanent position in food production," the city official said. "Please see that he is kept away from machinery of any kind. If he causes any problems, contact security."

A cool hand took Trenton's, and he turned to find Simoni standing beside him. "I'm so sorry," she said. She led him to the elevator. "Let's get something to eat. Things will look better tomorrow. I promise."

Trenton felt numb. His own mother had done this to him. She had ruined his life, betrayed him. The elevator door clanged open, and Simoni stepped inside. Trenton began to follow her but then stopped.

"I'll meet you later," he said, shock turning to anger. "I have to get something."

"Get what?"

He turned away. "I left my gloves at the tilapia tanks."

"Get them later," Simoni said. "They'll be there in the morning."

The elevator gate began to close, and the security officer reached out to stop it. But Trenton shook his head. "Go on without me. I'll catch up."

As he walked back toward the fish tanks—in particular the tank with the unusually large filter box—his hand went to his tool belt.

15

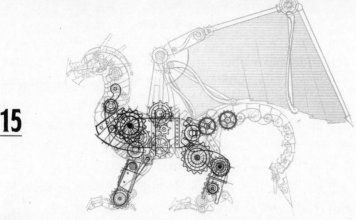

Trenton waited for Kallista in the dark basement, wondering for at least the hundredth time if he should leave. He was committed to giving her the pieces he'd found—at least, he was if she would agree to his conditions—but it was clear that something had gone wrong since the last time he was here. His eyes turned again to the door he'd followed her through into her father's shop. Or where the door *had* been. Now there was only a blank metal wall.

He'd run his hands over the entire length. There was no crack, no mark, no sign that the door to Leo Babbage's workshop had ever existed. What did that mean? Had someone discovered the hiding place, destroyed the tools, and walled it over? It didn't seem like it could have happened in the few weeks since he'd visited. The wall didn't even look new. But what other explanation was there?

He'd climbed the stairs to the shop with the soaped-over windows. He'd gone so far as to pull himself out of the basement and check the front of the store to make sure he was in the right building. Yes, this was definitely the shop he'd followed Kallista into, but just as definitely, there was no longer a door.

A shadow passed by the window, and he pushed himself against the wall in case it was a security officer. The shadow disappeared, and he started to relax, when the window suddenly flew open and someone burst through it. The figure hit the floor, rolled, and came up holding a heavy wrench and a sharper-than-normal-looking screwdriver.

"One move and you'll be pulling this out of your lungs," she snarled.

"Kallista," Trenton said. "It's me."

With her long legs and gangly arms, he'd never expected that she could move so fast.

She blinked in the dim light. She lowered the tool slightly but didn't put it away. "What are you doing here? Shouldn't you be picking potatoes with the redhead?"

Trenton tugged at his apron. He hadn't bothered going home after recovering the metal pieces from the tilapia tank, and his clothes were still damp. "You have big problems. Someone sealed off your father's workshop."

Kallista's eyes darted to the wall and back again. "I don't know anything about a workshop. This is my father's empty store. There's nothing here but dust."

"What are you talking about?" Trenton asked. "Last time I was here, you—" He paused, looking around. Could someone be listening to their conversation? He stepped forward until he and Kallista were only a few inches apart. "Did security find out?" he whispered.

"Not unless *you* told them." She pressed the tip of the screwdriver against Trenton's chest. "What are you doing here? Think you can trade information about me to get out of pulling weeds?"

Trenton had a brief flash of guilt, remembering his conversation with the woman from the city. He *had* been willing to trade information if it meant getting a mechanic job. But things hadn't worked out that way. He hadn't mentioned any names.

And he'd come here to help. Now Kallista was threatening to stab him with a screwdriver.

"Figure out your father's code on your own," he said, pushing the tool away. "I'll just return what I found." He turned and walked toward the window.

"You found something? What? Where?" Kallista ran after him. "I've been looking all over, searching for patterns, doing mathematical calculations."

Trenton eyed the screwdriver, and Kallista lowered the blade. "Sorry," she said. "It's just that security has been snooping around—asking questions at work, coming by the shop at all hours. When I saw you enter the window, I assumed you were working with them." She chewed her lower lip. "Did you really find something?"

Trenton considered not telling her, but what was the point? He patted his apron. "I found what your father hid. If they've discovered the shop, we probably shouldn't talk here, though."

"Turn around," Kallista said.

"So you can stab me in the back?"

Kallista put the screwdriver into her tool belt and at least tried to look a little guilty. "I wouldn't have stabbed you— much. Now face the back wall. I have to do something."

"Do *what?*" Trenton asked, but he faced the spot where the door had been while Kallista moved around behind him. He heard a soft click, and the metal wall he'd so carefully searched rose rumbling into the ceiling.

"I don't believe it," Trenton said. With the wall up, he could see small tracks set into both sides of the room and the edge of the thick metal plate above him. When it had been down, though, the illusion was perfect.

"Did you really think my father would have left his belongings unprotected?" Kallista asked. "Or that they wouldn't have forced open the door and taken everything after he died?"

Trenton hadn't considered that, but now it seemed obvious. Why else would she leave such valuable equipment where anyone who climbed through an unlocked window could find it?

"But the wall was up the first time you brought me," he said.

Kallista opened the normal workshop door and turned on the lights. "When I climb through the window, I can trigger the door to open. I didn't this time, because I saw you go inside. My father built the wall. He installed alarms and traps all over the place. Be glad the wall was down when you got here. If you enter the wrong code in the door twice, everything inside the workshop goes up in flames."

Was she serious? He honestly couldn't tell. He followed her into the workshop, and she shut the door.

"So?" she said, facing him. "What was the clue? What did you find?"

Trenton took a deep breath. "I'll show you on two conditions."

Kallista's eyes narrowed.

"First," Trenton said, "we work on this together."

"Absolutely not," she said. "My father left this—whatever it is—for *me*."

"Funny, then, that I've found the first two clues."

The two of them glared at each other.

"I thought you didn't want to get involved," she said.

He shrugged. "Let's just say I've changed my mind."

Kallista's lips narrowed. "You're a farmer. Not a mechanic."

"I'm a mechanic who's been forced to farm. And my conditions are not negotiable. Either I'm in or I'm gone."

Kallista's hand slipped toward the handle of her screwdriver.

"Don't even think about it," Trenton said. "Your father left more than one piece this time. I brought one of them, but you'll never see the other two unless you swear we're a team."

It was a bluff, but it worked.

"Fine," she said. "What's the second condition?"

Trenton had been thinking about this ever since he'd taken the pieces from the tank's box, but how could he say what he had to? "I know he was your father, but . . ." He touched the cool metal inside his apron.

Kallista's face drew in on itself, and her shoulders pulled forward as if to protect her from a blow. "But *what?*"

There was no easy way to do this, so he spoke as quickly as he could. "I won't hurt other people. If this *thing* he was working on is dangerous—if it's some kind of weapon, or if it could injure other citizens—you agree that we destroy it."

"My father never hurt anyone," Kallista said, her voice cold.

"Maybe not on purpose. But he blew up that apartment building. He killed himself and a lot of other people."

"That's a lie!" Kallista shouted. Her face was nearly white except for two spots high on her cheeks, which glowed like coals. "My father was the best mechanic I've ever known. He understood every piece of equipment in the city. He wouldn't have blown up a water heater any more than he would have let his tools rust."

Trenton knew it had to be horrible for her to admit what her father had done. But if they were going to work together, she had to face the facts. "People died. *That's* not a lie."

Kallista folded her arms across her chest. "Name one."

"One *what?*"

"Name one person who died in the explosion," she said. "Everyone knows that Leo Babbage blew up an apartment building and killed a bunch of people. The chancellor tells the story over and over. So give me the name of one person who died in the explosion."

Trenton opened his mouth, then shut it. "Well, I don't know specifically, but I'm sure—"

"*Are* you?" She paced around the workshop. "After my father died, I was in shock. I couldn't understand how he could have made such a huge mistake on such a simple project. I'd never seen him so much as strip a bolt or put a gear on in the wrong direction. I couldn't help but think about the people who had died in the explosion. Finally I decided I had to track down the family members of the survivors to apologize."

"But it wasn't your fault," Trenton said. "You didn't cause the explosion."

"No. But I was the only living relative of the person who did. It's what my father would have done if he could have. I spent three weeks trying to locate the relatives of the people he supposedly killed. Guess how many I found."

Trenton shook his head.

"None," Kallista said. "Not one father, mother, sister, or brother of any person who died in that explosion."

"Impossible," Trenton said. Estimates ranged between twelve and twenty people killed. With that many deaths in a population the size of Cove's, Kallista should have been able to find a dozen relatives the first day. "Where did you get the list of victims?"

Kallista took a socket driver from the wall, turned it in her hands, and put it back. "Funny thing about that. After the explosion, there was a scorched building, broken walls, and lots of gossip about my father and all of the people they say he killed—a friend of a friend, an aunt's sister's nephew once removed. But there *was* no official list of victims' names. I went to the chancellor himself to request the names, and you know what he told me?"

The hairs on Trenton's arms stood up. "What?"

"He said the accident was hard enough on the families and that I should leave them alone. He refused to provide a single name of anyone who died in the explosion." She turned to stare at him, her eyes like pieces of flint. "You know what else was missing? Bodies. I got there within minutes of the explosion—it was the building next to ours. Not one body was ever pulled from the wreckage."

"But your father's . . ."

A single tear trickled from the corner of Kallista's eye. "They told me I wouldn't want to see what was left of him."

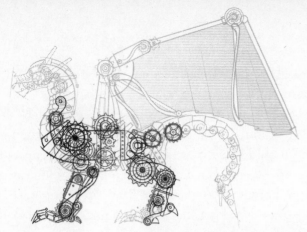

16

Trenton tried to take in everything Kallista had told him, but it was too much. None of it made any sense. "You think the city pretended that your father and those people died?"

"I don't know," Kallista said, wiping away the tear with an angry brush of her hand.

"Why would they do that?" It seemed far more likely that she'd twisted the story to ease her pain. He couldn't blame her. "If your father didn't die in the explosion, what happened to him?"

"I don't know," Kallista said. "I don't know if the explosion was real or set up. I don't know how my father died. Maybe the chancellor was telling the truth; maybe none of the victims' families wanted to talk to me." She clenched her hands. "But can you see now why it's so important that I find out what my father was working on?"

"Yes," Trenton said. Hoping he wouldn't regret it, he reached into the pocket of his apron and took out the three pieces he'd found in the metal box. One by one, he laid them on the worktable.

Kallista's eyes gleamed.

"Do you know what they are?" he asked. "The tubes look like they fit into the curved piece."

"They do." Kallista took the first tube out of a box under the workbench and set it beside the other two. "That's what the ring cut into the top of each tube is for." She inserted each of the tubes into the curved piece. They fit in place with a soft click. When she inserted the last one, all three of the tubes extended out and down like curved fingers.

"Is it some kind of weapon?" Trenton asked. Maybe Kallista's father knew someone was trying to kill him and he wanted to protect himself.

"I don't think so." Kallista turned the U-shaped piece over. With the tubes inserted, a pair of threaded bolts had popped out from the back of the curve. "This is part of something bigger," she said, handing it to him. "Something else connects here, and this hole in the middle is for another star driver. It's designed so that the tubes can all be drawn in or pushed out at the same time."

"It's light," Trenton said. The curved piece was almost a foot across and solid to his touch. It should have weighed as much as a pipe wrench, yet he could easily lift it with one hand. "This isn't iron or steel. Definitely not brass or copper."

"It's called an alloy," Kallista said. "My father was researching metals lighter and stronger than we have now."

Different kinds of metals? This was much more than changing the size of the gears in a machine or tweaking a chain drive. "Then he *was* an inventor." The word popped out before he realized what he was saying. He clapped a hand to his mouth. "I'm sorry. I didn't mean it."

If someone had called his father a name like that, Trenton would have been livid. But Kallista didn't flinch. "My father didn't think that *inventor* was a bad word. He said the human mind was built to look for better ways of doing things." She took the device from Trenton and placed it on the workbench. "He used to tell me how there were things no one else knew about the city."

"What kinds of things?" This probably wasn't a conversation he should be having. His father would frown on this kind of talk, and his mother would throw a fit. But wasn't it his mother's fault that he was here in the first place? If she hadn't gone to the chancellor, he'd be happily fixing a steam plant or a coal feeder.

"He never told me," Kallista said. "I got the feeling he was afraid that knowing could get me into trouble. Or maybe he didn't think I was old enough." She ran a hand across the shiny metal, clearly proud of her father's work. "Where did you find these, anyway?"

"In the filter box of one of the fish tanks. The pattern on the first tube matched the shapes of the tanks I was working on. You're lucky I was assigned there."

"It wasn't luck." Kallista went to a cabinet and took out several boxes of hexagon-shaped nuts. She began trying them on the ends of the bolts. "You know, my father never told me he loved me. He was a terrible cook. I've done all the laundry, made the meals, and cleaned our apartment for as long as I can remember. But he taught me to read when I was three. I knew how to use and take care of every one of his tools by the time I was five. Most importantly, he taught me that you make your own luck. He never left anything to chance."

"You're saying he knew I'd get assigned to food production and work on the fish tanks?" Trenton asked.

Kallista rolled her eyes. "He was a mechanic, not a psychic. He left these for *me*. I don't work on level one as much as I do on three, but I would have figured it out." She found the correct nut, threaded one onto each bolt, and nodded. "Was there any kind of message or clue on the fish tank?"

"Not unless it was underwater, and I'm not about to go swimming again to find out."

Kallista wrinkled her nose. "I was going to say something about your unique aroma," she said with a grin. "I'll think about the fish tank. You keep an eye out for anything else out of the ordinary. In the meantime, I need to go to level three to find the next piece."

"Why three?" Trenton picked up the metal piece and studied it for more markings. "Did you find a clue?"

"I found two," Kallista said with a cocky grin. "The first tube was on the mining level. The rest of the pieces were on the food-production level. That leaves the city and level three."

Trenton snorted. "Not very scientific. What are you going to do, wander around those levels until you find strange, unclaimed parts? And technically, the first tube was halfway between levels three and four. It could have been scooped up in the mines or fallen down from above."

Kallista snatched the piece back from Trenton. "My father used to play a game with me where he'd hide something and I had to find it. When I was little, he made it easy, like an apple on top of my bedpost. Later, I had to follow a series of hints. I'm sure he set up the first tube to be found when and where it was. I'll bet that if you'd looked closer, you'd have discovered a timer set to release the tube onto the belt at a certain day and time."

"But the chute was too small for an adult to climb up," Trenton said. "He couldn't have fit inside."

"Which means he had to drop it in from above—from the coal-burning plant. Clearly he wanted me to figure out that the power plant was where he'd hide the next piece of the puzzle."

That sounded like a huge stretch. "You got this all from the fact that I found the first piece on the feeder belt?" Trenton asked.

"That. And the bolts." Kallista tapped the two bolts sticking out from the back of the piece.

"What about them?" Trenton asked. The bolts didn't look like anything special.

Kallista spun the nuts she'd taken from the cupboard. "The threads on these are much wider than on most bolts. They're used in only a couple of places. And it just so happens that one of them is the power plant connected to feed belt eleven."

Trenton was stunned. She knew the exact types of bolts used in a specific power plant?

Kallista grinned at his reaction. "I might have had one other small hint." She turned around the box she'd taken the nuts out of. There, printed in clear bold letters, were the words *Coal Plant 11.*

Trenton gaped before bursting into laughter. "You are such a faker! I can't believe I fell for that. *It just so happens that one of them is the power plant connected to feed belt eleven.*" He shook his head. "How are we going to get to level three?"

Kallista pulled the device toward her. "*We?*"

"We figure this out together. It was part of the deal."

Kallista sighed. "Fine. Meet me here tomorrow night at seven. Bring a coat."

• • •

Trenton was quiet at dinner that night.

"How was work today?" his mother asked. "Your clothes smelled strange."

"Clyde and I had a contest to see who could inhale the most plankton," Trenton said.

His father quirked his eyebrows. "Your mother says you came home later than normal. Is everything all right?"

Trenton glanced at him from the corner of his eye. Did his father know about his mother's visit with the chancellor? "I had a meeting with a woman from the city about my transfer."

His mother stiffened.

"How did it go?" his father asked.

All afternoon, Trenton had been thinking about how he would handle this moment. He could call his mother out by telling her what he'd learned. But what would that accomplish? According to the woman from the city, the decision was final. If he said anything now, it would only cause another argument.

"It was denied," he said.

"Oh." His father pushed his food around with his fork. "I'm sorry. I know how much you were looking forward to being a mechanic."

Trenton looked directly at his mother. "They felt that food production was a better career path. They thought that working with machines would be dangerous for me—and for the city."

"Did they?" his mother said, her face expressionless. "I'm . . . sorry too."

Trenton's father looked at the two of them as though sensing something was wrong.

"They were probably right," Trenton said. "If I were given access to complicated equipment, who knows what kind of trouble I'd get into?"

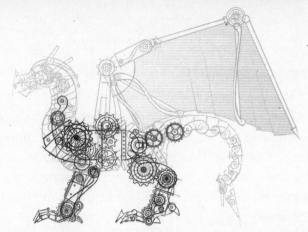

17

The next day, Trenton stepped off the elevator and found Clyde once again writing something on his slate. "What is that?" he asked, walking over.

Clyde jumped up and wiped his slate before Trenton could see what was on it. "Just taking notes on stuff we've been learning." Trenton eyed him curiously, but Clyde turned away without meeting his gaze. "Come on. We're working on alfalfa today."

They joined the group of students they'd been assigned to work with and followed their instructor to rows of shelves stacked with growing trays. The students were assigned to remove the plants from the trays, place them in vats to be dried, and reseed the mats.

The trays smelled much better than the fish tanks, and there was no slime to fall into, but even working in a nicer place Trenton couldn't stay focused. He kept thinking about what his mother had done. Did she think he wouldn't find out? Did she even care if he did?

"You feeling okay?" Clyde asked, handing Trenton a tray. "You look ready to throw someone into the algae pond."

Trenton realized he was scowling and forced himself to relax. "Yeah, I just have a headache."

He had to get his mind off his mother. She might be able to keep him out of mechanic training, but she couldn't stop him from fixing and building things. It was what he loved, who he was. As he emptied grass into the dryer, his thoughts drifted to what Leo Babbage had been working on.

It still seemed like a weapon. The finger-shaped extensions were sharp enough to do serious damage, and the curved piece could be mounted on a grip of some kind. But violence was a serious crime, and Kallista said that her father tried to obey the law. Plus, the parts were a lot of work to go through when something as simple as a knife or a hammer could be just as deadly.

Was it a farming tool, then? He looked at the hydroponically grown plants around him and laughed out loud as he imagined himself showing up for work with the tool strapped to his arm.

"What's that?" the others would ask.

"Mechanical hand," he'd say, opening and closing the metal fingers. "Just the thing for grabbing that stubborn catfish out of the pool and pollinating hard-to-reach pear blossoms."

At lunch, he set down his plate of food and pulled out his slate, sketching the device from memory. Three curved points—for grabbing? Stabbing? Holding? A mechanism that extended and retracted, and . . . *what*? What attached to the back?

Maybe a pole. He drew one on his slate, but it didn't look right. He changed it to a mechanical arm. He sketched hydraulics that opened and closed the extensions, and then a joint to pivot up and down. He added another joint in the center of the arm and made it gear driven so the arm could rise and lower separate from the end. It really did look like a mechanical hand. Except in his drawing, the tips didn't look like fingers at all. Or like weapons.

They looked more like . . .

"You draw even worse than you farm," a voice said.

Trenton lifted his head to find Clyde watching over his

shoulder. He tried to hide his slate, but Clyde had already seen the drawing. "I was just, um, you know, figuring something out."

"No offense, but you kind of stink at drawing." Clyde erased the slate and began sketching. In half the time it had taken Trenton, Clyde drew the mechanical arm.

It was perfect, exactly how Trenton envisioned it. "I didn't know you could draw."

"Drawing doesn't make anything or contribute to the city." Clyde handed him back the slate and shrugged. "You still want to work on machines?"

Trenton looked away.

"It's nothing to be ashamed of. Just because the city says you can't work on machines anymore doesn't mean you can't think about them. You can't be punished for what goes on inside your head." Clyde looked like he was going to say more, but at that moment, Simoni came over and sat down with a plate of cheese and fruit. Clyde lifted an eyebrow and took his food a few feet away.

"Is that how they get coal out of the mines?" she asked, cutting her cheese into neat cubes.

"Huh?" Trenton asked.

Simoni pointed her knife at the slate. "That's what you were drawing, wasn't it? A coal-digging machine? Looks like those claws would do a good job. Is that how they do it?"

Claws. That's exactly what he'd been drawing. The curved points did look like claws. Attached to the end of a strong enough arm, they'd be able to rip coal from deposits in mountain walls and put the chunks into mining cars.

Was that what Kallista's father had been designing, some type of mining equipment? Surprisingly, the idea disappointed him a little.

"Are you listening to me?" Simoni asked.

Trenton realized she must have continued talking while he was lost in his thoughts. "Yes," he said, searching his brain for any trace of her last words. "You were talking about, um, mining equipment, and . . ." He glanced at her plate. "Cheese?"

Simoni's brow wrinkled. She flicked a square of cheese in his face. "No. I was *not* talking about *cheese*. What's wrong with you today? Clyde says you've been in a trance all morning."

"Sorry. I've been distracted." Trenton put his slate back into his apron pocket, then pushed his food around with his fork. "I've been wondering about what I'll do now that my transfer request was denied."

"I *knew* it." Simoni's expression softened. "Farming isn't so bad. You need to stop moping and do something fun. A bunch of us are going to have a picnic in the orchards tomorrow after work. Want to come?"

If Angus had been jealous before, how would he react after hearing that Trenton and Simoni had gone on a picnic together? He liked the idea. "Absolutely."

He tried to focus on his work the rest of the afternoon, but as soon as his shift ended, he raced home, did his homework, and changed clothes to meet Kallista. She had said to bring a coat, but he didn't have one. He'd never needed one in the perfectly adjusted temperature. Even if he had, wearing it would have raised too many questions.

He couldn't think of any reason a coat would be necessary anyway. The city was warm, and level three even got hot from burning coal and the steam-powered plants. The suggestion was probably just Kallista's odd sense of humor. He could see her laughing her head off as he trudged through the hot, humid air, sweating like a pig in a coat. He finally compromised by tying an extra shirt around his waist, just in case.

When Trenton came out of his room and headed for the

front door, his mother was sitting in her wheeled chair, folding clothes. "Where are you going?" she asked.

"Out," Trenton said without looking at her. He briefly considered adding, *To put the citizens of your precious city in danger*, but thought better of it. Instead he turned his back and said, "I won't be home for dinner."

She rolled toward him. "Is there something you want to talk about?"

Holding the doorknob, Trenton finally met her eyes. "Is there something *you* want to talk about?"

They stared at each other until his mother looked away. Guilt gnawed at his stomach. Why should *he* feel guilty? She was the one who'd destroyed all of his hopes and dreams. If she'd minded her own business they wouldn't be in this situation.

He hurried outside before either of them could say anything more.

When he arrived behind the shop, Kallista was already waiting. She was dressed much the way she'd been the day he'd mistaken her for a boy—a long black coat, gloves, and boots. This time, though, her top hat had been replaced by a brown leather cap and welding goggles pulled up on her forehead.

She eyed his clothes and twisted her mouth. "Told you to bring a coat."

Trenton frowned. "I've been to the third level. It's not cold."

"Fine," she said with a hint of a smile. "Don't say I didn't warn you." She tossed him a pair of goggles like her own, along with a flat leather cap.

"What are these for?" he asked.

"You'll see." Kallista said, jogging down an alleyway. Trenton expected her to turn right toward the center of the city. Instead, she headed left.

"Where are you going?" He hurried to catch up with her.

"The elevators are that way," he said, jerking a thumb over his shoulder.

She glanced down the street in both directions. "The elevators have guards. Or do you happen to have a pass to the third level? If so, that would have been good to know."

Trenton followed as she ran across the street and ducked into the shadows of a clothing store. "I assumed *you* had one. You said you work on equipment in the lower levels."

"You really are naïve." She snorted. "You think just because I've worked on different levels that I can take the elevators anywhere I want? Unless your job assignment is there, you need a work order to leave the city. No work order, no elevator."

This area was mostly shops, and since they all closed at seven o' clock, the streets were nearly empty and the streetlights dimmed. The darkness made it easier to hide, but the lack of people made the two of them stand out. Every time someone came into view, Kallista ducked out of sight. The more she ducked and ran, the more frustrated Trenton became.

"If you don't have a pass, what's the point of all this?" he asked. "The elevators are the only way to get to the next level."

"Is that right?" she asked with a mysterious gleam in her eyes.

They continued toward the edge of the city, where the buildings were smaller and more spread apart, until they were so close to the bare stone of the mountain wall that Trenton could see the tool marks where the rock had been broken away.

Kallista stepped into the doorway of a closed vegetable market and knelt. She pulled a piece of chalk from her pocket and handed it to Trenton. "Draw Cove."

He took the chalk. "What do you mean?"

Kallista tapped the sidewalk with her gloved hand. "Draw it.

Right here. I want to see how much you know about the place you live."

"Okaaay." Trenton didn't see the point, but he hunched down and started by drawing a circle on the sidewalk. Kallista brushed away the shape before it was even halfway complete.

"I didn't ask you to draw a map of the *city*," she snapped. "Anyone can do that. We've lived here our whole lives, haven't we? I want you to draw Cove from the side. The way you'd see it if you cut the mountain in half."

Trenton stared at her. He'd never thought about viewing Cove from the side. He put the chalk to the cement and paused. "They don't teach that in school."

"They don't teach a lot of things in school—one of the many reasons my father never sent me," Kallista said. "It's about time you got a real education."

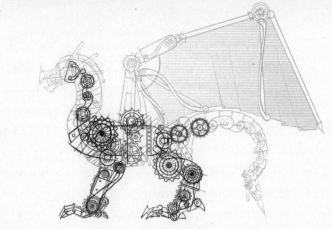

18

Trenton squeezed the chalk until his fingers turned white. He tried to start the sketch several times but kept pulling back. "How am I supposed to draw something I've never seen?"

"You say you're good with machines," Kallista said. "Don't tell me you can't form a picture in your mind. Imagine the mountain the way you would a machine, then draw it."

She was right. Working on things required you to envision how the pieces fit together. He could see each level on its own from above; he just needed to reorient them in his brain. He started by making two sloping lines that met at the top—the sides of the mountain. Next, he drew the first level across the mountain about halfway down, then the city level below that, then the power-plant level, and finally, the mining level at the bottom. He labeled them: one, two, three, and four. He definitely didn't have Clyde's drawing talent, but he thought he'd done a decent job.

Kallista put her hands on her knees and nodded. "Keep going."

What else was there? He studied the drawing. He'd forgotten the elevators—of course. He need to add one for each of the four quadrants of the city. He drew four shafts running from the top level to the bottom. Good. But something was still missing.

He mentally reviewed each level. The first level: food

production. The second level: housing, businesses, schools, and parks. The third level . . .

He nearly slapped his head. Of course. He'd missed the feeder chutes that brought coal and ore up from the mines to level three.

Now that he was thinking about Cove as a whole, there also had to be steam pipes running up from the lower levels to the power-generation plants. He didn't know exactly where the chutes were in relationship to everything else. So he guessed, sketching lines in several places across the city.

"How's that?" he asked, sitting back and admiring his work.

Kallista snickered, and Trenton tensed.

"Actually," she said in a conciliatory tone, "it's probably better than most people could do."

Trenton stared at his drawing. "What's wrong with it?"

Kallista took the chalk. "For one thing, it's all out of proportion." She wiped away the sides of the mountain with the sleeve of her coat and redrew them. Instead of running from one side of the mountain to the other, the levels now filled less than a fourth of the mountain's width. She then extended the sides of the mountain down farther until even the lowest level was barely a third of the way down from the mountain's top.

She eyed the drawing critically and nodded. "My dad could have done better, but this is close enough. If the mountain were hollow, the way you drew it, the whole thing would have collapsed under its own weight long ago. Also, your levels are too close together. Fifty feet of rock, minimum, separates each section to keep one level from falling into the other. And there are stone pillars—here, here, here, and here—left in place to help bear the weight of the rock." She drew four thick lines in each of the four sections of the city. Sixteen total.

"I've never seen any pillars," Trenton said, thinking she was making fun of him.

Kallista rolled her eyes as if she were trying to teach a clumsy baby to walk. "You also haven't seen the masses of pipes, drains, and struts running through all four levels. Not to mention the wires running from the power plants to the conversion stations like the one you built your swing on. That's because they're all hidden." She pointed to their right. "Haven't you ever wondered why there are only a few buildings as tall as that?"

Trenton stared at the structure she was pointing toward. Most city buildings were two or three stories, tops. But now that he thought about it, each quadrant had four buildings that reached all the way to the top of the level. They were bigger around than the average building.

"So the pillars are hidden inside those," he said, feeling like someone had just revealed an extremely impressive magic trick he hadn't even realized was going on until that moment. "But why are they hidden?"

"Probably because buildings look better than a bunch of big columns of rock sticking up everywhere. Of course, there are also holes drilled all over the place to run pipe and wires and such."

Trenton nodded excitedly, feeling his heart race. "We can climb through the holes."

"Not even," she said. "There's barely enough room for the pipes. Every time there's a leak or a wire goes bad, they have to fish the whole thing out. It's pretty dumb."

"Then what was the point of telling me this?"

Kallista puffed out her cheeks and exhaled. "Because I thought you'd actually be interested in what's around you."

"Okay," Trenton said. "It *is* interesting. But how does it help us get down to the next level?"

Kallista drew a tube that ran straight up the center of all four levels before angling to the edge of the mountain. "You left out something that you see every day. Something kind of, I don't know, important, because it keeps us alive."

"The air-exchange pipe," Trenton blurted. How had he forgotten about that? It's what gave them the air they breathed. Running through all four levels and, at more than a hundred feet across, it was plenty big enough to climb down. "If we could get inside it, we could go to any level we want."

"We *could*," Kallista agreed. "Except A, there are iron grates between every level, and B, even if you managed to get inside, which is all but impossible, the exhaust fans are so strong, they'd suck you up like a pea through a straw and chop you into itty-bitty bloody pieces."

"*Then how are we supposed to get down?*" Trenton exploded. Kallista had to be the most irritating person he'd ever met.

She put her finger to her lips. "Listen."

Trenton took a deep breath and tried to control his temper. Tilting his head to the side, he listened. At this time of the evening, with businesses closed and most people inside eating dinner, the city was nearly silent. There was nothing to hear except . . .

There *was* something—a swishing sound. As if someone nearby were blowing through lips pressed almost close enough together to whistle. He looked around. The noise seemed to be coming from the mountain wall. Glancing up, he spotted a metal shaft running the length of the wall and through the ceiling.

"The pipe at the center of the city draws the bad air out," Kallista said. "The fans inside it create a huge suction. That's why no one is allowed to get too close to it. What most people don't realize is that the air coming from the outside is sucked in through vertical ducts located around the outside of each level. It just so happens that the ducts are almost exactly the right size for kids like us to climb in—both up and down. And the vents take all of about five minutes to unscrew."

"We're going to crawl inside an air duct?" Trenton asked.

"It's not too bad," Kallista. "I've done it before. Every ten feet, you can hold on to brackets and rest."

Trenton ran his fingers through his hair. "We'll be climbing through air from . . . *outside?*"

"Don't worry," Kallista said. "It's filtered before it ever gets to us." She folded her arms wrapped in her long black cloak. "But it *is* a bit cold."

• • •

She hadn't been kidding. The air blowing through the vent was so icy that the metal duct almost hurt to touch. Climbing down a few feet behind Kallista, he tried to keep his arms and legs from shivering. "W-why is it s-so freezing?"

"The air comes from the top of the mountain," Kallista called up. "My father says that there's something called *snow* up there almost year-round. It's like crystals of frozen water."

Climbing down the shaft was hard work. But even with the exertion, by the time they managed to work their way down to the third level—by pressing their backs against one side and their knees on the other—Trenton could barely feel his fingers. The hat and goggles protected his head and eyes, but his second shirt did nothing against the bitter-cold air that ran down the shaft in a constant gale.

Removing the vent from the outside had been a simple matter of removing the screws. It took Kallista longer to get the second vent off from the inside because she had to twist the screws out with a pair of pliers and then hammer them when they were unscrewed too far to grip. When the two of them finally climbed out on the third level, he was pretty sure he knew what it felt like to be an ice cube.

Kallista watched him stomp his feet and rub his hands. "Maybe next time you'll take my advice."

Trenton shivered, waiting for the warm air of level three to thaw him out. "M-m-maybe next t-time you'll t-t-tell m-me w-why."

"Some people learn from being told. Others need to experience things for themselves," Kallista said. "I get the feeling you're in the second group." She quickly screwed the vent back in place, then looked around. "I think the plant we want is that way."

Trenton followed her through a maze of square buildings and rumbling equipment. Unlike the food-production level, which had bright lights and pleasant smells, or the city, which had shops and parks, level three looked rough and smelled worse. The buildings were boxy and plain, and the warm, damp air stank of smoke and oil. Gears ground, chains clanked so loud they made his ears ring, and random flames occasionally shot into the air.

"Everything you dreamed it would be?" Kallista asked, glancing back at him.

Trenton grinned from ear to ear. "Even better."

This was the most amazing place he'd ever seen. His head swung left and right, taking in row after row of powerful machinery. The smell of oil was like perfume to him, and the clanking equipment was music to his ears. If he'd had any doubt of where he was supposed to be, this visit put an end to it.

Kallista watched him ogling the buildings and grinned. "How did a gearhead like you end up in food production?"

Trenton thought about telling her to mind her own business

before deciding that it didn't matter if she knew the truth. "My mother told the chancellor that I'm too dangerous to be allowed near machines."

She stopped and stared at him. "Your *mother*?"

Trenton shrugged.

"Why? What kind of danger could you be?" She shook her head. "What did you say to her when you found out? If one of my parents did that, I'd—I don't know what I'd do."

Listening to the rumble of a nearby engine, Trenton thought about how he could be learning to work on it, if only his mother hadn't gone to the chancellor. "I didn't say anything. She doesn't know I found out. At least not for sure."

"Are you kidding?" Kallista put her hands on her hips. "You *have* to talk to her. Tell her how you feel. Tell her—"

"It's not that easy," Trenton complained, cutting her off. He shook his head. "She's kind of messed up. From an accident, a long time ago." He wasn't sure why he was telling Kallista this when he didn't even know her that well, but he had to tell someone. "If I say anything, it could make things worse."

Kallista ran her fingers through her hair. "I'd give anything to talk to my mom or dad, even if it was only to argue."

"She's *not* your mom," Trenton said, feeling embarrassed and angry. "She's mine, and I don't want to talk about it anymore. Can we just go?"

Kallista turned around, and the two of them walked silently until they reached a large plant with two smokestacks rising out from the top. Although he'd never been inside one, Trenton knew it was a power plant. He'd read all about them. Coal was fed from the mines below up into a furnace that heated water into steam-powered massive pistons.

Kallista leaned against the wall and peeked around the corner. "Once we go inside, keep walking and look like you know what you're doing. Don't make eye contact with anyone unless you absolutely have to."

They waited until a couple of workers exited the building, then ran to the entrance. Trenton couldn't help stopping to stare. He could actually feel the rock vibrating under his feet from the pounding of the huge pistons.

Kallista reached for his goggles and adjusted them. "Take out a wrench or something. And try not to look like you just got your first taste of candy."

He tried to stop smiling, but it was hard. After his transfer request had been denied, he never thought he'd see an actual power plant. "What are we looking for?"

"No idea," Kallista said. "Some of my father's clues were easy to figure out when we played games, and some were really hard. The only consistent thing was that I always knew them when I found them."

"What do we say if someone stops us?" Trenton asked, watching a couple of workers moving around on the other side of the gate.

Kallista licked her lips. "Let's hope that doesn't happen."

Her hope didn't last long. They had barely walked through the front gate when footsteps sounded from behind them.

A uniformed man stepped around the corner, stopped, and eyed them. "What are you kids doing here?"

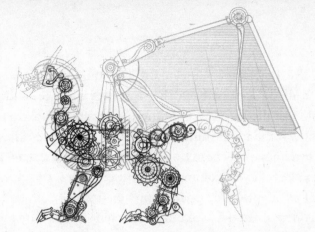

19

Trenton felt his throat seize up. He glanced at Kallista, but she was scowling at the ground.

"I asked you what you're doing here," the officer said.

Trenton held out his wrench. "We're here to, uh, make repairs. On the plant gears."

The man narrowed his eyes. "Where are your badges?"

Kallista took a badge out of her pocket and handed it to the officer.

He studied it for a second. "Says you're a repair tech in the city."

She swallowed. "I work on equipment wherever I'm sent."

The officer eyed her long coat and gloves. "You have a work order?"

She shook her head.

"Didn't think so." He pushed up her hat. "I know you. You're the inventor's kid. Babbage."

"Her name's Kallista," Trenton said.

The officer turned to him. "I recognize you, too. You're the kid who built the swing that nearly shut down the city. Marshal warned us to be on the lookout for you. Said you were apt to be up to no good." He looked from one of them to the other. "What a pair. Don't imagine you'd like to tell me how you got here with no work order."

"We took the elevators," Kallista said. "How else?"

"Really?" The man jeered. "Show me your pass."

Kallista looked back the way they'd come, and Trenton could tell she was deciding whether or not to make a run for it. That was the worst thing she could do. The officer knew both of their names *and* where to find them. Trenton gulped and tried to explain. "I was holding the work order and the elevator pass, but I accidentally dropped them when we got off, and they fell down the shaft. They're probably somewhere in the mines."

Kallista gawked at him.

The security officer didn't seem nearly as impressed. "We'll see about that." He waved at a man working inside the plant. "You know anything about these kids being sent to do repairs?"

The man shrugged. "Not my department. You'd have to ask the plant manager."

"Where is he?" the officer asked.

"*She*," the worker said. "This way." He turned and climbed a set of metal stairs.

The security officer waved a hand for the two of them to go ahead of him. "After you."

Trenton leaned toward Kallista, his feet clanking on the steps as they walked side by side. "What are we going to do?" he whispered.

Kallista frowned. "A couple of months of retraining, I'd guess. The marshal doesn't like me."

"That's it?" Trenton hissed. "Your plan was to climb down here and hope we didn't get caught?"

"I didn't hear you come up with anything better," Kallista said.

Trenton hung his head. This kind of thing was what always got him in trouble. He was a hard worker. He had good intentions and enough talent to do anything he set his mind to, but he didn't think things through. Maybe his mother had been right all along; he wasn't a good gear. He did things without considering about how they would affect everyone else. Being put in food production, where there were fewer things he could mess up, probably *was* best for him—and for the city. And now even *that* assignment might be lost.

At the top of the stairs, a narrow catwalk gave a clear view of the plant below. Even with as much trouble as he was in, Trenton still couldn't help but be fascinated by the equipment spread out beneath him. He scanned pressure gauges, feeders, rods, gears, and pistons and calculated how each piece worked, why it was placed where it was, and how the whole process might be improved.

No, he told himself. That was the kind of thinking that had gotten him on the wrong track. Instead of thinking of different ways of doing things, he needed to train himself to understand how and why things were done the way they were. He needed to stop trying to *fix* the machine and enjoy its magnificence.

"Wait here," the worker said. He knocked twice on a door, then went inside.

Trenton's mouth felt dry, and his stomach burned. Soon the security officer would know for a fact that they were lying. He'd take them up to the city offices. They might end up in the same locked room he'd been in when he swore that he'd never get in trouble again.

"I'm sorry," Kallista whispered. "I shouldn't have made you come with me."

"You didn't *make* me come," Trenton said. "If anything, I forced you to bring me." Looking into her wide eyes, he saw that she was at least as scared as he was. Why wouldn't she be? He'd been thinking about what getting caught could mean for him, but, no matter what happened, at least he had parents to support him. The only thing she had was her father's tools. If the authorities discovered the hidden room, they'd take those, too.

A few minutes later, the door opened and the worker stepped out. His eyes went from the security officer to Trenton and Kallista. "Miss Huber will see you."

Trenton followed the security officer into a small room. He'd expected the plant manager's office to be filled with tools. Instead, the walls were lined with shelves holding more books than Leo Babbage's workshop had—instructional manuals, books about parts, equipment documentation, and a broad selection of books on math, engineering, and science. Outside of the school, Trenton had never seen so much paper in one place in his life.

Sitting behind a metal desk was a woman with hair nearly as short as Kallista's, but while Kallista's hair was jet black, the woman's was mostly gray. She had a broad, open face with bushy eyebrows and a smear of grease down one cheek. Her arms were as thick as Trenton's father's and as heavily muscled.

"What do you want?" she asked, looking up from the work she was doing on her slate. Her tone was gruff, and her cold, blue eyes made it clear that she didn't like being interrupted.

The security officer coughed into his hand. "These, uh, kids say they were sent down to fix some something. Is that true?"

Miss Huber's brows drew down until her eyes all but disappeared. She pushed aside the slate and stared at the officer. "Does this look like the kind of place where children would be sent to 'fix something'?" She glared at Trenton's wrench and growled. "What are you planning to do with that, adjust my chair?"

The officer narrowed his eyes. "That's what I thought. Just making sure before I haul them to the security building."

"Do what you want with them." The woman waved one hand. "Get out of my office."

"Wait," Trenton said as the officer took him and Kallista by the arms. "This is my fault. Kallista has nothing to do with it. I was mad that I didn't get sent to mechanics school, so I tricked her into bringing me here by faking a work order."

She stared at him, dumbfounded. "No, you didn't."

"Yes, I *did!*" Trenton shouted. He was in trouble no matter what. It didn't make sense for both of them to suffer. He hated the idea of anyone finding the workshop and seizing the remaining pieces of whatever Leo Babbage had been working on. "It's my fault. Arrest me. Retrain me. Do whatever you want. I'm a bad cog; you already knew that. But let Kallista go."

"Oh, you'll get retraining," the officer said. "Both of you. And a lot more than that. Wouldn't be surprised if the two of you end up sweeping coal dust before the year is over." He grinned, seeming to enjoy the thought. Yanking them both by the arms, he dragged them toward the door.

Miss Huber popped out of her chair. "Wait."

The officer paused inside the doorway.

"What did you say the girl's name was?"

"You don't need to worry about her," the security officer said. "I'll handle things from here."

The manager marched around her desk and seized the man's shoulder, nearly lifting him off the floor. "You'll do nothing in my plant unless I tell you to."

What was she doing? A second ago, she didn't seem to care what happened to them.

"What's the girl's name?"

"I—that is—it's Babbage, ma'am," the man sputtered. "The inventor's kid. I have to take her in."

"You're not taking them anywhere unless I say so." Miss Huber's eyes turned into ice chips.

The officer tugged at his cap. "But they're trespassing, and off the city level without a pass. It's my job to arrest them."

"Who says they're trespassing?" Miss Huber asked.

"Y-you did," the officer said, clearly confused.

Trenton was confused too. What did this cranky old woman care about what happened to them?

The manager released the security officer and planted her hands on her hips. "I said nothing about trespassing. You wanted to know if these children had been sent for. I asked if this looked like the kind of place where kids would fix things. Obviously it is. How did your feeble brain not make the connection?"

The officer let go of Trenton and Kallista. "You're saying you *did* send for them?"

"Of course, you babbling fool!" the woman roared. "How else would they have gotten here? Are you telling me that your people would have let them get on an elevator and come all the way to my plant without the proper passes? What would your commander think of that?"

The man's face went white. "No. Of course not."

"Then I suggest you leave," Miss Huber said. "Get back to your rounds. We have work to do."

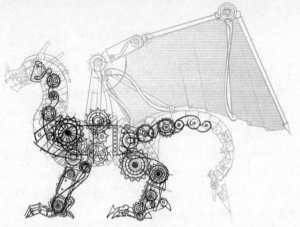

20

renton watched as the flustered security officer stomped out of the room and slammed the door behind him. He glanced at Miss Huber, nearly as terrified to be left alone with the rough-looking woman as he would have been to be dragged back to the city.

"Put that wrench away," the woman barked, "unless you're going to use it."

Trenton quickly shoved the tool into his belt.

"Thank you for helping us," Kallista said.

Miss Huber waved her hands and scowled at the two of them. "What are you *really* doing here?"

"I always wanted to see a—" Trenton began, but quickly shut his mouth at the woman's stony stare.

Kallista twisted her hands together. "My father wanted me to. I believe he left something in your plant for me—some kind of message."

The big woman pushed Kallista's goggles up and studied her face. "You look like Leo, and even more like your mother. I see it in the eyes and mouth."

"You knew my parents?"

"Natch. Everyone knew them." She patted Kallista on the shoulder. "I was so sorry when your mother passed. And then your father . . ."

"I still think about him all the time," Kallista said.

"Of course you do, dear." The woman walked behind her desk, placed her hands flat on its metal surface, and eased herself into the chair with a soft groan. "Sit," she said jabbing a blunt finger toward a couple of chairs stacked in the corner.

Trenton and Kallista took the chairs and sat down. Trenton still couldn't believe the woman had backed their story. "Why did you lie for us?" he asked.

Miss Huber pursed her lips and gave a look that under any other circumstances would have sent him running. "Lying takes you from the little pot of hot water to the cauldron of boiling water. I do not do it, nor do I recommend it."

Trenton slouched in his seat. "But you told the guard that you sent for us."

"I did nothing of the kind," she said, slamming her palm on the desk. "I told the featherbrain that you were sent here. Is *that* a lie?"

"No," Kallista said. "My father sent us."

Trenton couldn't help but smile. The plant manager was scary, but he had to admit that she was also smart.

Miss Huber frowned, a deep crease forming between her brows. "Do I want to know how you managed to get past security to reach my plant?"

Kallista shook her head.

"I thought not." The woman busied herself writing on her slate for several minutes until Trenton began to wonder if she'd forgotten that he and Kallista were there. He thought about coughing but was too scared.

"Your father was a *different* kind of man," Miss Huber finally said. "I can honestly say that this plant would not be running today, at least not as well as it is, if it weren't for his work."

Kallista leaned forward. "He repaired things here?"

Miss Huber chuckled. "*Repair* is the wrong word. Child, your father studied machinery the way a doctor studies the human body. He could walk into a plant, tap on this, listen to that, examining each and every moving part. He could tell you exactly what was out of sorts and how to get any machine running smoothly again. I'd venture to say he worked on half of the equipment in the city. No one ever asked Leo Babbage for *his* pass when he came and went."

Trenton couldn't believe how this woman was describing Kallista's father—the same Leo Babbage he'd always heard about, the crackpot inventor who'd killed himself by taking silly chances. The two stories didn't add up.

"If he was such a good mechanic, why did he work in a little repair shop? Why wasn't he assigned to be the head of maintenance?" he asked.

Kallista gave Trenton a dark look, but Miss Huber nodded. "I suggested that very thing more times than I can count. And I wasn't the only one. If he'd stuck to machines, he *would* have been in that position long ago."

Kallista took off her goggles. "What do you mean, *if he'd stuck to machines?*"

"As I said, Leo was a different man." The plant manager looked at the ceiling and sighed. "Most people who turn to working with machinery do so because they find engines easier to understand than people. Your father, on the other hand, saw through the workings of the human mind as easily as he could analyze a squeaky driveshaft."

"What's wrong with that?" Trenton asked, wishing he could understand people like he did machines.

"Just that he thought he could fix people the same way he fixed equipment. He didn't understand that you can't straighten bent motives with a hammer. You can't repair broken relationships with a wrench. He could see what people were thinking, but when it came to dealing with them, he was all thumbs."

Trenton glanced at Kallista out of the corner of his eye, wondering how she was reacting to all of this talk about her father. She unbuttoned her coat and wiped the perspiration from her forehead.

"My father wasn't very good at telling people how he felt. He, um, had a hard time in social situations."

"That's putting it gently," Miss Huber nodded understandingly. "He angered people in powerful positions because he saw through their stories. He angered them even more because he was far too blunt in pointing out their mistakes."

Kallista stared at her hands. Miss Huber seemed to realize the effect of her words. "Don't look so glum, child. None of us is perfect. Those who believe themselves to be without flaws are the worst of the bunch. Your father understood that he wasn't good at expressing himself with words. So he did it with actions, which brings us back to why you are here. You say you think your father left you something, yes?"

"The year before he died, he was working on a . . . project of some kind."

Miss Huber folded her meaty hands beneath her chin, her eyes serious. "This *project*. What do you know about it?"

Trenton held his breath, hoping Kallista would be careful. How much did they really know about this woman? Could they trust her? She could be working with the chancellor. The whole thing with the security guard could have been a setup.

If Kallista shared any of his doubts, she didn't show it. "He wouldn't tell me. But I think he wants me to find out now. He left clues for me." She leaned toward the desk. "Do *you* know what his project was?"

The plant manager's brows lowered until her eyes nearly disappeared. She seemed to consider her words carefully before speaking. "I think I may. Not precisely *what* he was working on, but *why* he was working on it. He came to me with a story that was so"—she waved her hands in the air—"so *outlandish*, so unlike Leo Babbage, that I couldn't believe he was serious. I told him so. But now I can't help wondering . . ."

"What was it?" Trenton nearly shouted. "What did he tell you?"

"Yes, what?" Kallista asked, both of them barely remaining on their chairs.

But Miss Huber shook her head. "No. He kept the project secret for a reason. I believe he regretted telling me as much as he did. Even if I knew the details, I wouldn't share them with you. He clearly believed that what he was doing was too dangerous to share. And so do I."

"Dangerous?" Trenton asked. "Like a weapon? You think he was trying to hurt someone?"

Kallista opened her mouth, but Miss Huber spoke first. "Leo Babbage was one of the gentlest souls I've ever known. I never saw him lay a hand on another person in anger. When I tell you that what he was working on was dangerous, I speak not of danger to others but to himself. He put himself into direct conflict with powerful people, and now . . ." She sniffed and shook her head. "I'm sorry. I can't help you."

"But he wanted us to come here," Kallista said. "He left something for us in your plant. I know it."

Miss Huber pushed her chair back from her desk and stood. "If he sent you here, I can only assume it was so I could tell you to stop your search. You may think you want to know what he was working on. But trust me, you do not."

Trenton bit the inside of his lip. He'd come here looking for answers. Now he was a little relieved they hadn't gotten them.

Kallista stood, her cheeks bright and her dark eyes glinting. "I don't *want* to know what my father was working on; I *have* to know."

"I'm sorry. I can't help you." Miss Huber walked to the door. "I'll have one of my staff escort you back to the city. Please don't come here again."

Trenton turned to leave, but Kallista refused to move. She glared at the plant manager. "You're lying. I know you are. My father left something for me, and I'm going to keep coming back until I find it. If you have me arrested, the first thing I'll tell them is that my father told you all about his project."

Kallista was shorter than the plant manager and weighed probably a third of what the woman did. But as Trenton watched the two of them glare at each other, he had no doubt as to who would come out on top in this battle of wills.

At last Miss Huber bobbed her head. "Very well." She crossed to a metal cabinet and knelt before it. The door had a series of dials and levers—it was a safe.

Miss Huber muttered as she worked the dials. "You're as stubborn as your father was."

"More," Kallista said with a smug grin.

Miss Huber pushed the final lever, and, with a loud click, the door swung open. She took out a cloth bag and set it on the desk with a clunk. "Several months before your father died, he gave me this package. He said that if anything happened to him, I should wait two years. If, during that time, his daughter came asking for the package, I should give it to her. If she did not come, or if anyone else asked for the package, I was to destroy it." She shook her head. "I thought it was a mistake then, and I still think so now. I wonder if I shouldn't have destroyed it the day I heard about his . . . accident."

"What is it?" Trenton asked. "What's inside?"

"I don't know," Miss Huber said. "He requested that I not open it, and I haven't."

• • •

The entire trip back to the workshop, Trenton thought about what the plant manager had said about Leo Babbage's project being dangerous. He didn't think the tough old woman could be scared of anything, but toward the end of their visit, he was almost positive he'd seen fear in her eyes.

What could be so dangerous that it scared a woman like her?

Kallista must have sensed his hesitation. "You don't have to stay," she said. "This was between my father and me. I won't blame you if you walk away."

Trenton eyed the package on the table. He knew he was walking a fine line between curiosity and stupidity, but he had to know what Leo Babbage had left behind. Maybe then he could decide whether to quit the search or keep going. He took a deep breath. "Open it."

Kallista reached into the bag. She took out another extending tube and a teardrop-shaped piece of metal that Trenton could instantly tell fit onto the bolts of the U-shaped piece. She turned the bag upside down above the workbench, and a small tube of paper fell out.

With trembling hands, she picked it up and unrolled it. "It's his handwriting," she said, quickly scanning the small sheet.

"What does it say?" Trenton asked, leaning over her shoulder.

She showed him the note. There was no mention of Kallista or a signature. Only two short lines.

Remember the time I took you to visit the house of the big guy's nine daughters? The hunger there has always bothered me.

Kallista shook her head. "Not even a *Love, Dad*."

"He didn't want anyone to know that it was a letter for you in case someone else got hold of it."

"Yeah," Kallista said. "That's probably it."

But Trenton thought he saw tears in her eyes. She looked away too quickly for him to be sure. "What does it mean?" he asked.

"I have no idea. I'll have to think about it. In the meantime, let's put these pieces together." She took the teardrop piece and fitted it into the U. Two nuts tightened the pieces together, and the last tube clicked into the back tip of the teardrop.

The entire thing was now more than eighteen inches long. With the three tubes in front and the one in the back extended, the pointed tubes held the device a good ten inches off the workbench.

"Look," Trenton said, pointing to the opening at the top of the teardrop shape. "See the gears and hydraulic connections inside? Whatever this connects to will have the ability to open and close the tubes, *and* rotate the whole thing forward and back. It's like a big metal hand."

"Not a hand." Kallista shook her head. "A foot. It looks like a . . ." She suddenly burst into laughter.

Trenton looked from her to the device, puzzled. "What's so funny?"

"Sorry," Kallista said. "It's just . . ." She giggled again, and Trenton couldn't help but join her, even though he had no idea what she was laughing about. She managed to stop giggling long enough to say, "It looks like my father built a metal chicken foot."

Trenton stared at the contraption. She was right. That's exactly what it looked like—a giant metal chicken foot. He quickly ran some numbers in his head. "If that's a foot, the chicken would have to be at least thirty feet tall." He clapped his hands to his mouth. "I'll have to tell food production to prepare for some really big eggs."

"Giant eggs!" Kallista hooted. "My father's secret project was providing enough scrambled eggs to feed the whole city."

They both laughed so hard they collapsed to the floor.

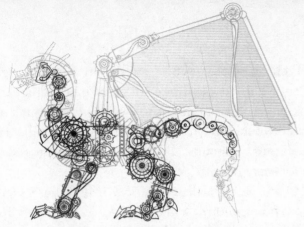

21

The next day, Simoni rushed up to Trenton as soon as he finished work. "Let's go," she said, handing him a leather satchel. "This is going to be so much fun."

"What's this?" he asked, hefting the satchel.

Simoni stopped, the smile disappearing from her face. "Tell me you didn't forget the picnic. You've been disappearing every day after work, but you promised."

The picnic. Of course. With his mind on giant chickens and the clue on Leo Babbage's note, Trenton had completely forgotten his promise to go to the orchard with Simoni and her friends today.

"I didn't forget," he quickly said. "I was just surprised that you already have the food." He hefted the pack, pretending it weighed more than it did. "What's in here, rocks?"

Simoni's smile returned. "You'll have to wait and see. But it's delicious. Come on." She broke into a trot. "Let's catch up with the others."

Trenton had been planning on going to the workshop to brainstorm about the clue with Kallista. Plus, he wanted to get another look at the foot. He had an idea that by calculating the size of the hydraulic line and the number of teeth in the gears, he might be able to estimate what it connected to as well as the strength of whatever powered it.

Still, he found himself getting caught up in Simoni's cheerfulness as she chattered about the latest gossip concerning the other food-production students. It turned out that two different girls liked Clyde—who'd have guessed *that*? Apparently Clyde was clueless. That much Trenton could have guessed. Another one of the students—a girl he didn't know well—had been caught smuggling fruit to her family and was sentenced to three days of retraining.

Walking beside Simoni in the fragrant orchard, Trenton realized he'd forgotten how much he enjoyed being around her. Unlike Kallista, who always seemed on the verge of punching him in the nose, Simoni was like a bright, bobbing flower.

"Here we are," Simoni said as they reached a group of eight others already gathered at a perfect spot to eat. The apple and pear trees were in bloom, and tiny petals covered the ground.

Trenton started to sit down before seeing that Simoni was giving him an expectant look. He glanced around quickly, wondering what he'd missed, and noticed the others had laid blankets out on the ground. Was he supposed to have brought a blanket? He should have thought to ask more questions.

"Inside the bag," Simoni whispered.

Trenton opened the satchel and saw a blue- and brown-checkered wool blanket. He breathed a sigh of relief. He spread it out beneath a couple of cherry trees.

Simoni grinned and sat down. "Thank you, kind sir."

"You're, um—welcome," he stammered.

As Simoni began taking food out of her bag, Trenton glanced at the other kids. A few of them had been in his school, although one graduated the year before. Several others he didn't know well; either they'd gone to different schools or he hadn't worked with them yet. Four boys and four girls all watched him.

"Are you just going to stand there?" Simoni asked.

"No. Uh, definitely not," Trenton said, stumbling over his words. He reached into the satchel and pulled out random items.

The meal included hard-boiled eggs, fresh breads, artichoke hearts, and a fruit salad with some kind of sweet and slightly nutty sauce. There were even little smoke-flavored sausages. If he could have done nothing at the picnic but sit and eat, it would have been perfect. The problem was, the others seemed to expect him to talk. And not just talk; he was supposed to say funny things.

Trenton had never been good at small talk. Ask him about a job or how to do something mechanical and he could speak as clearly as anyone. But when it came to jokes or amusing stories, he didn't have a clue. And he was pretty sure the others wouldn't see the humor of a giant chicken foot.

"How do like your training?" asked Arthur, the second-year student.

"Good," Trenton said, desperately trying to come up with something that would make them laugh. "A couple of days ago, I fell in the plankton tank."

The girl by Arthur frowned. "Plankton? How disgusting."

Not the reaction Trenton had been hoping for.

"You should have seen my shirt when I got home," he tried. "It was totally green."

The comment was met with complete silence. Knowing he needed to come up with something—and quickly—he remembered the clue on Kallista's note.

"I have a question for you all," he said. "Where do the nine daughters of the big guy live?"

"The big guy?" asked one of the other boys. "You mean the chancellor?"

"No one could have nine daughters," said a girl with long, nearly white hair and a pointy nose. "That's against the law."

Trenton shifted on his blanket. "Oh, no one in the city. It's a riddle. You know, like a clue to figure out. If someone gave you a note telling you to go to the house of the big guy's nine daughters, where would you go?"

"Nowhere," said Arthur. "Obviously, it would be a trick, since no one in Cove has ever had—or will ever have—nine children, sons or daughters."

Simoni smiled politely at Trenton. "So what's the answer to the riddle? Where is the home of the nine daughters?"

As everyone waited expectantly for Trenton's response, it occurred to him that he didn't actually know the answer. "You guys think about it for a while. I don't want to spoil it for you."

"Well, that was . . . *fun*," Arthur said. The group rather pointedly turned away from Trenton and Simoni and began a discussion about their various jobs in food production.

Trenton released a sigh of relief, grateful to have the awkward conversation ended.

"Let's go for a walk," Simoni said, disappointment shadowing her face.

As Trenton followed her through row after row of trees, he glanced at one of the grain silos that ran all the way to the ceiling—and counted three more. He immediately knew why they were there.

"The pillars," he said.

Simoni stopped to see what he was looking at. "The what?"

He pointed to the nearest silo. "Did you know that each quadrant has four stone pillars? They help keep one level from crashing down on the next."

Simoni squinted. "I don't see any pillars."

"That's because they're hidden inside the silos." He looked up and noticed several discolored spots on the stone ceiling by the silos, almost as if the rock had been patched. Maybe something had been attached to the ceiling there at some point?

"If you say so." Simoni shrugged. "Now, stop staring and come this way. I know a great place behind the hay bales."

Trenton followed her, but he couldn't stop staring at the rock above them. Now that he was looking for discolored spots, he noticed more and more of them.

"Isn't this perfect?" Simoni asked, pulling him down to sit beside her in the hay.

"Sure," he said. "A little itchy, though." He looked to his left and spotted the biggest mark yet. Something must have been attached to the ceiling, but he couldn't imagine what.

"What are you looking at?" Simoni asked.

Trenton pointed to the dark spot. "I'm wondering what used to be attached to the rock up there—probably a long time ago. This was the original level where our forefathers founded Cove."

Simoni pulled back. "Are you giving me a history lesson?"

"No." Trenton tore his gaze away from the ceiling. "I just thought it's, you know, *interesting* to understand more about where we live."

Simoni shook her head. "Remember what I told you about Clyde being clueless that someone liked him?"

"Sure," Trenton said.

"He's not the only one." Simoni moved closer and took his hand in hers.

• • •

By the time Trenton got off the elevator at level two, he was still in mild shock.

Simoni looked at him as they stepped through the gate. "You didn't mind holding hands?"

He swallowed hard. "No! I mean, I liked it. I'm glad you,

and me, that we . . ." He could feel his face turning redder and redder, so he quit trying to talk.

Simoni smiled and gave his hand a squeeze. "Good," she said. "Next time, don't be so clueless," she called over her shoulder, before running off.

Clueless, Trenton thought as he walked back toward his apartment. That's what he'd been, all right. *Simoni likes me.* How long had she felt that way? And why hadn't he realized it? He'd liked her since the second grade. But he didn't think she'd ever looked at him that way.

He checked his pocket watch and wondered if he had enough time to see Kallista and still get home on time. Maybe, if he hurried. He glanced around to make sure no one was watching, then started to jog.

Halfway to the repair shop, a uniformed figure stepped out of an alley. Trenton skidded to a halt.

"I know what you've been doing," a familiar voice said.

"Angus? Why are you wearing that security uniform?"

"It's my assignment." Angus gloated. "I'm in training to be a security officer. I've been watching you, and I know what you're up to."

Trenton tried to swallow, but his throat refused to obey. "You do?"

Angus closed in until the two of them were only inches apart. "You don't think anyone has seen the two of you sneaking around, but *I* have. And now the other officers will be keeping an eye out for you—and for her." He clenched his jaw. "I'll bet you're on the way to see her now."

Ice filled Trenton's chest. What had Angus seen? How long had he known? "It's not what you think."

"Let me guess," Angus said. "She feels alone and asked you to help her. You had no idea what you were getting into. But now you're interested, and you think I'm going to let you get away with it." With the sleeve of his uniform, he furiously polished his badge. "I'm not backing off. I'm going to do something about you two."

"What are you going to do?" Trenton asked, dreading the answer.

"I'm inviting her over for dinner."

"Wait, what?" Trenton thought he must have heard wrong.

"I'm inviting her to dinner," Angus said. "And if that's not enough to convince her I'm much better than you, I'll take her to the city offices. Introduce her to the chancellor himself, maybe. *You* can't do that, can you?"

Trenton stared at Angus. Was this some kind of joke? "Why would you take her to the meet the chancellor?" Maybe "take her to dinner" was some kind of security code term for retraining.

"Look," Angus said, his voice bordering on desperation, "I've always liked her. I don't know why she'd want anything to do with you."

Trenton wondered if he'd passed out at the picnic, if this was all part of a dream. "How do you even know Kallista?"

"Who?" Angus asked.

Trenton shook his head. "Who were *you* talking about?"

"Simoni, of course," Angus said. "I know you like her, and the two of you are never going to happen. You may as well give up now."

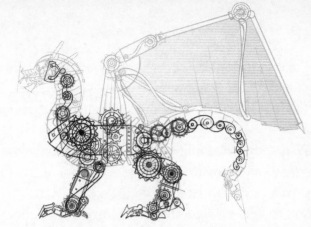

22

Trenton watched Angus disappear down the street, heart still thudding. *Simoni*. Angus had been talking about Simoni the whole time. Part of him wanted to burst into relieved laughter, and part of him wanted to burst into tears. He considered heading home and going to bed early, but he really wanted to find out what Kallista had learned.

He had just reached her shop when, for the second time that day, someone surprised him by stepping out of an alley. This time, he actually jumped, a squeak forcing its way between his lips.

Dressed in a knee-length leather jacket covered with brass buckles and a hat made almost entirely of springs, gears, and wire, Kallista edged up beside him and hissed, "I saw you talking to that security officer."

Trenton put his hand to his chest. "Does everyone have to jump out of the shadows?" He stared at her outfit. "What's with the hat? Did a clock explode on your head?"

"Forget the hat." She glanced anxiously around. "Who was the security officer? Does he know what we're doing?"

"No." Trenton thought through what she'd said and tilted his head. "How did you know about what happened with Angus? Have you been following me?"

"You know his *name*?" She narrowed her eyes. "What did he want?"

Trenton tried to get his breathing back under control, but it wasn't easy. "I think he wanted to take you on a date."

"What?" Kallista's cheeks reddened. "What are you talking about?"

Trenton released a laugh that felt far too close to panic. "It didn't have anything to do with you. He likes a girl we went to school with and wanted some dating advice."

Kallista arched an eyebrow. "From *you*? I've never pictured you as much of a ladies' man."

"Really?" Trenton asked, feeling more than a little offended. "It so happens that I was at a picnic after work today. With a girl."

Kallista's eyebrow lowered. "What girl?"

"Sorry." Trenton huffed. "It's private."

"Whatever," she said. "It was probably that redhead you were talking to at graduation. I didn't come here to talk about your love life."

"What *did* you come here to talk about?" Trenton asked. "Why were you following me?"

Kallista interlaced her fingers and cracked her knuckles. "I figured out my father's clue. I was waiting to tell you, but apparently you had better things to do."

"Seriously? You solved it already? Who's the big guy, and where do his daughters live?"

"Come on. I'll show you." Kallista started toward the shop. "I have a few minutes until I have to leave."

"Where are you going?" Trenton asked, but Kallista was already halfway down the alley. He followed her through the window and into her father's workshop, where at least a dozen books were spread across the counter. He picked one up and flipped through it before realizing the pages were filled with stories about make-believe animals and fictional people. He dropped the book like a burning coal.

Kallista clucked her tongue against the roof of her mouth. "I told you; they're from before Cove was founded, so they aren't illegal."

Maybe that was true, but Trenton had never seen books about imaginary creatures—not even at the school library—and he felt uncomfortable around them. It was one thing to alter a machine a little; it was another thing entirely to make up stories or pictures of things that had never existed. That was *creativity*, pure and simple. He wanted nothing to do with it.

Kallista sat on a stool. She picked up a thick book and opened it to a drawing of a man wearing what looked like a bedsheet. "This is the 'big guy' my father was talking about. His name is Zeus."

Trenton had never heard the name. "Who is he?"

"A Greek god." Kallista shifted from one foot to the other, clearly excited. "My father was big into mythology, stories made up a long time ago about a bunch of gods and goddesses that lived in a place called Mount Olympus."

So far, none of it made any sense. Trenton was pretty sure they'd learned about the Greeks in school, but if they'd ever covered this *mythology* stuff, he didn't remember it. He leaned over to see the picture more clearly. "What's that he's holding?"

"A lightning bolt," Kallista said with a grin. "The thing about nine daughters sounded familiar, so I started looking through my dad's books. It wasn't until I saw this picture that I remembered he used to call Zeus 'the big guy with the lightning bolt.' And then I remembered that in the stories, nine of Zeus's daughters were known as the muses. They're the ones we're supposed to go see."

Trenton tilted his head. "We're supposed to go to *Mount Olympus?*"

"No. See, Zeus lived on Mount Olympus," Kallista said. "But his daughters didn't. They lived in a temple on Mount Helicon."

Was she messing with him? Trenton couldn't tell. "So, we're going to a temple?"

"In a way." Kallista flipped to another section of the book, which she'd marked with a screwdriver. "In the note, my father said that he took me to visit the house of the nine daughters. Of course, we never went to Mount Helicon, but I finally figured out what he meant. The house of the nine daughters was the temple of the muses." She tapped a picture of a rectangular building with large, stone pillars.

"I still don't get it."

Kallista laughed. "I didn't either at first. So I did a little more research. Turns out that the Greek word for the muses' temple is *Mouseion*—which also happens to be where we get the English word for—"

"*Museum*," Trenton said. "He hid the next piece in the museum."

Kallista nodded. "We used to go there all the time. He used to say that the best way to know someone is to see what they focus on from their past."

Trenton looked at the mechanical clock in the corner. It was almost seven thirty. "The museum closed half an hour ago."

"Exactly why we're going now," Kallista said. "I want to look around without anyone watching us."

• • •

Trenton rubbed his palms on the front of his pants as he followed Kallista. The road to the museum, which was normally filled with pedestrians and people riding bicycles, was now almost deserted. The lights were dim, and even the trolley had stopped running.

"Maybe we should come back tomorrow."

Kallista shot him a dark look. "I'm getting the next piece tonight. If you don't want to come, feel free to leave."

"I want to go with you." Trenton checked the time. "It's just that my parents were pretty upset about how late I came home last night. If I'm late again, they'll throw a fit."

"Is it them you're worried about getting in trouble with? Or your girlfriend?" Kallista took long, quick strides.

"*Girlfriend?*" Trenton caught up with her. "You mean Simoni? What does she have to do with anything?"

"So it *was* Red," Kallista said without looking back. "Clearly it was more important to spend time with her after work than help me look for clues."

Trenton's legs were shorter than hers, so he had to jog to keep up. "Are you mad about something?"

"I'm not mad," Kallista snapped. "Learning what my father was doing is important to me. I thought it was important to you, too. But if your mind's on some girl, I don't know that I can trust you."

"You can," Trenton said.

They stopped by a wall, and Kallista peeked around the corner to make sure no one was in sight before quickly crossing the street. She shoved her hands into the pockets of her coat. "When that security officer caught us yesterday, you tried to take the blame. Why?"

The abrupt change in topic caught Trenton off guard. He shrugged. "I guess I didn't see the point in both of us getting in trouble."

Her eyes darted toward him, then away. "Did you feel sorry for me?"

Trenton had expected Kallista to take more of the back routes that she seemed to know so well, but she was walking straight toward the museum. What was she thinking?

"No, I don't feel sorry for you," he said. "Well, maybe, a little. What does it matter?"

Kallista slammed a fist into her palm. "It matters to me. I already have too many people feeling sorry for me, the poor little orphan girl, daughter of the lunatic inventor. Poor little thing never went to school. Never had a proper upbringing. I don't want anyone else feeling sorry for me, so if pity is the reason you're doing this, I don't want your help."

"I don't feel sorry for you. Not like that," Trenton said, wishing he'd stayed home. "Half the time, I don't even like you. You're a know-it-all and a pain in my neck. You have a terrible temper, and you do things without thinking. The only reason I'm doing this is because I want to know what your father was building."

Kallista stopped and looked at him. "You think I'm a pain in the neck?"

"Sometimes," Trenton said, bracing himself in case she was going to punch him again.

Instead, she grinned. "Excellent. Let's get inside the museum."

Trenton rolled his eyes. He really needed to stick to machines.

Although the building was clearly closed, Kallista marched straight up to the doors as if she belonged there. She knocked, waited for a minute, and jiggled the knob.

"You know it's locked, right?" Trenton asked, sure they'd be arrested any second.

Kallista pulled a pair of wires out of her hat. "Good thing a 'clock exploded' on my head." She slid the wires into the knob and fiddled with the lock.

"You're seriously going to break into a city building?" Trenton asked. "Do you have any idea how much trouble we'll be in if we get caught?"

"More trouble than we'd get in if someone found out we climbed down the air vents to the third level? More trouble than we'd get in if they found out we were assembling parts Leo Babbage left behind?"

"How do you know there isn't a guard on the other side of that door?"

Kallista knelt down to get a better look. "We knocked, and no one answered. Besides, if someone stops us, we'll just say we're solving the city's food problems by building a giant chicken."

Trenton couldn't help snickering. "Did your father teach you how to pick locks?"

"He was a repairman," Kallista said. "You'd be amazed how often people lose their keys or lock them inside their homes. Can I help it if the skill also comes in handy for breaking into other places?"

A few seconds later, a clicking sound came from inside the knob, and Kallista swung the door open. Trenton had been in the museum many times, both with his school classes and his family. Then, it had mostly been boring. Now, with the overhead lights out and the only illumination coming from the displays, it was a little bit creepy.

"What are we looking for?" he whispered.

"I don't know," Kallista said, walking softly along the hallway. "The second part of the note said, 'The hunger there has always bothered me.' That could be taken literally, or it could be more misdirection to throw off anyone else who might read the note."

"Great," Trenton said. "I'll keep an eye out for a green salad."

Kallista made a face. "Ha-ha."

Hunger, Trenton thought. The museum had plenty of that documented. The starvation of the people who founded Cove often showed up in their paintings and writings. Technology-caused pollution had destroyed crops, and disease had made most animals inedible.

Kallista moved along one wall, tapping her fingers every so often. Trenton assumed she was looking for a secret compartment. After a few minutes, she climbed the stairs leading to the podium with the *Book of Chancellors* on it.

"What are you doing?" Trenton shouted, pulling her back.

"What does it look like I'm doing?" She yanked herself out of his grasp and began flipping through the pages of the ancient volume. "Looking for clues."

"You aren't supposed to touch that."

No one but the current chancellor was allowed to touch the book, but Trenton found himself glancing over her shoulder as she turned to the very first page. And there it was—the actual handwriting of the very first leader of Cove. Three full paragraphs describing people nearly starving to death that first year as they struggled to get the farms up and running—how they built the first fish tanks and planted seeds.

"I worked on that," Trenton said.

Kallista gave him an amused look. "*You* worked on the *Book of Chancellors?*"

"Of course not. I worked on the first fish tank ever built here. It's where I found the parts your father hid."

"Good for you." Kallista turned the book to the current page and hopped off the podium.

"There's one thing I don't understand," Trenton said, following her.

"How to be quiet while searching?"

"Very funny." Trenton went to the display cases containing

the writings of the original settlers. "According to these, the people who founded Cove had no food. So where did they get the seeds to plant and animals to breed?"

"What are you blabbering about?" Kallista asked, annoyed.

Trenton rapped on the glass covering a painting of stick-thin people planting seeds in the first hydroponic troughs. "Up on level one, they have almost every kind of plant and animal you can imagine. But according to the *Book of Chancellors*, they were starving. How did they get all of the seeds and healthy animals they have now? Also, how did they survive when—"

"Look," Kallista said, cutting him off.

Trenton moved down to the display case she was staring at. It contained a document written by one of the city's founders. The paper was roughly fourteen inches wide by twenty inches tall. Over time, the ink had faded and smudged a little on the corners.

"What does that look like to you?" Kallista asked, pointing a finger at the bottom right corner.

Trenton leaned in to get a better view. "There's something under it."

Kallista gripped the side of the case and pried the metal from the glass.

"What are you doing?" he said. "That paper is extremely fragile. There has to be a better way to open the case."

Kallista yanked on the case until it came lose. After pushing up on the glass, she slipped two fingers inside to tweeze whatever was beneath the letter. Trenton held his breath as she slid it out. Only when she managed to get the second document free did he let himself exhale.

"What are you doing?" he shouted. "Do you know what's going to happen when someone discovers what you did to one of the most cherished documents in history?"

But Kallista wasn't listening. The paper she was holding was roughly the same size as the document in the case, but it was folded into fourths. By the time she unfolded it, the document was nearly three feet wide and four feet tall.

Trenton stepped toward her. "What is it?" he asked, his mouth dry. "It looks like plans . . ."

The words died in his mouth as he leaned closer and saw what was on the paper. It was a set of plans, all right—the schematics for what her father had been working on. What *they* had been putting together.

It was a machine, but not only a machine. It *was* a weapon—just like he'd feared. But not only a weapon. It was . . .

Well, he didn't know exactly *what* it was. If the plans had been drawn up by anyone other than Leo Babbage, Trenton would have considered them a joke. But if there was one thing he'd learned about Kallista's father, it was that the man did not seem to have possessed a very refined sense of humor.

The plans were no joke. They were real. Though why he would have drawn them up and what he expected his daughter to do with them was beyond understanding.

The plans on the page—shown in surprisingly great detail— were for building a creature that looked like it had come directly from the pages of one of the storybooks in Leo Babbage's workshop. Trenton studied the powerful, clawed legs, the broad wings, and the sharp-toothed mouth.

"What is that thing?" he whispered.

Kallista held the plans up, eyes filled with wonder. "It's a dragon."

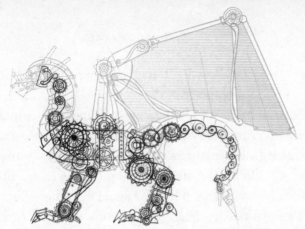

23

Trenton paced the workshop, running his hands through his hair. "I don't know why you're still wasting time on this."

"It's *my* time," Kallista barked, looking up from her slate. "I can do what I want with it."

It had been over two weeks since they'd found her father's plans, and Trenton couldn't believe she was taking them seriously. He'd stopped by before work to see if she'd finally given up on the project. Clearly she hadn't.

He dropped onto a stool and rested his elbows on the workbench. "So many things are wrong with this; I can't begin to count them."

Kallista stared at him, her lips narrowed.

"Fine. I'll count them." He held up one finger. "First, you're talking about something out of a *story*." He swept his hands over the books Kallista had spread across the workbench. Each was opened to a picture of what Kallista called a *dragon*. Apparently her father had a thing for the make-believe beasts because there were more than a dozen pictures of them burning buildings, devastating cities, and soaring through the air. "They aren't real," he sputtered, amazed that he had to say it.

"*They* aren't," Kallista said. "But this one *can* be. It *will* be. I'm going to build it."

"With what?" Trenton held up another finger. "That's my second point. You want to build this *creature*, but all you have is a foot. *One* foot. You don't even have a pair of feet. What good are the plans with no parts?"

Kallista shoved aside her slate and unrolled the plans, which she and Trenton had pored over for hours. "The parts are listed here, along with instructions for how to put them together. My father wouldn't have left the plans if there weren't already parts to go with it. All I need to do is figure out where he hid them."

Trenton put his head in his hands. "Do you hear how you sound? We're talking about a thirty-foot-tall steam-powered . . ." He couldn't bring himself to say the word.

"Thirty-three feet, six inches," Kallista said. "A thirty-three-foot *dragon*."

"Exactly." Trenton curved his fingers into claws. "It's one thing to hide a few talons inside a mattress or under a sink. It doesn't make any sense, but at least it's possible. Do you honestly believe there's a metal head taller than you and that it's hidden somewhere in the city where no one's noticed it for a year?" He pulled the plans toward him. "I have no doubt that your father drew these up. And who knows—it could even work. But he clearly didn't get a chance to finish making the parts."

Kallista took the plans away from him. "If he didn't finish making them, *I* will."

They'd been over and over this. He nodded toward the map she kept updating on her slate. "How many smelting plants have you checked now?"

She looked away. "Six."

"And how many have the ability to make the metal your father machined the pieces from?"

Kallista didn't answer. She didn't need to; he'd seen the map. She'd taken every repair job on level three that she could get, and she'd visited every plant with the ability to turn ore into metal. She'd carefully asked questions at each one, looked around for anything unusual, and checked their finished products. Not one had the ability to make anything other than steel, iron, copper, or brass.

Trenton got up from the stool and touched her shoulder. "Are there any other plants left to check?"

She shook her head.

"Then why do you keep trying?" he asked. "Even if you could find the place he had the metal smelted, and even if you figure out a way to make the parts, where would you build it? There's nowhere in Cove you could assemble a giant *dragon* without people noticing. Even if you could, what would you do with it? Can you imagine what the chancellor would do if he walked out of City Hall and saw a dragon flying overhead?"

Kallista's lips pulled up a little. It wasn't much of a smile, but it made Trenton happy anyway. "I'd dive-bomb him," she said. "Knock that monocle right out of his eye."

Trenton chuckled. "We could breathe flames on him and melt his stupid walking stick to slag."

"*We?*" Kallista folded her arms. "I thought you didn't believe in making the dragon."

He raised his hands. "I don't. But if you *did* manage to build it, you couldn't fly it by yourself. Look at the plans—two seats, one in front of the other, and two sets of controls."

Kallista looked over the plans. "I could change that if I combined the wing stick control with this one and added an extra foot pedal here."

"It would never work. The person in front has to control the direction, legs, and head. The one in the back handles altitude, tail, coal feeder, and flames. No way could one person handle all of that at the same time."

Kallista shook her head. "I could automate the coal feeder, and who cares about the tail?"

"You think you can improve on your father's design?"

Soon the two of them were lost in discussions of wing strength, landing options, and a hundred other nuances. Trenton had no doubt that Leo Babbage had been crazy when drawing up the plans, but he was a crazy genius. Trenton had never seen a machine this complicated—or this brilliant. How the man had come up with the idea in the first place was beyond him. That didn't change the fact that it was a useless design that could never be built.

He glanced from the plans to his pocket watch—he was late for work. How had the time passed so quickly?

"I gotta go," he said, jumping up from his chair. "Seriously, though, stop wasting your time on this."

"I'm *not* wasting my time," Kallista said. "My father built those parts somewhere, somehow. I *will* figure it out. All I need are better maps."

"Where are you going to get them?" Trenton called, running across the basement to the window.

Kallista slapped her hand on the workbench. "I know just the place. The city offices."

Trenton stopped halfway through the window and looked back. "You are not breaking into City Hall."

She only grinned, and Trenton shook his head. Like father, like daughter.

But if she was going, so was he.

"Don't go until I get back from work," he said before boosting himself into the alleyway behind the shop.

He ran all the way to the elevator. By the time he reached it, the car was empty.

"The other students went up fifteen minutes ago," the security officer said. "You're late."

"Thanks for letting me know," Trenton muttered. Fidgeting

the whole way to the top level, he checked his pocket watch. This was the second time in a week he'd been late. One more time and he'd get a permanent mark on his employee record. That could have an impact on what position he ended up with after his training.

As much as he hated the idea of being a farmer, there was no changing his future. If he had to be stuck in food production, he didn't want to end up processing plankton or cleaning up after cows for the rest of his life.

The moment the gate opened, he raced to potato processing, where he was assigned for the day. As he ran panting to his station, he realized something was wrong. Instead of the usual joking, everyone worked with their heads down, their attention focused on the potatoes they were peeling. Trenton looked for their teacher, wondering if this was about him being late, but there were no adults in sight.

"Where have you been?" Simoni asked, yanking him into line next to her and handing him a bag.

"Sorry," Trenton said. "I couldn't find my . . ." He thought furiously. "My apron. It fell behind my bed last night." His lying skills had improved considerably since meeting Kallista, which probably wasn't a good thing. Glancing over his shoulder, he asked, "Has anyone noticed?"

"No," Simoni said. "Everyone's been focused on Clyde."

"Clyde? Why?" Trenton asked. He looked around, but his friend was nowhere in sight. "Where is he, anyway?"

Simoni wiped her eyes with the back of her glove. "Security took him on the way here. Everyone's saying he's been sent to retraining."

Trenton's stomach went cold. "What did he do?"

Simoni pulled a potato from the bracket suspending it in the water and shoved it into Trenton's hands. She looked quickly around and whispered, "He was caught being creative on the way up in the elevator. I saw him writing something on his slate, but I didn't think anything of it. He's always taking notes. The security officer running the elevator must have seen something more because he snatched the slate out of Clyde's hands before he could erase it."

He remembered how Clyde had fixed the schematic of what Trenton now understood was a dragon's foot. He knew what Simoni was going to say next. "It was a drawing, wasn't it? A *creative* drawing?"

Simoni nodded and fought back a sob. "They pulled him out of work and took him back down the elevator. None of us could do anything to stop it." She shook her head. "Why would he do something like that?"

"I don't know," Trenton said, squeezing the potato until he thought it would burst. But what if Clyde felt the same way about drawing that Trenton felt about building things? What Clyde had done couldn't be half as bad as what Trenton and Kallista had been doing.

Putting his head down, he tried to push thoughts of Clyde and the dragon out of his mind and concentrate on bagging potatoes. By the time lunch rolled around, he'd picked more potatoes than anyone, even though he'd started late. But even working hard wasn't enough to stop him from thinking. If anyone here deserved retraining, he did.

As the other kids headed to lunch, Trenton tucked his gloves into his apron and walked in the opposite direction.

"Where are you going?" Simoni asked.

"I'm not hungry. I'm going to take a walk."

Simoni hurried to join him. "I'll go with you."

Together they went past the greenhouses and around the fish tanks to where the rock wall marked the edge of the level. There, they turned right and continued the same circuit Trenton had been slowly walking over the last few weeks.

"You come out here a lot," Simoni said. "I see you during lunch and after work."

Trenton hadn't realized she'd been paying any attention. "This is the original level of the city. I've been looking the spot where the founders first tunneled into the mountain."

"Why?" Simoni brushed her hair over one ear and shivered. "They sealed that off. Otherwise the outside air would have poisoned us."

"I know," Trenton said. "But there has to be some sign of where the entrance used to be. I can't help wondering about those people. I know they built the city to get away from creativity and inventions. But weren't they being creative themselves by building all of this?"

"Don't say that," Simoni said, squeezing his arm. "Do you want to be sent to retraining too?"

"No." Trenton shook his head. "But I can't stop myself from wondering how it all started."

"You should go to the museum. They have lots of information about the men and women who founded the city."

Trenton groaned. He'd found information in the museum, all right. But not the kind she was thinking of.

Simoni reached down and took his hand in hers. "You think differently from most people."

"I don't mean to. I guess my brain just doesn't work like everyone else's. I'm curious about things. I'm trying to change, though."

"I wasn't saying it's bad," Simoni said. "I mean, obviously we have to be careful of where curiosity can lead us. Creativity and change are what got us into the situation we're in now. But you're right; the people who designed the city must have had *some* curiosity, or they never would have come here to escape the sickness, right?"

Trenton met her eyes. "Yeah. They must have."

"The important thing is to keep those kinds of thoughts in here," she said, tapping his head. "If Clyde had kept his pictures in his mind instead of putting them on his slate, he wouldn't have been arrested."

At the thought of Clyde, who was one of his few friends, Trenton felt guilty all over again. He hoped everything would be okay.

"Ebony's pretty broken up," Simoni said. "She really likes Clyde, and I think he likes her."

"Yeah?" Trenton asked.

Simoni nodded. She moved closer, and their shoulders brushed together. "I know this is a bad time to ask, but I have to know. Do you like me?"

Trenton nearly tripped. "Yeah. Sure."

"Like or *like?*" She looked at him with her deep-green eyes, and he could barely breathe.

Unable to speak, he nodded.

Simoni stopped and turned toward him. "Angus wants to be more than a friend with me. He says so all the time. He's cute, but not nearly as interesting to talk with as you."

Was she saying he *wasn't* cute?

"Do *you* want to be more than friends?" she asked.

"I . . ." Trenton swallowed hard, and for some reason, Kallista's face popped into his head. That was dumb. He and Kallista were barely even friends, and definitely nothing more. "I'd *like* that."

"Good," Simoni said. "I'd like that too."

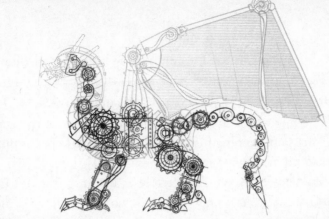

24

Having skipped lunch, Trenton was starving that night, and he couldn't stop worrying about Clyde. Part of him wanted nothing more than to eat dinner and go to bed. But he knew Kallista would be more than happy to break into the city offices on her own. With her heavy-handed tactics, she'd probably rip the whole place apart if he wasn't there to stop her. Also, his father would be home from the mines any minute, and his parents had been giving him odd looks lately.

Running through the kitchen, he saw that the table was already set.

"You aren't staying for dinner?" his mother asked.

"Can't," he said, grabbing two pieces of bread and shoving a chicken breast between them. "I have to study with some friends."

"What friends?" his mother asked. "Do I know them?"

"Probably some of them." He yanked the door open and shot through. "Don't wait up."

"Your father and I want to talk with you," his mother called after him. "You keep coming home so late."

He slammed the apartment door—pretending not to hear her—and raced out before his father could arrive home. Trenton had a pretty good idea what his parents wanted to talk about. *That* was a discussion he hoped to put off as long as possible.

Kallista was waiting for him outside his apartment building with her top hat on and a pack slung over one shoulder. She folded her arms, eyeing the slapped-together sandwich. "You're late."

"Why does everyone keep telling me that?" he grumbled around a bite.

"Maybe because you're terrible at keeping track of time." Kallista spun around and walked down the street. "Which is almost as bad as talking with your mouth full."

Trenton finished his sandwich and brushed his hands on his shirt as he ran to catch up. "What's in the pack?"

"Things we may need."

When they turned up Main Street, Trenton felt as exposed as he had the night they broke into the museum. It was one thing to sneak through back alleys. It was something much different to sneak into the most important building in the city.

As they passed through the shadow of a building, Kallista turned to look at him. "Is everything all right? You look tense."

He ran his fingers through his hair. "My friend was arrested today for drawing a picture."

"What a danger to us all." Kallista sneered. "I'm surprised the magnificent machine that is our city hasn't stopped functioning completely."

Trenton didn't feel like arguing. Mostly, he felt sick over Clyde's arrest. "Are you sure you want to do this? I've explored almost all of level one over the last few days, and there's no place there your father could have built anything as big as the dragon. You know the city better than I do, and I'm guessing you've explored most of level three by now. All that leaves is the mines, and no one could build anything down there without the miners noticing. What do you hope to find on a map?"

"If I knew what I was looking for, I wouldn't have to find

the map. I told you, my father didn't do anything without a reason. He wants me to figure out where he built the pieces."

"You keep saying that," Trenton said. "But if your father did everything for a reason, why did he design a mechanical dragon in the first place?"

"To make you ask dumb questions," Kallista sniped.

She was smarter than that. She was only pretending not to understand.

"You know very well that there's no possible reason for designing a thirty—no, a *thirty-three-and-a-half*—foot dragon inside a city built in a mountain. What could we possibly do with it? It would be like giving a steak to a man with no teeth."

They paused outside the main city square. Even with the offices closed, plenty of people were coming and going. And standing right in front of the entrance to City Hall, was not one, but two security officers.

"Looks like we need another plan," Trenton said.

Kallista tilted the top hat forward on her head. "I'm going around back to find another entrance. Since you're obviously toothless, you can stay here and gum your steak."

Why did he bother hanging around with her when he could be with Simoni, who was so much nicer? Biting back a nasty response, he followed her around the outside of the square to the back of the building. He secretly hoped there was no back entrance so he could say something witty about listening to him more often. Unfortunately, they found a single metal door, and no security in sight.

At least Kallista didn't say anything rude before pulling out her picks and going to work on the lock. But she did appear to be smirking as she worked. Apparently the locks on City Hall were stronger than the ones at the museum. As the minutes passed, Trenton grew increasingly anxious. Did the officers spend all night at the main entrance? Or did they occasionally make trips around the building, where they would discover two kids trying to break in?

"What's wrong?" he whispered. "Why can't you open it?"

"Because some annoying boy keeps whispering in my ear," she snapped.

Trenton bit the inside of his cheek, shifting from foot to foot. His eyes swept left and right, waiting for someone to come around a corner. Sweat dripped down the back of his neck, soaking into his shirt.

"If you don't stop that dancing, I'm going to shove one of these picks up your nose," Kallista said.

It was all Trenton could do to not yank the hat off her head and stomp it flat. "Clearly you inherited your father's social skills."

She took the picks out of the lock and shoved them toward him. "You want to try?"

"I don't know how," Trenton said.

"Right. Because my father didn't teach *you*; he taught *me*." Kallista was so angry that her hands shook. "Maybe he didn't teach me how to talk nicely or make friends with other kids. Maybe he didn't teach me that it isn't polite to say whatever I think. And maybe those things make me a bad person. But he *did* teach me everything I know. And even though he never said he loved me, I loved him."

She brushed at her eyes, and Trenton felt terrible.

"I loved my father, and I trusted him," she said. "I'm sick of having you tell me that he was sick or wrong or a killer. Either you trust him too, or you walk away right now and you don't come back. I won't listen to you say another word against him."

She glared at Trenton, tears streaming down her face.

Trenton dropped his head. "You're right. I've been a jerk."

He shoved his hands in his pockets. "I'm sorry. I won't say another bad thing about your dad. I want to stay, and I want to help you. But if you want me to leave, I'll go."

They stared at each other for several seconds; the whole time, Trenton was sure she'd tell him to leave. With all of the bad things people had said about her father, how could he have added to her pain?

Kallista lowered the picks. "I don't want you to leave."

"I want to stay," Trenton said.

She smiled. "I'm glad."

Two minutes later, the lock clicked open.

Tiptoeing through the halls, they peeked into room after room. They were able to eliminate most of them quickly. They had only desks, slates, and personal items—nothing of interest. A few of the rooms had filing cabinets, but the papers and slates inside weren't anything they needed.

They came across several maps, but none any more detailed than what they already had. At the end of one hall was a door that looked more solid than the others. Trenton tried the knob, but it didn't turn.

"Locked," he said.

That was odd. None of the other offices they'd checked even had locks on the doors, which made sense; theft was extremely rare in Cove. The idea of being a thief made Trenton feel guilty that he was the exception to the rule, but he tried not to think about that. After all, they were here to look, not take anything. At least that's what he told himself.

"It's not just locked; it's triple locked," Kallista said.

Trenton studied the door. The knob itself was locked. Plus there were two dead bolts, one at the top of the door, and another at the bottom.

Kallista pulled a mining helmet out of her pack. "Someone

really doesn't want us to get in there." She lit her helmet lamp and examined the locks under the bright light. "Guess what, though. We aren't the first ones to try getting in here."

"What?" Trenton knelt beside her, and she pointed to several faint lines in the metal.

"See these scratches? They were made by lock picks. You don't get those from using a key. Someone's picked this before."

"Do you think it was . . ."

"My father wasn't the only one who could pick locks," Kallista said. "But he's the only one I can think of who might have picked a locked door inside City Hall."

It didn't take her nearly as long to open this door as the last one, maybe because she'd seen how the other lock worked, or maybe because it had been picked before. Either way, she'd been working on the knob for only a minute or two when the lock clicked open. The ones on the top and bottom went even faster.

She pushed the door, and Trenton stared at what was inside. He pressed his tongue against the roof of his mouth, which suddenly felt too dry. "Are those what I think they are?"

Kallista walked into the room and shined her light across shelf after shelf of books, paintings, pencil sketches, and reams of paper covered with tight lines of handwriting.

Feeling sick to his stomach, Trenton stepped forward and looked at a few of the drawings. He'd been hoping to find schematics. Instead he found portraits and landscapes, paintings of people with wings on their backs, and some paintings that were nothing but blobs of color arranged in odd and unsettling ways.

Turning away, he thought he saw someone standing to his right and was shocked to see the figure of a woman made of stone, hands raised above her head as though she were reaching for something. There were dozens more figures carved out of stone—some people, some animals, and a few of the fantasy creatures Kallista's father had liked.

"They're called *sculptures*," Kallista said. "My father told me about them."

Trenton had never seen so much creativity in his life. His hands trembled, and he thought he was going to be sick. "What's it all doing here?" he asked in a shaky voice.

Each of the items in the room had a tag attached to it. Kallista turned one of the tags around and shined her light on it. Block letters read *Helen Karnoff, confiscated 3/35*. They checked several of the other tags. All of them had the name of the person the item had presumably been taken from and the date it was found.

"I guess now we know what happens to things like the drawing your friend made," Kallista said. "They get locked away here, where they can't affect the citizens of our great city."

How could she be so calm in the face of so much unapproved material? Trenton felt trapped by the abominations surrounding him. The room was packed from wall to wall. Some of the art was covered with so much dust that it could have been there for decades.

Kallista picked up a stack of fragile-looking pages, blew the dust from them, and studied the writing. "I think this is what my father called *poetry*."

"Where did all this paper come from?" Trenton asked. His lips felt numb, as if the creativity in the room was suffocating him.

"A very good question." Kallista studied the pages. "This is much higher-quality paper than the stuff my father made from hay."

Trenton had no idea how there could be this much paper. But then he thought about all of the trees in the orchards of level one. The branches were pruned regularly, and surely some of the tress were replaced now and then. What did they do with the leftover wood?

"Most of this stuff is really old," he said. "The paper must come from food production. But if they had the ability to make this much paper back then, why force everyone to write with chalk and slates now?"

Kallista put the pages back on the shelf. "Do you know what a printing press is?"

"I think so," Trenton said. "Metal blocks with letters on them get lined up in the right order, then you rub on ink and print a page. Isn't that how books are printed?" He took a deep breath, reminding himself that the things in the room couldn't hurt him.

Kallista nodded. "My father told me about when the printing press was first invented. He called it one of the most important steps in the democratization of knowledge."

Trenton wrinkled his brow. "The what of what?"

"The democratization of knowledge. The printing press allowed people to share ideas more broadly than they ever could before. Scientists could share ideas with lots of other scientists. Scholars could distribute their work widely and cheaply. Stories, textbooks, and religious materials were all available to anyone who could read."

That made sense. But he still didn't see what she was getting at. "We still have books."

"But who prints them?" Kallista asked. "And who writes them? City officials. We have printing presses, but without paper, what good are they? As long as the city controls the paper, they control the communication. From the looks of this room, that wasn't always the case. But at some point, the city seized all of this and started limiting paper to control the flow of knowledge."

Trenton started to shake his head. Why would the city want to stop people from writing things or printing books? Why would they want to stop people from sharing what they knew? Yet, as he stared at pile after pile of paper and books, pages, and paintings, he couldn't think of any other reason to withhold paper.

Walking toward the back of the room, he noticed a painting that was nearly as tall as he was. "Your father would have loved this one," he said, staring at a great green beast shooting a stream of fire at a crowd of people fleeing in terror. It was so real looking that he could practically feel heat coming out of the frame.

"He would have." She touched the edge of the frame. "I wonder . . ." Grabbing the huge painting, she pulled it from the wall. "See if there's anything behind it."

Trenton squatted down and looked, but all he saw was dust and shadows. "Nothing there," he said.

Then he looked more closely. Was there something pushed into the corner? "Hang on." He reached as far as he could, and his fingers closed around a dark leather binding that had been nearly invisible leaning against the wall. "I see something," he said, grabbing the item and tugging.

It was a book, nearly two feet by two feet, bound in old, dark leather.

Kallista leaned the painting against the wall, and together they opened the book. Inside was a series of maps drawn in extreme detail.

"What was it doing back there?" Trenton asked.

"Someone hid it. Someone who knew I'd look there."

They turned from one page to the next. The maps were the best they'd seen, but they showed no hidden rooms, nothing Trenton and Kallista hadn't already explored.

"Looks like we're out of luck after all," Trenton said. He started to close the book, but Kallista gasped.

"Wait," she cried, pulling the book back open. She pointed to a line of barely legible writing in one corner. It was so small that Trenton was surprised she'd noticed it at all. He leaned over the book and squinted at the tiny print.

"A-M-E . . ." He turned to Kallista. "Amelia," he read. "It says Amelia. What does that mean?"

Kallista's voice was so quiet that he could barely hear her. "It's my mother's name. My father left this for me. It's another clue."

With his head turned, Trenton noticed something new. He ran a finger along the inside edge of the first page. It was rough.

"Point your light here," he said.

Kallista twisted the helmet, and under the bright light, they could clearly see a tiny shred of paper sticking out from the binding where another page had been. No, not one page. Two.

"Someone tore two pages out," Kallista said.

Why would they do that? What did it mean? All at once, Trenton remembered Mr. Sheets's words in the elevator the night Trenton had found the first tube.

"Most folks think of the food-production level as one, the city proper as two, power generation as three, and mining as four. What they're forgetting is—"

Trenton's father had cut the man off, and Trenton had forgotten all about it until now. But he didn't need to hear the rest. Suddenly everything he'd wondered about the first level made sense—the marks on the ceiling, the fact that he couldn't find any sign of an outside tunnel.

"Food production isn't level one," he said. "There are two more levels *above* it."

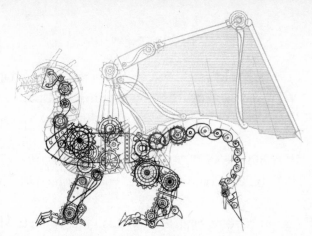

25

The next morning, Trenton came out of his room, lost in thoughts of the hidden levels. He and Kallista had decided to climb the air vent that night, an idea that both excited and terrified him at the same time. When he stepped into the kitchen, his father and mother were waiting for him. His father had not yet left for work, which meant this was serious.

"We'd like to talk to you," his father said. "Have a seat."

Trenton's stomach dropped as he took his place at the breakfast table.

His mother wheeled herself to the table and spooned some eggs onto her plate. "You've been going out a lot lately."

Trenton nibbled on a piece of toast, but his appetite was gone. "I've been, um, you know, doing homework and stuff."

His father stared at him from across the table, and Trenton's heart thudded against his ribs. Did they know? Had someone seen him coming out of City Hall the night before? Had Angus been spying on him?

"Is there anything you want to tell us?" his father asked. "Something going on in your life we should know about?"

The toast formed a scratchy lump in the back of Trenton's throat. "Like what?"

Trenton's mother glanced at his father before returning her eyes to Trenton. "Mrs. Patsy came to see me yesterday."

The snoopy old neighbor lady down the hall. What had she seen? What had she heard? How much might the old woman know? He looked from one parent to the other, trying to read their faces.

"What did she say?"

"That you've been coming and going with a girl," his father said.

Trenton tried to swallow the bread but choked. Mrs. Patsy had seen Kallista. She knew he was working with Leo Babbage's daughter. Did she recognize her? Had she told the authorities? He imagined security officers searching Kallista's father's shop at that very moment. For everything he'd said about the dragon, the idea that the plans—and the foot—might be destroyed made him shake with anger.

"When can we?" his mother asked.

"What?" Trenton asked, realizing he'd missed something.

Trenton's mother laughed. He looked from one parent to the other. Instead of being furious, they both seemed happy. What were they smiling about?

"When can we meet this girl?" his mother asked. "And why haven't you told us anything about her?"

"What are you talking about?" Trenton asked, more confused than ever.

They wanted to meet Kallista? Did they want to question her?

Trenton's father chuckled. "You're a little young for a girlfriend, aren't you?"

"Of course," his mother said. "But he's not too young to have a friend who's a girl. I met you during my first year of mining training. You looked so cute in your mask and hat."

Trenton slumped back in his chair, finally able to breathe.

They didn't know what he'd been working on, and they thought Kallista was his *girlfriend*.

"What's her name?" his father asked, digging into his food.

"Her name?" Trenton's mind spun. How many Kallistas could there be in the city? Even if they didn't recognize her first name, they were bound to ask for her last name, and if they learned it, the conversation would go in a completely different direction. Desperately, he blurted, "Simoni."

"The girl from school," his mother said with a delighted smile.

His father nodded. "The redhead. I knew it."

"Have some more eggs," his mother said, piling food on his plate, although he hadn't touched what was already there. She put a finger to her chin. "Why don't you invite her to dinner tonight?"

"Dinner?" Trenton froze with a fork of eggs halfway to his mouth. "Tonight?"

His mom wheeled away from the table and opened the pantry. "You never bring any of your friends home. We think it's time you did. Tonight is beef and potatoes night. I know just the recipe I'll use."

"Sounds wonderful," his father said. He got up from the table, patted Trenton on the shoulder, and grabbed his helmet and mask. "I look forward to meeting her."

Trenton dropped his fork onto his plate. How had he ended up agreeing to bring Simoni home to meet his parents? Especially on the same night he was supposed to climb the air vent with Kallista? He almost wished they'd discovered what he was really up to.

• • •

They'd moved from harvesting potatoes to asparagus that morning. Picking was easy, but they also had to wash and trim the spears and then band them into bunches.

An hour before lunch, Clyde returned. Dark rings circled his eyes, and his mouth twitched every so often. Trenton started toward him, but Clyde shook his head and quickly took his place in line to Trenton's right.

Several instructors walked over, but when they saw that Trenton and Clyde were working quickly, they moved away.

As soon as the teachers were out of earshot, Trenton whispered, "How are you?"

Clyde gave a tired smile and nodded. "I've been worse. Can't remember when exactly, but I'm sure I must have."

Simoni leaned toward them. "How did you get released so quickly? I was afraid they'd keep you longer."

"I told them it was an accident," Clyde whispered. "That my mind was wandering and I didn't realize what I was doing. Since it was my first offense, they went easy on me."

As Clyde cut a handful of spears, his hands were shaking ever so slightly. His fingers were swollen and seemed to move stiffly.

"What did they do to you?" Trenton asked.

Flexing his hands slowly, Clyde grimaced. "I'd rather not talk about it." He grinned, but it was a shadow of his former smile. "Everything's kind of a blur right now, and I think I'd like to keep it that way."

Trenton thought back to the drawings and paintings locked away in City Hall. Maybe Clyde's slate was stored there now. For the first time, Trenton wondered what was so terrible about a drawing. Who did it hurt? How did drawing a picture make the city run any less smoothly?

He was so caught up in his thoughts that he completely

forgot about the fact that he was supposed to invite Simoni to dinner until everyone began putting away their tools for lunch.

"Coming?" Simoni asked. "Or are you going on a walk again?"

Trenton looked up to find that he was the only one still working. He considered asking Simoni to dinner later, but the longer he put it off, the harder it would get. Trying not to meet her eyes, he said, "I, um, was wondering if you, uh . . ."

Simoni pressed her lips together. "If I what? Is something wrong?"

Clyde, who was beginning to act a little more like his old self, moved toward them, and Trenton turned his back, trying to shield his conversation with Simoni.

He took a deep breath and plunged forward. "Do you have any plans for tonight?"

She paused with her gloves halfway into her apron pocket. "I don't think so. Why?"

Clyde leaned toward Trenton and whispered, "Go for it."

Trenton picked up a handful of asparagus and scrubbed vigorously. "I was talking to my parents, and they were saying how they never get to meet my friends. And, well, my mom's making something special for dinner, so . . ."

Simoni looked expectantly toward Trenton. Heat spread from his cheeks to the tips of his ears. *This* was why he preferred working with machines. Getting your finger caught in a chain was infinitely less painful than asking a girl to dinner.

"He wants you to have dinner with his family," Clyde said, as if that would somehow help things.

If his friend hadn't just returned from a terrible twenty-four hours, Trenton would have punched him.

"Is that what you're asking?" Simoni said.

"Actually, it was my parents' idea. They want me to ask if you'll come to our house for dinner tonight."

Simoni frowned. "You make it sound like having me over is some kind of punishment."

Trenton realized he'd been grimacing. "No. It's not. I mean, I *want* you to come." His ears felt hot enough to burst into flame any second.

"Do you really?" she asked, studying him like she'd be able to spot a lie instantly.

"Yeah." Trenton looked down at the asparagus spears he'd been cleaning. He'd practically destroyed them. "Only if you want to. You don't have to. If you have something else tonight, I totally understand."

"I'd love to come," Simoni said, bouncing up and down on the balls of her feet. "What should I wear?"

Trenton was at a complete loss. He shrugged. "Uh, regular clothes, I guess."

As Simoni hurried to tell her friends, Clyde clapped Trenton on the back. "Smooth."

• • •

Talking to his parents was awkward. Half the time, Trenton didn't understand what they were trying to say. Talking to girls was hard. They seemed to speak a language he didn't understand, full of hidden meanings and implications that sent the conversation going to unexpected places. Except for Kallista. She was the one girl who always said exactly what she was thinking.

But sitting at the dinner table with Simoni and his parents, Trenton felt as if he were juggling balls of all different weights and sizes and failing miserably. Simoni and his mother clearly both spoke *girl*. They said something, then smiled in a way that made it clear that they both understood things Trenton didn't have a clue about. And his mother and father spoke *parent*, giving each other meaningful glances throughout dinner and laughing for no reason he could find.

Trenton was left trying to contribute while knowing that at least half of the conversation was going over his head.

"How are you enjoying your training?" Trenton's mom asked.

Simoni finished chewing a small piece of potato, then patted her lips with her napkin. "It's very interesting. I had no idea the city had so many plants and animals in production. The orchards smell like perfume."

"How's Trenton adjusting?" his father asked. "Not trying to rebuild water pumps, is he?"

His mother scowled at that, but Simoni laughed. "He's the hardest worker in our group. All of the teachers are impressed with him. And he stays after work a lot to explore."

His mother cut a piece of meat. "He arrives on time?"

Trenton held his breath.

"Of course," Simoni said without missing a beat. "Sometimes he gets there before I do."

Trenton gave her a grateful smile. But even though things were going better than he had feared they might, he didn't think he could take much more stress. He felt like an appliance being examined on a shop floor. He gulped down the rest of his meal and wiped his mouth.

"Well, we'd better get going."

"Already?" his mother asked. "What about dessert?"

Simoni folded her napkin and pushed back from the table. "Thank you for the meal and the conversation. But we both have a lot of studying to do." She smiled at Trenton. "Are you going to walk me home?"

He looked at the clock. Twenty minutes until he was supposed to meet Kallista.

"Of course he will," his father said.

"Yeah, okay," Trenton said. "One minute." He ran into his room, where he snatched up an old sweater and work gloves.

"I hope we get to see you again soon, Simoni," his mother called as she and Trenton walked out the door.

As they headed down the apartment building stairs, Simoni glanced at his sweater and gloves. "Expecting a storm?" she joked.

"I've been feeling a little chilly lately," he said. "I might be coming down with a cold."

Simoni placed a hand against his forehead. "You don't feel feverish."

Outside his building, Trenton noticed a uniformed figure watching them from down the street.

"Angus," Simoni said. "He thinks that just because his dad is someone important, I should gush all over him." She took Trenton's hand deliberately, and Angus disappeared from sight.

They walked for several minutes in silence. Trenton wanted to hurry, but Simoni appeared content to stroll slowly along.

"Your parents seem nice," she said.

"They're okay. My mom was a lot more cheerful than she usually is." Was that because he'd brought a girl home, or because she thought he'd given up on machines? Her response would definitely have been different if he'd invited Kallista.

When they reached Simoni's apartment building, she stopped and turned to him. "I was surprised when you asked me over."

Trenton kicked his feet in the dirt. Simoni was nice and smart and funny. And she was one of the cutest girls he knew. So why did being with her make him feel so awkward? "I'm glad you could come," he said, realizing he meant it.

She stepped forward and gave him a quick peck on the cheek before running into her building. Trenton felt his face turn beet red.

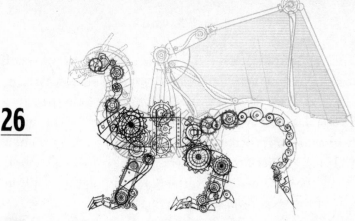

26

As soon as Simoni was out of sight, Trenton broke into a jog. He was already five minutes late, and the vent was at least ten minutes away. Running down the street, he caught movement out of the corner of his eye.

So Angus hadn't gone away after all.

No surprise. If one thing characterized Angus—other than his strength—it was stubbornness. Trenton slowed to a walk, forcing Angus to drop back, then ducked between a pair of shops and sprinted through the alley. He turned right, before Angus could see him, ran into another alley, and hurried inside the back door of an apartment building and out the front.

He waited across the street for several minutes, watching to make sure he'd lost Angus, before racing as fast as he could to the vent. He expected Kallista to be fuming when he got there. When he didn't see her, he thought maybe he'd lucked out and she was running late too. As he got closer, he saw that the vent was propped in place, but not screwed in.

He yanked it from the wall and stuck his head through the opening. From somewhere above, he could hear banging and shuffling. "Kallista!" he yelled.

The clanging stopped for a moment, then started up again. How could she have left without him? He squirmed into the opening and pulled the vent against the wall behind him.

Climbing up the shaft was more difficult than going down. If he released the pressure of his knees from the sides too early, he started to slide back down. He tried to hurry but knew that if he wasn't careful, he could end up slipping all the way to the mines.

He was making progress, though. Kallista was taller than he was, so it was harder for her to wriggle up. He was also more nimble. By the time he reached the light shining through from the vent of the food-production level, she was only a few feet ahead of him.

"Wait up," he called.

"I'm surprised you came," she said, continuing to climb.

Trenton ground his teeth. "What are you talking about? I told you I would."

Kallista grunted and pushed herself faster. "Didn't think you'd be able to break away from your date."

Trenton paused at that. She'd seen him? He forced himself up the vent more quickly. "It wasn't a date. My parents wanted to meet some of my friends." His knee slipped, and he had to reach out a gloved hand to catch himself. "Besides, why do you care if I asked Simoni to dinner?"

"I *don't* care," Kallista said. "Ask your whole neighborhood to dinner if you want. Just do it on your own time." One of her feet slid on the cold metal and clipped Trenton's ear. Either that or she had kicked him intentionally.

"I didn't have a choice." His arms and legs were beginning to ache, and he was working so hard that the cold air actually felt good. "Our snoopy old neighbor told my mother she'd seen me spending time with a girl."

Kallista stopped, catching her breath. "What did you tell them?"

Trenton rested his head against the side of the duct. "What could I tell them? That I've been building a dragon with Leo

Babbage's daughter? I told them it was Simoni, and then they insisted that I ask her to dinner."

"You could have told me you'd be late," Kallista said, her tone softening a little.

"Didn't have a chance. Besides, it was only, like, fifteen minutes."

An odd rumbling sound drifted down to them, and they both stopped talking. It came again, an echoing roar, like an engine revving.

"What is that?" Trenton asked.

"How should I know? I've never been up there," Kallista said. He could almost hear her eyes rolling.

They waited several minutes for the noise to come again. When it didn't, they continued climbing. A thought occurred to Trenton. "Do we know how high up the filtration system is?"

"It should be past the first level," Kallista said. "The *real* first level. But it's possible they moved the filters down after those levels were sealed off. We'll find out soon enough."

They climbed in silence. The higher they went, the more uncomfortable Trenton felt. They were about to leave the only world he'd ever known and would be that much closer to poisonous air.

"Why do you think they sealed the levels off?" he asked. It seemed like something they probably should have considered before climbing up.

He could hear Kallista panting above him. Was she as exhausted as he was? "Probably lots of reasons," she said.

He noticed she didn't suggest any, his brain seemed all too capable of coming up with possible explanations. What if the top levels were contaminated? What if they were unstable? Maybe they'd been sealed off because mutants had gotten inside. He and Kallista could be heading into an ambush right now.

Kallista stopped. "Should we go back?" It was the first time she'd ever suggested quitting. Apparently, she had the same kinds of thoughts he did.

Another weird, rumbling noise would send them both scrambling back down the shaft. But wasn't it a matter of time before they tried again? Their curiosity would be too much.

"Let's keep going," he said. "But if we see, hear, or smell anything weird at all, we're gone."

Kallista continued climbing, but at a much slower pace. Sometime later, she paused again. "I think I've reached another vent," she said softly.

That was a good sign, wasn't it? If the air on this level was bad, they'd have sealed off this vent to keep it from contaminating the levels below. Of course, that didn't mean there wasn't something else equally dangerous waiting for them.

"Can you see anything through the vent?" he asked.

"No. It's completely dark. The only reason I know it's there is because I can feel the grill." Trenton listened as Kallista fished around in her pack. A moment later, he heard a click, and bright light filled the duct. The flame on her miner's helmet flickered and jumped in the rushing air.

She pulled out a pair of pliers and began unscrewing the vent. "It feels like they're rusted in place," she said, struggling to get the screws to turn.

Now that they'd stopped climbing, the cold air began to work its way through his sweater and gloves. His ears felt like icicles stuck to the sides of his head. At least Kallista blocked some of the air. She had to be freezing. The pliers chattered against the screw as her hands shook.

Just as he was about to suggest they climb down to warm up, the vent fell out of the wall with a clang, and Kallista whispered, "I g-g-got it." The light of her helmet disappeared as she stuck her head through the opening. Her voice floated down to him. "W-w-wait there f-for a m-minute. I'll s-see if it's safe."

Trenton crouched in the duct, trying to decide how long to wait for her to return. What would he do if he heard a thud? Or even worse, a scream? What if something had taken Kallista, and she couldn't call for help? Right now she could be—

"Come on up," Kallista said. "It's okay."

Trenton's arms and legs were cramped, and his hands were numb as he started climbing again. He nearly fell twice before reaching the vent. Kallista held out a hand and pulled him through. The air wasn't as cold as inside the duct, but it wasn't nearly as warm as the city. As he stood there shivering, Kallista turned around, and her helmet lit up a series of tall dark shadows.

"What are those?" he asked, squinting up at the shapes.

"Machinery and buildings, probably," Kallista said. "This must have been their old manufacturing and power level."

The two of them walked deeper into the darkness, the only light coming from the flame on Kallista's helmet. Everything was covered in layers of dust. Except for the hiss of the lamp and the sound of their own footsteps, the entire level was silent, making it far too easy to imagine ghosts or bloodthirsty creatures waiting to jump out at them.

"What if your light goes out?" he asked.

Kallista patted her pack. "I brought enough fuel to last for days."

"I hope you're not planning on staying *that* long," Trenton said, but Kallista was barely listening.

They passed what might have been an old power plant, then a factory. Bits of rusted metal and pieces of abandoned equipment were scattered across the floor.

"Do you think your father came here?" Trenton asked.

"I know he did." Kallista pointed to the ground.

Although the rest of the floor was covered with dust and debris, a path was clear where someone had walked repeatedly.

"This way," she said, following the path deeper into the maze of buildings.

They'd been walking for ten minutes before something caught Trenton's eye. "What's that?" He pointed to a nearby building. It was an old foundry, where metal was produced and cast into shapes. Although the rest of the equipment was covered with years of dirt and rust, the machinery there looked almost brand-new.

"This is it," Kallista said. "This is where he was working."

The two of them hurried through an open metal gate maybe twenty feet across and into a large open courtyard. Just inside the gate was a switch. Kallista pushed it up. Nothing happened. She pulled it back down. Still nothing.

"Hang on," Trenton said, noticing a crank below the switch. He tried to turn the handle but could barely budge it. Using two hands, he bent down and shoved. The handle finally spun around, and a rough *put-put-put-put-put* filled the air. The sound slowed, nearly stalled, then rose to a smooth and steady rumble. "Try it now," he said.

She pushed the switch up again, and one light after another turned on until the foundry and courtyard were lit up so brightly that Trenton had to squint.

"Look," Kallista said, pointing to a gleaming gold-colored pile. They walked to an immense stack of metal sheets, beams, and rods. "The alloy," she said, brushing off a slight layer of dust.

They looked up from the pile at the same time to find a message painted on the wall. The letters were large and blocky but perfectly easy to read.

"If you have come this far, know that you are now in extreme danger."

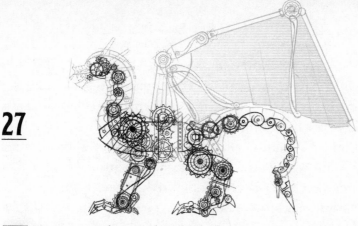

27

Trenton stared up at the words, bumps rising on the backs of his arms that had nothing to do with the cold. "What did he mean by *extreme danger?*"

"I don't know," Kallista said. "But look at all of this stuff. I knew my father wouldn't have given me the plans if there was no way to build the dragon. Look at the steam pipes. And here's part of the coal feeder." She picked up a foot matching the one they had and held it over her head, dancing around. "The second foot! Our dragon has two feet!"

"Stop it!" Trenton shouted.

Kallista lowered the foot and glared at him. "What's wrong with you? We've finally found what we've been looking for. I'd guess that at least half of the parts we need are here, and we can make the rest with the equipment my father left behind."

"What's wrong with *me?*" Trenton yanked at his hair with both hands. "Your father was working on this, right here where we are. For some reason, he never finished the dragon. But he did manage to leave us a note warning us that we aren't just in danger—we're in *extreme* danger. And now he's dead. Are you not connecting the dots?"

Kallista looked up at the words her father had painted, probably not long before he died.

"Yeah," Trenton said. "*Extreme danger.* Before we get all yay-for-our-team, shouldn't we figure out what he meant?"

191

"I'm sorry," Kallista said. She set the foot down. Trenton thought it might have been the first time he'd ever heard her apologize. "I was just so excited. I mean, my father left all of this for me. It was his way of showing he loved me."

"I know," Trenton said. "I'm excited too." He waved his hands in the air. "This is like a dream come true for me. All of the machinery I could ever want to study, tinker with, repair . . . not to mention a steam-powered dragon that might actually fly. I could live the rest of my life up here and never get bored. But at the same time, that message terrifies me."

He didn't know what dangers her father was talking about. Didn't know if they'd be able to put the dragon together, and if they managed to, he couldn't imagine they could actually make it fly. Security would probably catch them and shut the whole thing down. But right there, at that moment, he felt happier than he'd ever been in his life.

"I've got to get back soon, or my parents will worry. But let's at least look around."

Kallista smiled, and Trenton couldn't help but smile back.

Along with everything else Kallista's father had left behind were several mining helmets. Trenton picked one up, dropped a handful of carbide pellets into the lower chamber, and added water to the top, the way he'd seen his father do it. It took him a moment to figure out how to adjust the drip of water onto the carbide, but once he did, acetylene gas began to hiss and he lit the lamp.

Together they explored the rest of the foundry. There were tools to shape metal, equipment to make more of the alloy, and a variety of molds to make everything from gears to ball bearings.

"I don't see any gas masks," Kallista said. "That's a good thing. It means he wasn't worried about the air."

"Your father knew how to make gas masks?" Trenton asked. He'd read about them—the early settlers of the city had worn them to survive outside, but he'd never actually seen one.

Kallista added carbide to her helmet. "He couldn't find any plans for them, so he adapted the masks used in the mines."

"By why? The air here is fine."

"It is," Kallista said. "But it wouldn't be if we had to go outside."

Trenton, who had been examining a set of calipers—a tool designed to measure the thickness of things—frowned. "Why would we ever do that?"

Kallista seemed surprised by the question. "My father said we'd have to someday. We could run out of coal. Disease could wipe out the food supply. There could be an earthquake. Leaving Cove was a topic he talked about a lot. He said it wasn't a matter of *if*, but *when*. When I was little, he spent a lot of time on gas masks. I don't know why he stopped."

The idea of leaving the city disturbed Trenton more than he wanted to admit. Cove was safe. It was home. Inside the city, he understood how things worked. Outside, *anything* could happen. The thought made him want to curl up in a ball and hide.

"Let's follow the path in the other direction," Kallista said. "I want to know how he got up here."

They turned off the generator and, with only the glow of their hissing helmets for illumination, followed the trail of footsteps leading away from the foundry. This level was laid out a lot like the city below—wide streets and buildings arranged in neat rows. Except that factories and heavy equipment took the place of apartment buildings. The ceiling was too high for them to see by the light from their lamps.

Trenton was fascinated by all of the machinery. Some of it looked familiar, but the rest was unusual enough that he had to resist the urge to run over and take everything apart to see how it worked.

"Why do you think they left all off this here?" Trenton asked. "Why not take it with them when they dug out new levels?"

"Maybe it was too difficult to move," Kallista said, craning her neck to look at a crumbling smokestack. "Or maybe the old equipment was worn out and falling apart."

That made sense. Why move worn-out machines when they could build new ones? Trenton looked at the trail, wondering how many trips back and forth Leo Babbage had taken and how many years he'd worked on the project.

"How do you think he found this place? Did he know that the levels were here all along, or did he discover the torn-out maps like we did?"

Kallista sighed softly. "He was always asking questions. It bothered most people. But I remember thinking he knew everything about everything. He loved to read, especially old books. He was gone a lot the last few years. This must be where he went."

"How did he come up here so often without being discovered?"

Kallista picked up a rock and flung it against an old metal tank; the impact made a loud clang. "That's part of what I want to find out. He was too big to climb through the vents."

Turning his head, Trenton spotted what looked like an opening in the wall. "What's that?" he asked, walking toward it.

As they got closer, he could see that it was a cave. Kallista leaned over to pick up a chunk of something black. "Coal," she said. "It's a mine entrance. They must have done their mining and power generation on the same level."

"I don't think so," Trenton said. He walked a little deeper

into the cave and stopped near a familiar sight—a coal chute disappearing into the ceiling. The feeder belt was gone, but he could still see the metal brackets where it used to be.

He ran his fingers over the stone surface of the chute. "They fed the coal through the ceiling here. So at some point, the power plants were above this level. They probably changed it into a factory level when they had to dig deeper. I'll bet that's how each of the levels started."

Looking around, it suddenly struck him that every level had once been solid mountain. "What did they do with all the rock and dirt they had to excavate?"

"There's a separate pipe inside the air exhaust," Kallista said. "Any unused minerals are ground to dust and spewed outside." She peered up the belt. "Do you want to see what's up there?"

"I don't know," Trenton said.

A cold draft blew down from the opening with a hooting sound, as if the spirits of everyone who had died in the outside world were calling down to him. Cold shivers ran from his scalp to the base of his spine, and all at once, he didn't want to go up there.

"The map had only two pages torn out," he said. "That must mean that the level above is where the settlers came in from the outside. What if they didn't seal the entrance tightly enough, or if leaks have formed over time? The air up there could be poisonous."

Kallista stared into the darkness and rubbed her arms. An odd rumble, which could have been the wind, or something else, echoed down the opening. "Why do you think they closed these levels?"

"Maybe that's what your father meant by extreme danger. There has to be a reason he chose to work down here."

Kallista nodded. "Let's go," she said. "We need to get back anyway."

They followed Leo Babbage's trail back the way they'd come, and a few minutes later discovered a low passage slanting into the ground. It was another coal chute—this one was surprisingly clean and going down instead of up.

"*This* has to be how he got here," Kallista said.

Trenton peered into the hole. "Maybe. But where does it go? I'm pretty sure that someone would have noticed a hole in the ceiling of the food-production level."

"There's only one way to find out," Kallista said. She sat down and scooted into the chute on the seat of her pants.

Trenton followed. It was sort of fun. The slant was steep enough they could slide almost the whole way. He expected the chute to end at the ceiling of what he had, until recently, known as level one. Instead, it ended abruptly at a little metal door.

"Careful," he said as Kallista reached for the door. "There could be a big drop on the other side."

Propping her feet against the sides of the chute, Kallista eased the door open. "What is that?" she said, peering into the dark. She sniffed. "It smells . . . weird."

Trenton recognized the smell immediately. He slid next to her and shined his light on a pile of small, yellow kernels. "Dried corn," he said. "We're inside a grain silo."

Below the metal door was a circular walkway. He and Kallista climbed out of the feeder chute and onto the walkway. When they pushed the door shut behind them, it was nearly invisible. Trenton ran his finger across the surface until he touched a hidden button that popped the door open again.

"How did he find this?" Trenton asked. "And who made it?"

"This is my father's work," Kallista said. "I'd recognize it anywhere. Somehow he discovered the chute above this silo and dug it out."

Trenton couldn't imagine how much time and patience that had required. He was coming to admire Kallista's father more and more. They shut the door and walked around to the opening on the other side of the silo. Looking out, Trenton saw a ladder leading down to the back of a barn.

"We can take the elevator down from here," he said.

Kallista shook her head. "I'll have to go back through the vent. I'm not allowed on this level."

Trenton laughed. "They only check your pass going up. The security officers assume that if you were allowed up, you're okay to go down. I'll grab you an extra apron and gloves. No one will look twice at you."

He started to climb onto the ladder, but Kallista clutched the back of his shirt. "I don't know what kind of danger we're getting into, but it's okay if you want to stop. I can build the dragon by myself, and I really think I can figure out a way to fly it alone. Not that there's anywhere to fly."

He reached up and squeezed her hand. "You said your father did everything for a reason. That means he purposely made the dragon to require two people. Maybe he thought you needed a friend."

Kallista bit her lip and nodded. "I've never had one." Then she pushed his hand away and grinned. "Hopefully it won't be *too* bad."

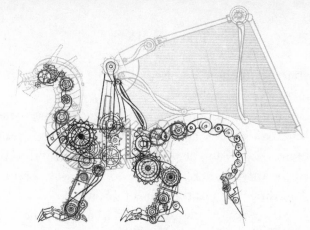

28

The next few months, Trenton found himself constantly running from one thing to another. The dragon was coming along faster than he could have hoped. But homework was ramping up as he neared his first-year halfway exams.

At the same time, he found himself spending more time with Simoni after work, taking walks around the orchards and sneaking treats to the farm animals. She made him laugh, and talking to her was getting easier. Even Angus appeared to have backed off.

The only thing less than perfect was the fact that Trenton was hiding a huge secret from her. Lying to her and to his parents about where he was going and what he was doing had become so common that he did it almost without noticing. Every so often, though, the guilt got to him enough that he'd consider telling Simoni about what he and Kallista were working on.

One afternoon as they walked through the trees, he pointed to the orchard and asked, "Have you ever imagined what it would be like to create something different, like a new kind of apple?"

Simoni smiled uncertainly. "Why would we need a new kind of apple when the ones we have are perfect?"

Trenton scratched his cheek. "I don't know. Maybe you could improve them. Like, what if you could breed an apple as tart as a cherry, or as juicy as a peach?"

Simoni punched him softly on the shoulder. "You're joking. Apples are crunchy, cherries are tart, and peaches are juicy. That's the way it's supposed to be. They all taste like what they are. If you started changing things you'd ruin them. Next thing you know, you'd have beans that tasted like potatoes or—or— beef that tasted like fish."

"I guess you're right," Trenton said. "Sometimes I just wonder if change is always bad, if things have to stay the way they are."

Simoni squeezed his hand. "Are you still upset about not being a mechanic? You know that all jobs are equally important, and you're becoming an excellent farmer. I wouldn't be surprised if you ended up getting the best test grades in the class."

Trenton squeezed her hand back. "I don't know about that. But being in food production is great. Especially since it means we get to work together. I'll bet Angus wishes he were a farmer right now."

Simoni smiled. "I'll tell you what. On your birthday, I'll make you a pie with peaches, cherries, and apples all together. Even if it's not the right day for those fruits."

"Careful," Trenton said. "If Angus hears you talking like that, he'll have you sent for retraining in no time."

As soon as he dropped Simoni off at the elevator—telling her he was going to make one last check on the plankton tanks—Trenton raced to the barn, made sure no one was watching, and climbed up the silo. He put on the sweater and helmet he'd hidden inside the secret door, then climbed up the coal chute and jogged to the foundry.

As soon as he got there and saw Kallista, he could tell something was wrong. She sat on the frame of the dragon's body, a deep frown on her coal-smeared face.

Trenton scrambled up the twenty feet of front leg to the belly of the dragon. "What's wrong, a part not fitting right?"

"Everything fits fine," Kallista grumbled. "But it doesn't work."

Trenton peered at the feeder Kallista had recently installed. It looked like a miniature version of the power plants on level three. Coal was pulled up from the bin and fed into the furnace, where flames heated pipes that then turned water to steam. The pressurized steam powered the pistons, which created power to run everything else.

"Let's see," he said.

Kallista let out an exasperated breath before pushing the button that lit the furnace.

Trenton watched the temperature gauge rise steadily as the coal burned in the furnace. Soon he heard pistons moving. As they churned, the feeder belt kicked into gear, adding more coal to the fire.

"It works perfectly," he said with a grin.

"No, it doesn't," Kallista snapped. "Look at the pressure gauge."

The needle was barely up to the halfway mark. Trenton frowned. He tugged a rod that would eventually be connected to the rider controls, when they got that far, and the mechanical wings unfurled from the sides of the dragon's body. He pulled another rod, and the wings moved up and down.

"The pressure isn't quite where we'd hoped it would be," he said, "but it's enough to power the wings."

Kallista slammed the rods back, folding the wings against the sides of the frame. "It does now. But the wings will never move fast enough to lift the dragon—not to mention lifting both of us. It will only get worse with the added resistance of the canvas."

"So we speed up the feeder." Trenton moved a lever, and the belt pulling coal from the bin increased to full speed. The pressure gauge moved up a few marks, but not nearly where it needed to be.

"It's not creating enough power," Kallista said, glaring at the gauge. "We'd need at least twice as much power to even consider flying." She spun the air valve shut, cutting oxygen from the furnace, and the engine slowly powered down as the flames went out.

"Hmm." Trenton scratched his head. Careful to avoid any hot parts, he climbed into the body and examined the entire assembly from underneath. "What's this open space for—the one between the coal bin and the furnace?"

"I don't know," Kallista said. "That's the way it was designed."

That didn't seem right. The rest of the dragon had been built to be as lightweight and efficient as possible. It had to be, if it would ever take off and keep itself in the air. He climbed up next to Kallista and held out his hand. "Let me see the plans."

Her brow furrowed. "I told you, that's the way it was designed."

"I know," Trenton said. "I just want to see if we missed something." He reached for the plans, but Kallista held them out of his reach.

"I didn't miss anything," she snarled. "I've been over the plans a dozen times. I've been up here doing everything while you and your *Simoni* waltz around the gardens."

Trenton felt like she'd slapped him in the face. He'd been putting in as much time with the dragon and Kallista as he could. It wasn't his fault that she didn't have any homework. Not to mention that she also had no friends or family, so she could spend every spare minute she wasn't doing repairs working on this.

"That's really how you feel?" he demanded, folding his arms across his chest.

She set her jaw. "Yes."

"Fine." He climbed down the leg. "Figure it out alone. I'm done."

Kallista climbed after him, the plans pinned under one arm. "What do you mean, you're done?"

Trenton jumped down. "Done. Finished. I'm sorry that I can't spend every nonworking minute up here like you do. But, yes, I do have other things in my life—like friends and a family. I've spent as much time up here as I can. I've lied to people I care about. I'm probably putting them all in danger by coming up here so often. And I did it to help you. If that's not enough, then I quit. Do it yourself. Your father should have designed his dragon for one person, because it's clear you can't keep friends."

Kallista stared at him, the color leaving her face. "Is that how you really feel?"

"Sometimes." Trenton's chest heaved. He picked up a pipe, then thew it away, knocking over a stack of brackets. "I'm doing as much as I can. I really want to see this succeed. But you have to understand that I can't give up my life for this project. I can't be a cherry and an apple at the same time."

"You're using *fruit* analogies?" Kallista raised an eyebrow.

Trenton snorted. "What do you expect from a farmer?"

Kallista unfolded the plans and handed them to him. "Maybe it *would* help to have a second set of eyes double-check my work."

Trenton took the plans and carried them to a nearby table. He studied the design as Kallista looked over his shoulder. She was right; the design did have an empty space between the coal bin and the furnace, with no indication of why it was there. Unlike the rest of the plans, which had been so carefully documented, the area for the power source was simply a blank space with the words "steam engine here" printed in small, neat letters, as if Kallista's father had meant to finish it later.

"Maybe we could add a second feeder."

"It wouldn't do any good," Kallista said. "At full speed, the belt is already sending as much as coal as the furnace can handle."

He turned the plans one way and then another. He had the feeling that he was missing something, but he didn't know what. "Could we squeeze in a second engine?" he asked, already knowing the answer.

"Yes, if we had room for a second coal feeder and another furnace," Kallista said. "Which we don't."

He knew that; he'd been grasping at straws. He could see why she was so frustrated. As good as Leo Babbage's plans were, it seemed he'd missed the one crucial thing that ruined the whole design.

"Let me think about it," he said, holding out the plans for her to take. "Maybe we can add some kind of oxygen pump to increase the burn rate."

"Keep them," Kallista said, folding her arms.

He blinked, sure that he'd misunderstood. "You want me to keep your father's plans?"

"You may as well," she said. "I have them memorized. When you can't come up here, study them down there. Who knows? Maybe you'll catch something I didn't."

"What if someone sees them?" Trenton asked.

Kallista scraped at the grease under her thumbnail. "Then we'd both be in really big trouble. So make sure no one does."

"All right," Trenton said. "I told my parents that I'd be home for dinner. But I promise I'll figure something out."

"I wouldn't be surprised if you did." She smiled and climbed back onto the dragon, humming.

Girls, Trenton thought as he headed home. *Just when you think you understand them, they do something that makes you realize you don't have a clue.*

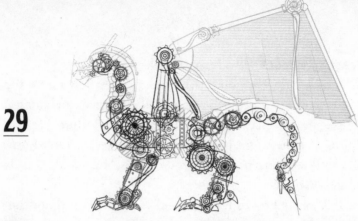

29

By the time exams arrived, the dragon was actually looking like a dragon. Trenton and Kallista had completed the segmented tail so it could swing left, right, up, and down. The head was attached—complete with orange eyes—and the operators' seats and controls were in place.

Unfortunately, neither of them had found a solution for the temperature problem. There wasn't enough pressure to control the wings and tail at the same time. The legs could move, although unsteadily. And the flames that were supposed to shoot out, hot enough to melt steel, barely made it up to the dragon's mouth.

Neither of them had said anything, but it was becoming clearer by the day that there *was* no solution. The design had a fatal flaw. Trenton didn't blame Leo Babbage. The numbers had probably looked right when he drew up the plans, but he never had a chance to test them before he died.

But this morning, Trenton couldn't afford to think about any of that. Not with midyear testing. With several pieces of new chalk and a freshly washed slate, he hurried to the elevator. For once, he was right on time. The students already gathered in the car were laughing and talking, but the talk revolved around what subjects they were worried about, and the laughter had a nervous edge to it.

"Are you ready?" Simoni asked as Trenton squeezed in beside her.

"I hope so," Trenton said with a forced smile. He wiped his hands on his apron.

The test had two parts. The first was practical; they'd do things like sheering a sheep, picking and processing only fully ripe fruit, and showing proper pollinating techniques. He didn't expect to have any problem with the practical half of the test. The more he worked in food production, the more he came to view it as just another set of moving parts to be figured out.

The second part was written. He'd gone over the practice questions with Simoni so many times, he practically had them memorized. Even Kallista had helped, quizzing him on the growth cycles of corn, wheat, and alfalfa while they installed the dragon's neck rings. Still, he couldn't help worrying that he'd missed something in his studies.

"How about you?" Trenton asked. "Nervous?"

"Are you serious?" Simoni held both hands out. They were shaking. "I'm terrified."

Trenton took her hands in his. "Don't be," he said. "You're so smart, you'll ace it."

When the elevator gate opened and they all piled out, a surprise awaited them. Mr. Blanchard stood in the same spot he'd met them on their first day of training, only now all of their other instructors had joined him. Standing beside him was Chancellor Lusk himself.

"We have a special honor today," Mr. Blanchard said. "Every year, our esteemed chancellor chooses one group of students to observe during their midyear exams."

Hushed whispers raced from student to student as the chancellor stepped forward. Trenton felt a sick twist in his stomach, remembering the last time the man had spoken to him.

"Don't look so worried," the chancellor told the students, resting his hands on his walking stick. "I won't be the one scoring your work. I couldn't tell a tomato seedling from an alfalfa plant if my life depended on it." He adjusted his monocle and winked. "Although I do a pretty mean job of milking cows."

The students burst into overly loud laughter, and Clyde shouted, "I'd like to see that."

"Perhaps you will," the chancellor said. "I've heard great things about this class, and I'm excited to watch young citizens who will one day oversee the plants and animals that keep our great city operating like the well-oiled machine it is."

He wore a fancy top hat with a working clock on the front. He tipped the hat to the students and said, "Young, energetic, well-trained people like yourselves make me proud to be your humble servant. Now go out there and show your parents, your teachers, and your city what you're capable of."

Mr. Blanchard began clapping, and the other instructors and students quickly joined in. They clapped so long and hard that the chancellor waved them to stop, and when they didn't, he finally took a graceful bow. Trenton clapped so hard his hands hurt. When he'd first started his training here, no one could have convinced him that he'd ever be proud to be a farmer, but at this moment, his heart swelled until he felt as if he were about to cry.

On the practical section of the test, Trenton did as well as he'd expected. He netted more catfish in sixty seconds than anyone else and correctly identified nineteen of twenty seeds—mistaking only the cantaloupe for honeydew, which the instructor admitted was an error even she might have made.

By the time they gathered for the written test, he felt much more confident. "How did you do on the practical?" he asked Simoni as they sat at a row of tables.

"Pretty well," she said. "Although I completely failed the

pollinating section, and my sheered sheep look like they've been attacked by a mad barber. But I passed the rest. Everyone's been saying you did the best in the class."

Trenton tried not to grin too widely. "I did okay."

Simoni clearly wasn't fooled by his act. She poked a finger into his side and said, "Don't let that head get any bigger, or it'll explode."

The exam questions were every bit as hard as he'd expected. He knew at least a few that he'd missed for sure. Anything relating to numbers was a breeze, but some of the *What would you do in situation* A-type questions threw him off. Still, by the time he turned in his slate, he was fairly confident he'd finished near the top.

When they finally turned in their slates, everyone was in a much better mood than when they'd arrived that morning—talking and laughing.

Mr. Blanchard stood and waved his hands. "Quiet. Everyone quiet. Please sit down."

Slowly, the students stopped talking and took their seats.

"I know you're all excited to have testing out of the way," Mr. Blanchard said. "And to be honest, so are the sheep." Everyone laughed, and several kids blushed. "Next, you get to have a delicious lunch, and then you will be released for a three-day break."

That announcement created such a loud cheer that Mr. Blanchard spent almost three minutes trying to calm everyone down again. When he could at last be heard, he raised a hand toward Chancellor Lusk. "The leader of our fine city would like to say a few final words."

All eyes turned to the front of the room as the chancellor stepped forward and faced the class. "I must say that I'm very impressed by what I've seen. I have great confidence I will not starve anytime soon."

A polite applause followed, which wasn't nearly as long as the one at his first speech. They were all tired, hungry, and ready to go home.

Clyde leaned toward Trenton and whispered, "*I'm* going to starve if they talk much longer."

"I know you all want to get to your fine lunch," the chancellor continued, "but first I would like to make two announcements." He held up his right hand, which was encased in a black silk glove, and raised a finger. "First, it pains me to say that it appears our city has a bent gear."

The room instantly silenced, and Trenton leaned forward.

"Several months ago a person or persons broke into one or more of the city offices. City property was vandalized, and historical documents—documents that belong to every one of you in this room as citizens of Cove—were damaged."

"No," Simoni whispered.

Students began looking at one another. Trenton tried not to meet any of their eyes. Did the chancellor know it was him? Was that why he'd chosen to observe this class? His chest seized, and his legs felt so weak, he didn't think he could stand if he tried.

"As horrendous as this crime is, we believe it is part of a bigger issue," the chancellor said. "Bent gears and cogs are encouraging the questioning of authority. I hate to say it in front of children, but it appears that creativity and free thinking are once again threatening our very existence."

His eyes slowly scanned the assembled students, and Trenton pushed himself back in his seat, trying not to look guilty. Beside him, Clyde was shaking.

"I'm sure no one here knows anything about this," the chancellor said. "You would have alerted someone immediately, of course."

"Yeah," several kids shouted.

"But I want to ask you all to watch for any suspicious activity. Security will be increased throughout the city, and, until we catch the culprit or culprits, an earlier curfew will be put in place. All citizens not required to work in the evenings must be home no later than nine p.m."

Unhappy grumbling filled the room, and the chancellor nodded sadly. "I know that a school break is a bad time for a curfew, but I'm sure you all understand the importance of finding these bad gears and cogs before they damage the magnificent machine of our city more than they already have."

Trenton wondered if Kallista had heard the news. The curfew would put a serious dent in the time they had to work on the dragon. They might even need to stop for a while, until security loosened.

The chancellor quickly held up another finger. "Second, on a more positive note, some of you may be aware that this year we are celebrating a very special anniversary of our city's founding. One hundred and fifty years ago, a group of sick and starving men, women, and children made the brave decision to leave the world that technology had destroyed. Using few resources, they dug into the side of this bountiful mountain we call home and founded a city of protection, a city of stability, a city where change would no longer endanger their lives or the lives of their families."

Mr. Blanchard led the room in a round of applause.

"As a part of the celebration," the chancellor said when the room had quieted down, "one week from today, a formal ball will be held in the assembly hall. Such events are typically restricted to adults, but in light of the fact that the curfew will put a bit of a damper in your break, we have decided to invite trainees to join us."

There was a moment of shocked silence, and then everyone began talking at once.

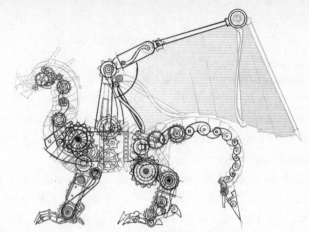

30

At the after-test feast, Trenton put food in his mouth but barely tasted it. How had they discovered the break-ins? Was it the bent frame in the museum? Or had someone noticed the pick marks on the locks at City Hall? They'd left the map book in the paper room in case someone else knew it was there, but maybe that had been a mistake.

What if someone looked through the pages and noticed the name of Kallista's mother? How long would it take them to track the break-ins to her? He wanted to go up and warn her right now, but he couldn't leave until after lunch.

"You seem quiet," Simoni said.

Trenton put a slice of cheese in his mouth even though he no longer felt hungry. "I'm just thinking."

"Something you want to tell me about?" she asked, a small grin on her face.

The cheese caught halfway down Trenton's throat; he had to cough to dislodge it. "No. I mean, it's boring stuff. Nothing you'd be interested in."

The grin disappeared, replaced by a look of exasperation. Across the table, Clyde was holding his hands out in a gesture Trenton didn't understand. Trenton looked around, wondering if he'd missed something.

Simoni pushed the fruit around on her plate. "It's too bad

about the curfew. I hope they catch whoever broke into the offices."

"Yeah," Trenton said, nodding vigorously. "Probably someone from North West. I've heard there are some really bent gears out that way."

"But the other announcement was pretty exciting, don't you think?"

"Sure," Trenton said.

Across the table, Clyde kept holding out his arms, shaking back and forth, then pretending to talk. What was he doing? It looked like he having some sort of fit.

Simoni put her hand on Trenton's and smiled sweetly. "Is there anything you'd like to ask me?"

Still distracted by Clyde's antics, Trenton only half listened. But it was clear that something was going on—something he had no clue about. "I, uh . . ." His mind raced. Clyde pointed from Trenton to Simoni.

"Oh," Trenton said, realizing what she wanted. "How did you do on the test?"

Clyde leaped from table, ran around, and yanked Trenton up by the arm.

"What is *wrong* with you?" Trenton asked. "Why were you waving your arms?"

"I was dancing," Clyde hissed.

Trenton stared at his friend, wondering if he'd eaten a bad fruit or something. "Okaaay. Why were you dancing?"

Clyde pulled him a few feet away and whispered, "Simoni wants you to ask her to the dance, you idiot."

Trenton stared at his friend. "I can't dance."

Clyde clutched his forehead as though he'd been struck with a terrible headache. "No one can dance. You just move your feet around to the music. Ability has nothing to do with it. Simoni wants you to ask her to the ball, but you're shoving cheese in your mouth and talking about tests. Are you really that dense?"

Trenton glanced at Simoni, who sat slumped on the bench.

"Maybe I am that dense," he said. "Are *you* going?"

"Of course," Clyde said. "I'm a dancing machine. My only problem is choosing which girl to ask."

Trenton shook his head. He walked back to the table and waited for Simoni to look up. She seemed especially intent on cutting her salad, although it was already chopped into tiny pieces. He coughed into his hand, wishing once again that girls were as easy to understand as machines. "Uh, can I ask you a question?"

Simoni looked up suddenly, as if surprised he was there. "Are you talking to me?"

He gulped. Why did she have to make this so hard? He folded his arms, unfolded them, and finally put his hands behind his back. "Would you, um, want to go to the dance with me next week?"

She bounced up from the bench and squealed. "I'd love to. What colors should we wear?"

• • •

Breaking away from lunch took longer than he would have liked. A bunch of kids were heading down to the park and invited him to join them, but he claimed to be too tired from the testing.

Simoni barely noticed when he left. She and a group of other girls were discussing dresses, hats, and a million other things related to the dance.

Fortunately, while security might have increased in the city, no extra guards had been assigned to food production. He made it inside the silo as easily as always. He expected to find Kallista working on the dragon, and he had a moment of panic when he reached the site only to find it dark. Then he remembered she would still be at work.

He turned the crank to start the generator and switched on the lights. Kallista had made a lot of progress since his last time here. Canvas stretched across the struts of one wing, and metal scales had been attached to the underbelly, making the dragon look more like a living creature and less like a machine.

He climbed up to the seats at the base of the dragon's neck and started up the furnace. A couple of minutes later, the engine kicked in, and the dragon vibrated beneath him. Taking a control in one hand, he lifted the dragon's tail, and the body shifted. They'd have to be sure to use the tail as a balance whenever walking or flying to avoid tilting too far one way or the other.

Moving the control, he flicked the end of the tail, sending a twenty-pound sledgehammer flying across the floor. In his mind, he could see himself and Kallista working in unison to make the great beast come to life. He imagined the wings unfurling, the legs pumping, the tail raised, and the rush of air as they—

The pistons stuttered, and the tail dropped to the ground with a clang of metal. Trenton shut off the furnace, and the engine wound down. He put his head in his hands. It was never going to happen. They'd put so much time and effort into a machine that would never work.

Unable to make himself spend any more time on the dragon, he climbed down and shut off the generator. The other kids would still be in the park, but he wasn't in the mood to join them, and he didn't want to talk about the colors of suits and dresses with Simoni. He didn't feel like going home, either, so he walked around the level, poking at bits of old equipment and examining machinery.

It might be fun to get one of the plants running again. He didn't know what kind, or what he'd do in it, but at least he'd be working on something that had the chance to operate the way it was supposed to.

A deep growling filled the air, and he froze in place. He looked around, trying to locate the source of the sound. Was it more equipment Leo Babbage had left behind? Something they hadn't found?

He heard another sound, like grating rock, and the rumbling came again. This time it sounded a little farther away. He waited, tilting his head and straining to hear, but after several minutes, the strange noises seemed to have stopped. He'd have to ask Kallista if she'd heard anything like them.

Noticing a nearby smokestack, he wandered into a power plant that—except for the layer of dirt and grime covering it— could have been the one where he and Kallista had met Miss Huber.

He looked longingly at the huge steam engine. What could their dragon do with that kind of power? This furnace didn't look in bad shape. It had a few dents and some rust, but no holes. He stopped and studied it. Something was different about the engine. Where the pistons and gears should have been was a long metal cylinder. A piece of equipment connected the furnace and the feeder belt that didn't belong there.

Adjusting his helmet light to point up, he walked closer. What was that connected to the feeder? It looked like some kind of processing machinery. But why would anyone process coal before feeding it into the burner? He reached for a bar above his head and started to pull himself up to get a better look, then paused, noticing a mark on the floor.

He dropped back down to get a closer look.

There, covered by a layer of dust much lighter than the rest of the level, was a set of footprints. Someone else had been in this power plant. Not recently, but definitely in the last year or two.

Right about the time . . .

"He was here," Trenton whispered. "Leo Babbage stood right here."

His heart began to race. Quickly he climbed back onto the equipment. It didn't take long to figure out that the first piece of machinery was a crusher. It crushed the coal before it went to the furnace. The crushed coal was then blown onto the flames. The blower case was open, as though someone had taken it apart to examine the inside. Trenton reached out to run his fingers through the black powder coating one of the blades but pulled back, noticing a streak in the dust—another set of fingers had done the same thing.

He moved past the furnace to where the steam pipes should have connected to the pistons and saw a large metal cylinder that stood open as well. A pair of rusty bolts lay on the ground next to a curved plate. Bracing himself with his hands, he leaned forward and peered into the opening.

What he saw there made no sense. Instead of pistons and gears, rows of thin metal fans were attached to a single shaft. In the dust outside the metal housing, someone had written the word "turbine."

All at once, Trenton realized what he was seeing, what Leo Babbage had seen before him. This power plant had once crushed the coal into a fine powder, then blown the powdered coal directly into the furnace. That made the coal so combustible it must have practically exploded when it hit the flames. And instead of moving pistons in the cylinders, which had to heat up and cool down with each cycle, steam was used to turn the fans.

His mind raced, calculating. This kind of engine would be so efficient that it could easily triple their current power production. The design took up much less space, too, allowing the engine to be bigger.

The empty spot in the plans was exactly the right size to install a crusher and blower.

Kallista's father had designed it that way all along.

Trenton threw his hands in the air and shouted, "Leo Babbage, you are a genius!"

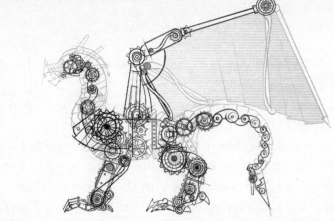

31

Trenton tightened the last bolt on the blower, checked the gasket to make sure it wasn't pinched anywhere, and sat back to examine his work.

"All done?" Kallista called from above.

"As far as I can tell," Trenton said.

He looked over the turbine assembly, wishing for the hundredth time that Leo Babbage had given them the designs for this instead of making them figure it out on their own. What if they'd built it wrong? If they blew in too little powder, the furnace wouldn't get hot enough. Too much, and the whole thing could explode.

"Why do you think your father didn't put the steam turbine in his plans? Why make us discover it for ourselves?" he asked, climbing up to sit next to Kallista.

"He did everything for a reason," she said.

Trenton shook his head. "You keep saying that, but that doesn't help unless we know what the reason was."

She tightened a fitting on the dragon's neck. "The bigger question is why isn't this technology being used in the city power plants?"

They'd gone around and around on this without finding a clear answer. Maybe the turbines and blowers had been forgotten over time. Maybe they didn't work as well as they were supposed to.

"Maybe it's dangerous," he said. "Maybe one of the plants blew up or something."

Kallista raised one corner of her mouth. "Do you really believe that?"

No, he didn't. Not only had he done the math himself, carefully measuring the equipment in every power plant on this level—all of which were built with the same machinery—but Leo Babbage had clearly wanted them to discover it. That alone told him that the process was solid.

"Well," Kallista said, running a finger across the power button. "Should we put it to the test?"

Trenton checked the time. The dance would start in a couple of hours. "Is there enough coal?"

"Fully loaded."

He took a deep breath. "All right. But we have to be quick. I promised Simoni I'd pick her up at seven. Are you sure you don't want to go?"

"To a *dance?*" Kallista puckered her mouth as if tasting a rotten apple. "I'd rather impale myself on a steam pipe and slowly bleed to death while the heat cooks my brain."

"Oh, that's real nice," Trenton said. "Way to encourage me for my big night out." He sighed. "Speaking of being out at night, I think you need to stop working on the dragon after curfew. Security officers are everywhere right now. I swear I saw a couple of them examining the air vents the other day."

"Ha." Kallista stuck her nose up. "The marshal's men couldn't catch me if I gave them a ten-foot head start and hopped on one leg. Besides, lately I've been spending the night up here and going down in the morning."

"I'll bet *you* smell fresh at work." Trenton nodded to the power button. "Let's do this. If we're going to blow ourselves up, we may as well get on with it."

Kallista grinned. "One . . . two . . ."

On "three," she pushed the button. Unlike before, a whoosh of flame appeared instantly as the furnace consumed the powdered coal in the primer. Within seconds, the turbines whined and the feeder belt started up.

The dragon vibrated harder than Trenton had ever felt it. His eyes went to the temperature gauge. The needle was climbing fast. *Too* fast? The pressure gauge was climbing too. The fans in the turbine kicked up to a pitch higher than anything he'd heard before. The dragon's eyes—which used to give a weak glow—cut through the darkness like spotlights.

His pulse raced as he realized this was going to work. Then he noticed the temperature gauge. The needle was almost all the way to the top, and the pressure readout was edging into the red.

"Turn it off!" he shouted, reaching for the button.

Kallista blocked his hand. "No. Listen. It's evening out."

Trenton held his breath. The turbines had gone from a deafening pitch to a steady roar. The pressure gauge held steady on the border between red and white. The temperature was a little high, but he could probably adjust that.

Slowly, he let himself relax, feeling a grin spread across his face.

"We did it!" Kallista shouted, bouncing up and down in her seat. "It works!" She turned the dragon's head to the left. It moved as if on a string. "Shoot out a blast of flames."

Trenton twisted the dial for the flames to halfway and hit the button. A blinding burst of fire hit the iron gate at the front of the foundry and melted it instantly. "Holy iron slag," he said, staring at the bubbling orange puddle. "Do you see that?"

Kallista nodded excitedly and gripped the controls for the

legs. The dragon lifted its front left leg, leaned precariously to one side, and turned before slamming it back down.

"What are you doing?" Trenton yelled, grabbing the edge of his seat.

"Trying to walk it," Kallista said. Gripping the levers in both hands, she made the dragon take first one step and then another toward the melted gate.

"Hang on!" Trenton shouted. "You have to use the tail as a counterbalance, or we'll fall over."

He pulled the control, lifting the tail off the ground, then shoved it left and right with each step Kallista had the dragon take. At first they moved out of sync, and he was sure they were about to tip over, but, after a few more steps, they started to get the hang of it. They walked the dragon out the front gate and turned onto the street.

With each crashing step, dust and rocks flew in the air. Could anyone could hear them from below? If so, they'd probably think the mountain was coming down on top of them.

But they were doing it. They were really doing it. They were riding on the back of a mechanical dragon the two of them had built with their own hands.

"This is amazing!" He hit the flame button, and a burst of fire shot out in front of them.

Kallista increased the speed, and the dragon began to run, leaping ten feet with each step, then twenty.

"Slow down," Trenton yelled, bouncing out of his seat with every step as he tried to keep the dragon balanced.

Kallista pulled the lever on her left and the wings began to extend.

"Stop it." Trenton reached for the lever, but Kallista knocked his hand away. With the wings fully spread, the length of their steps had gone from twenty feet to forty.

She looked back at him, her eyes agleam with excitement. "Let's fly!"

"No," Trenton said. They weren't ready for this.

They had too many things to test first. They were going too fast. Keeping the tail under control was getting harder and harder, and something sounded off with the hydraulics in the left leg.

He looked ahead and realized they were heading straight for a building. "Look out!" he screamed.

Kallista turned around and gasped. She tried to pull to the right, but it was too late. They couldn't turn fast enough, and there was no time to stop.

Knowing it was their only chance, Trenton yanked up on the flight lever. The wings changed angle and began to beat. The dragon jumped, landed hard, jumped again, then launched into the air. He watched the building disappear inches beneath them. The dragon's tail caught the top edge of the wall and blew it to bits.

"We did it!" Kallista shouted. "We're flying!"

Trenton looked down. Lit by the beams shooting out of the dragon's eyes, buildings and equipment blurred past below. He pulled the lever back a little more, and they rose higher into the air.

"My father's plan worked. It *worked!*" Kallista yelled, throwing her arms above her head.

Trenton had never been so scared in his life, but he couldn't help grinning. The cold air whipped against his face, bringing tears to his eyes, and he realized his entire body was shaking.

"How are we supposed to land?" he asked.

"I have no idea," Kallista said. "But isn't this great?"

It was more than great. It was amazing. This is what he lived for—to see something he'd built with his own hands work the way it was supposed to. To build something new, something . . . important. As much as he enjoyed farming, *this* was what he had been born to do. There was no doubt of that in his mind.

"You'd better turn around," he said. "We need to get back and figure out how to land this thing."

Kallista pushed a pedal with her foot, and the dragon banked to the right. The wing struts creaked, and Trenton moved the tail to act as a rudder. They heard a ripping sound, and Trenton whirled around to see the canvas on the left wing rip off one of the struts.

For a moment they evened out, but the cloth continued to tear away. At the same time, the canvas on the right wing shredded off of one whole section.

"Get us down!" she yelled. "The wings are coming apart."

Trenton pushed the flight lever forward, and the dragon began to descend. But not evenly. The wings shuddered, and the dragon swerved left, then right. Canvas was ripping all over now. The dragon was dropping too fast. Bits of shredded cloth flew into the air behind them.

"I can't steer us!" Kallista screamed.

Trenton shoved the stick all the way forward, trying to get to the ground more quickly, but the head went down, and the rear came up. He pulled back on the flight lever, forcing the tail down to act as a brake.

Kallista managed to pull the dragon's head up, but it was no good. They were coming in too fast, shaking like a ball bearing in a tin can, and Trenton could barely keep himself from falling out.

They hit the ground with a thud. Kallista worked to move the feet as fast as possible, but they were out of control. Something snapped, and the dragon tilted to the left. Trenton's hands were ripped from the controls, and he was thrown from the seat.

He saw the ground coming up to meet him, and then everything went black.

• • •

"Trenton, can you hear me?"

He heard a faraway voice but couldn't understand it. The world seemed to be spinning around and around, and he thought he was back on the gear trying to make the swing.

"Be sure to duck before the beam hits you," he muttered before passing out again.

Sometime later, he felt something cold and damp press against the side of his head. He opened his eyes, but the world was a blur.

"Don't try to sit up," a voice said. He recognized it.

"Kallista?" Where was he, and why did he feel like he'd been run over by the trolley? He started to sit up, but a wave of pain ran through his head and his neck.

"I told you not to do that," Kallista said.

He blinked, and a street filled with pieces of broken machinery came slowly came into focus. "What happened?" he asked. "Where are we?"

"We crashed the dragon," Kallista said. "You were thrown out. You're lucky you didn't die." She wiped her eyes. "It's all my fault. I should never have tried to fly it."

"Help me up," Trenton said.

She put her arms around his neck and back, helping him up to a sitting position. He stared at the mass of twisted beams and pipes. "Was it the . . ." He couldn't remember the right word at first but knew he should. "Was it the turbines?"

"No," Kallista said. "It was the wings. The canvas wasn't strong enough. It tore."

"Oh. Well, that's good." He tried to nod but instantly regretted it. "Wait." He stared at the mess of machinery in front of him and started to recognize parts. "Is that the dragon? Is it ruined?"

"I can fix it," Kallista said. "But I don't care about that right now. Only that you're okay. I never would have forgiven myself if I'd killed you."

"How about next time, we wear helmets," Trenton said. "And we add harnesses to hold us in our seats. Did your father have a reason for not including those?"

She laughed shakily. "Now you're starting to sound like the Trenton I know. You were unconscious so long, I worried you might never wake up."

"Unconscious?" Something clicked in Trenton's mind. "How long was I out? What time is it?"

"You've been sleeping for almost five hours," Kallista said. "It's just after eleven."

Eleven!

"Oh no," he groaned. "I missed the dance."

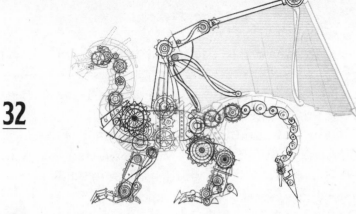

32

Trenton had been out of the hospital for almost two weeks, but Simoni still wouldn't talk to him. He'd tried talking to her in the elevator, during training, and after work, but she always went out of her way to be in a group of girls who made it clear that he wasn't invited to be part of their conversations.

Shoving his hand into the pockets of his apron, he joined Clyde and walked toward the orchard where they would be picking cherries that day. He paid no attention to a security officer who stepped up to them until a far-too-familiar voice said, "Guess you don't think you're all that special now that Simoni's dumped you."

"What are *you* doing here?" Trenton demanded.

Angus grinned, looking far too pleased with himself. "Got reassigned to this level."

"You mean your *father* got you assigned here," Clyde said.

"Watch your mouth, or you may end up back in retraining, *artist*." Angus put a hand on Clyde's chest, but Trenton slapped it away. The two of them glared at each other. Angus was much bigger than Trenton, but even though his father was the head of security, Angus would get in trouble for starting anything.

Angus sneered. "Simoni wants nothing to do with you anymore."

Trenton nearly laughed. "Thanks for letting me know. I had no idea."

"You're a loser," Angus said. "I would never have abandoned Simoni like that."

"Guess it's too bad that she didn't ask *you* to the dance, then," Trenton said, but his heart wasn't really into the insult. The sad fact was that Angus was right. Trenton didn't know how to fix things between him and Simoni.

"Come on," Clyde said. "Let's go."

As they turned toward the orchard, Angus shoved Trenton in the back, making his sore ribs scream. "I'm assigned here every day now, and I know what you're doing."

Trenton froze but tried not to show his shock. "What are you talking about?"

"You think I don't know what you're up to?" Angus glared. "I *know*. And I'll be watching you every day from now on."

Trenton walked away, but he could feel Angus's eyes on him.

Was he telling the truth? Did people really know that he was working on something? He thought he'd been careful. But if Angus knew, who else might?

As the morning went on, Trenton spotted Angus watching him pick cherries, Angus always in the distance, always watching. How much did he know? How much had he seen?

"He's trying to steal your girl," Clyde said. He seemed to be eating two cherries for every one he picked.

Trenton dropped a handful into his bucket. "What are you talking about?"

"Angus," Clyde said, tossing a couple more cherries into his mouth. "He knows you want to get back with Simoni, so he's trying to stop you."

Was *that* what Angus had meant? Was it possible that he

didn't know anything about the dragon after all? Trenton felt a huge weight lift from his chest. He glanced toward Simoni, who was picking several rows away.

"I told her I'm sorry."

Clyde gave him a pitying look. "That's not enough. She worked on her dress for a whole week. She planned dinner with her friends. She even dyed a pair of shoes to match your suit. And you left her hanging." He smiled sadly with juice-stained lips. "Girls don't forgive that kind of thing. You may as well start looking for a new sweetie."

Trenton set his filled bucket on a stack and grabbed a new one. "I broke two ribs, sprained my neck, and got a concussion. What was I supposed to do, drag myself to the dance?"

Clyde popped another handful of cherries into his mouth and chomped away, then spit the pits out one after the other. "My friend, if I'd had both of my legs cut off, I would have found a way to make it to see my girl that night. This was, like, a once-in-a-lifetime thing. She won't get to go to a city ball again until she's eighteen."

Their instructor strolled toward them and snapped his fingers. "Less talking, more working. And stop eating the fruit. A good citizen works for the benefit of everyone. He does not take that which has not been assigned to him."

"A good citizen is also hungry," Clyde said to Trenton. "How can it not be lunchtime yet?"

Trenton clenched his jaw and concentrated on his work. How could Simoni blame him? It wasn't his fault he'd been unconscious for the entire dance. You'd think she'd understand that. She wasn't the only one ignoring him, either. He didn't know if she'd told everyone to stay away from him, or if they were jealous that he scored the highest on his combined tests. Lately, no one but Clyde wanted anything to do with him.

"What would *you* do in my situation?" he asked Clyde, who was again sneaking cherries. "If you liked Simoni and you . . . you know, didn't get to the dance?"

"You mean other than drown myself in the plankton tank for losing the cutest girl our age?"

Trenton grimaced. If he'd had any other friends he could go to for advice, he would have asked them. "Assuming the plankton tank wasn't an option, what would you do?"

Clyde swished a cherry pit from one cheek to the other before spitting it at the nearest tree trunk and missing by a foot. "Hmm, tough one. If it were me, I'd probably find another girl. Preferably *not* one of Simoni's friends. But you're not exactly a hot commodity these days, so that might not work. I guess I'd suggest trying to talk to her."

It was all Trenton could do to keep from hitting Clyde over the head with his bucket. "I've been trying to talk to her for *two weeks*. She won't listen."

"You should probably start with telling her the truth." Clyde scratched his belly.

"What truth, that I'm an idiot? I think she knows that."

"No, tell her what really happened that night."

Trenton froze with his hand reaching toward a branch. "What do you mean?" Did Clyde somehow know about the dragon?

Clyde glanced at Trenton and quickly looked away. "How you really hurt yourself."

"I fell out of the barn," Trenton said. "What more could I tell her? That I'm a total klutz? I think she probably knows that already."

Walking over until he and Trenton were only a few inches apart, Clyde whispered, "No one believes that story. Except maybe the doctors who patched you up."

His gut cramped, and he felt like he was going to throw up. "Why not?"

Clyde looked at him as if he'd lost his mind. "Seriously? You were alone in the loft of a barn on a night two hours before a big dance and tripped over a bale of hay? Even *I* could have come up with a better story than that, and I'm the worst liar I know. Why didn't you say you fell down the stairs of your apartment building or something?"

"My apartment's on the first floor," Trenton said. Not to mention the fact that after the crash, Kallista had barely managed to get him into the silo and down the ladder. They'd never have made it through the elevator without security asking questions.

"What *really* happened is none of my business. All I'm saying is this: if there's one thing a girl hates more than a guy who stands her up for a formal dance, it's a guy who lies about why he did it."

"Time to break for lunch," their instructor called.

Clyde covered his mouth and burped. "Funny. I'm not all that hungry anymore."

"Disgusting," Trenton said. He looked at Simoni and knew what to do. Clyde was a slob at times, but, in this case at least, he was also right. Trenton ran to catch up with Simoni. She'd surrounded herself with a group of girls, but he forced his way through anyway. "Clyde says you don't believe that I fell from the barn loft."

Simoni folded her arms and stared at him without a word. She didn't have to talk; her expression said everything he needed to know. He tried to think of a creative story that could make everything right, but lies had gotten him into this situation, and it didn't seem like they'd get him out of it.

"Can I talk to you privately?" he asked.

She narrowed her eyes, practically turning his blood to ice.

"Give me five minutes," he pleaded. "If you don't want anything to do with me after that, I won't talk to you ever again."

She turned to her friends. "Go on," she told them. "I'll catch up."

Once they were alone, Trenton's mind went blank. He shuffled his feet, trying to think of how he could possibly tell her everything that had really happened.

Simoni tilted her head. "You need five minutes to look at your shoes?"

There *was* no good way to explain what had happened.

"I really did have a concussion," he said. "And obviously my ribs are broken."

"This isn't about that."

Trenton looked up. "It isn't?"

"It's not even about missing the dance." Simoni shook back her hair. "I heard that the food was terrible, and the band was worse—a bunch of old-people music."

Trenton stood there, completely bewildered. If she wasn't upset about the dance *or* his accident, then *what?*

Simoni stared at him; he felt as if her green eyes could drill right into his brain. "You've been lying to me."

Trenton opened his mouth to contradict her, but she held out a hand.

"Not only about the dance—although that was a lie too. But about everything. You've been lying to me ever since we started training. Don't you think I've noticed how often you 'forget' something and have to go back for it? How often you say you'll stay behind to work a little longer? Nobody studies as much as you claim to, yet your parents wonder how you're doing in school because you're never home."

And he thought he'd been so clever. Cold sweat dripped down his back. "I don't know what to say."

She smiled and shook her head. "Don't say anything. You can keep your secrets. That's fine. I won't even ask what they are." He started to relax—was it really going to be this easy? "Or you can keep me. But you can't keep both."

Trenton's throat tightened and his eyes burned. Simoni was a good person, and he'd been a jerk to her. Telling her about the tube, the workshop, Kallista, the dragon—that wouldn't be enough. She'd never believe him, not unless she saw it all herself.

But could he be sure she wouldn't give him and his secret away? It all came down to one thing: did he believe he could confide in her or not?

"You want to know you can trust me," he said. "I get that. But I need to know that I can trust you too."

"Of course you can trust me." Simoni stepped closer. "Don't you know that by now?"

Trenton bit the skin on the back of his thumb. "If I'm going to show you what I've been doing, you have to swear to me you won't tell—not anyone. If you decide you don't want anything to do with me, I'll understand. But I'm not the only one involved in this. You can't tell a soul even if you never speak to me again."

Simoni nodded. "I swear."

"Okay," Trenton said hesitantly. He hoped he was doing the right thing. If he was going to do it, it had to be now, before he changed his mind. "I'll tell Clyde to cover for us while we're gone. This could take a while."

• • •

Losing Angus took some work, but Trenton knew the level well enough to evade anyone who hadn't spent every day of the past six months there. When they reached the silo, he covered Simoni's eyes with a blindfold made from a potato sack and led her up the ladder. If she really wanted to figure out where they were and then lead someone here, she probably could, but it was the best he could do under the circumstances.

"Where are we?" Simoni asked as they climbed out of the shaft. She hugged herself inside Trenton's sweater. "It's so cold."

"Just a little farther." Holding her hand, he led her to the courtyard in front of the foundry where he and Kallista had been repairing the dragon. It still had a few issues, but the metal was so strong and light that the damage from the crash hadn't been nearly as catastrophic as they'd expected.

When they reached the melted gate, he had her stop while he started the generator and turned on the lights.

Simoni sniffed. "It doesn't smell like we're on level one anymore, but we didn't go down the elevator."

"Yeah, that's the thing," Trenton said. "This is going to be hard to believe, but a lot of what we've been taught our whole lives isn't true. Level one really isn't the first level. There are actually two levels above it."

With her eyes still covered by the sack, Simoni turned toward him and Trenton hurried on.

"And you know how we've been told that we use slates because there isn't enough paper? That's a lie too. People used to have plenty of paper. There's a whole room filled with books and paintings in City Hall."

"How do you know any of those things?" Simoni asked carefully.

Trenton sighed. "It's a long story, and I'll tell it all if you want. But the thing you need to know is that I would never do anything to hurt you or anyone else. I'd never hurt the city. I've come to love food production, and I especially love working with you. But there's also a part of me I can't get rid of, a part that needs to know things. Needs to understand things."

He gripped her hand, hoping he could find a way to make her believe. "Remember that day I made the swing, trying to impress you?"

Simoni smiled a little. Trenton hoped that was a good sign. "That's why you did it? To impress me?"

"You said you were bored, so I decided to build something you'd like. I know it was probably a dumb idea, now. But I didn't then. After that whole mess, the chancellor was going to send me away for months of retraining, until they discovered that I wasn't the cause of the power outage—it was a jam in the feeder belt of a power plant." Trenton rubbed the back of his hand across his mouth, hoping he wasn't making a huge mistake. "I found out that the thing jamming the belt was a part of something bigger. Something a *lot* bigger."

He walked behind her and untied her blindfold. "Anyway, one thing led to another. One part fit another. And the next thing I knew, a friend and I had built . . . *this*."

He pulled off the blindfold. Simoni looked up, her eyes growing wider and wider. She held her hands to her mouth. "What is it?"

Trenton tried to swallow, but a lump blocked his throat. "It's a steam-powered dragon."

"A *dragon?*" She stared up at it with wide eyes. "What's that?"

"It's a creature from old books," Trenton said. "It's a machine that actually walks and flies. Well, it flew once, but then the canvas on the wings tore. That was the night of the dance. I didn't have a helmet, and I got hurt when it crashed." Simoni continued to gape, and Trenton began to get nervous. "So, um, what do you think?"

She opened her mouth, closed it, shook her head, and then managed, "I thought you were seeing another girl."

Trenton laughed. "I'm pretty sure this is a boy dragon." He rubbed his palms on his shirt. "There is a girl, but not like that. We're building this together."

He studied her face, trying to gauge her reaction. "Are you still mad?"

"No," Simoni said, taking his hand. "Not anymore. I'm glad you told me the truth. I just . . . I need to think for a while."

"I totally understand," Trenton said. "I helped build it, and it's even hard for me to believe it's real. But you'll keep your promise not to tell anyone. Right?"

She looked over with an expression he couldn't read. "You can trust me."

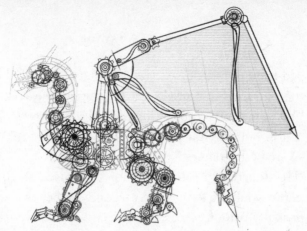

33

The following weeks were the best Trenton could remember. With no more lies between him and Simoni, they'd never gotten along better. Angus was still a pest, but he was so focused on Simoni that Trenton had no problem losing him when he needed to get to the silo.

The dragon was coming along great too. The repairs were complete, and they'd finished the scales on the outside of the framework. Kallista was happier than he'd ever seen her.

The only thing missing were new wings. They'd searched every fabric shop in the city but found nothing strong enough to withstand the force of flight. Metal would be strong enough, but it was far too heavy and not flexible enough for the wing movement they needed.

On a Saturday morning, with nothing to do, he and Kallista were killing time.

She sat in the backseat of the dragon, shooting fire at random things. "Ladon's bored. He wants to fly."

Trenton looked up from the floor, where he'd been bleeding air bubbles out of the hydraulic system. "Ladon?"

"That's his name."

Trenton shut the bleeder valve and frowned. "Since when?"

"Every dragon needs a name." Kallista leaned across the front seat to point the dragon's head at an old metal chair and slapped the fire button. A stream of flame engulfed the chair, leaving nothing but a single leg sticking sideways out of the ruins. "You can't just keep calling him *dragon* forever."

"Sure, but why Ladon? Why not Deathfire or Windfury? Those are better names."

"He doesn't look like either of those," Kallista said. "*Deathfire* would be for a mean dragon with beady eyes and flaring nostrils. Windfury has anger issues. Ladon was the dragon from Greek mythology who guarded the golden apples of immortality. Our dragon will guard us. He's powerful, but he's also smart, and kind."

Trenton looked at the puddle of melted goo. "Not if you're a chair."

"The chair had beady eyes. Ladon didn't trust him."

Trenton opened his eyes wide, and they both laughed.

"So," Kallista said. "How are you going to get him wings?"

"How am *I*?" Trenton climbed up the front leg of the dragon. With the coal powder burning, he had to be careful about staying well away from the furnace. Even when it was completely enclosed, the furnace's the orange glow showed through the metal ribs.

He popped himself into the front seat and made the dragon move forward and backward in a little dragon dance. "Don thinks *you* should figure out what to use for wings. He says it's only fair because I figured out about the turbines."

Kallista waggled the tail back and forth in time to the dance. "His name is *Ladon*, not Don. And he says I put most of him together, so the least you can do is find the parts."

Trenton tilted his head as if listening to something. "Did you hear that?"

"Hear what?" Kallista said. "Is Ladon telling you it's time for lunch?"

"Shut off the turbines."

She closed the air valve, and as the fire went out, the same growling sound came that he'd heard before.

"Sounds like an engine, maybe," Trenton said. "Have you heard it before?"

Kallista shook her head. "It's probably just wind echoing in the air ducts. We can hear it more clearly here because we're closer to the top."

Trenton wasn't sure. It didn't sound like the wind to him.

"I think we need to explore the top level," Kallista said.

Trenton stopped listening for the sound. "I thought we agreed that going up there isn't safe."

"Maybe it's not," she said. "But we've searched everywhere else for wing fabric. That sound could be a clue telling us the final piece of the puzzle is up there. My father did everything for—"

"A *reason*," Trenton said. "I know." He rubbed the back of his neck. "In all this time, you've never gone up there without me?"

Kallista shrugged. "I thought about going a few times, but . . . I don't know. Knowing it's so close to the outside—that so many people starved or died from the poisoned air—it would feel like entering a graveyard. But we have to at least look."

"When?" he asked.

She took a deep breath. "There's no point in waiting."

He had been afraid she would say that. "I guess it would be okay. If we're careful."

As they climbed down the dragon and lit their helmets, Trenton tried to occupy his thoughts with things he wanted to adjust on the dragon and what they were learning in food production. But his mind kept slipping back to the feeling he'd had looking up into the dark feeder shaft, and to Kallista's words.

It would feel like entering a graveyard.

As they walked into the mine shaft, he shivered and wished

he had a heavier coat. They stopped outside the feeder chute they'd discovered the first time they were on that level.

"We keep an eye on each other up there," Trenton said. "If either of us starts to feel sick, we leave."

She nodded. "I'll go first."

Trenton thought he should probably at least argue with her, but as scared as he felt, he didn't know if he could have led the way.

This chute wasn't nearly as steep as the ones below, and not as long. Before he was ready, Kallista stopped crawling. "We're here."

Trenton reached a hand near her ankle so he could pull her back if anything happened. "Do you see anything?" he asked.

She crawled a little farther, then paused for several seconds before saying, "There's something wrong."

"What do you mean, *wrong?*"

But Kallista was already climbing out.

"What do you mean *wrong?*" Trenton hurried after her, his heart racing. As he emerged from the mouth of the shaft, he found Kallista kneeling a few feet away. He turned toward her, and his helmet illuminated a shadow on the rock floor.

"What is it?" he asked, rushing to her side.

She stuck her hand into a groove cut into the stone so deep that she could reach inside it nearly to her elbow. The huge gouge was at least twelve feet long. Trenton ran his fingers along the edge—smooth, as though made with an extremely sharp tool. Scattered across the floor were pieces of rock blasted into glittering shards, some as long as his arm.

Trenton sucked in a breath. "What is this?"

"I don't know," Kallista whispered. "But there are more. Lots more."

Looking to his left, Trenton saw two more grooves as deep

and long as the first. He stood and slowly turned around. The rock floor had been blasted and gouged as far as his light reached in every direction. It was as if some giant had used a pickaxe to attack the city.

"What happened here?" he whispered.

Kallista lifted her head. "Do you smell that?"

Trenton sniffed. Other than rock and dust, he didn't smell anything. He began to say as much but sniffed again. This time, there *was* something. He couldn't tell what, but for some reason, it reminded him of the factories on level three.

Kallista got up and started off into the darkness.

"Where are you going?" Trenton said, trotting behind her. "Whatever did this could still be out there."

But Kallista had already found what she was looking for. A wall came into view. "There."

Trenton squinted, trying to understand what he was seeing on the wall, which looked oddly distorted. At first he thought it was simply a trick of the light from his helmet, but the closer they got, the more obvious it became that that wasn't the case. Something—or someone—had *twisted* the rock wall into strange and terrible shapes. In some places, the stone looked like it had run like water before turning into rock.

Kallista rubbed the wall, then pulled back and examined her fingers. Their tips were black. At some point a fire had raged here. Smoke—that was the smell. After who knew how many years since the level had been abandoned, the smell still lingered. How big would a fire have to have been to leave that much soot? But it couldn't have been hot enough to melt the stone itself, could it?

Trenton's heart pounded against his ribs, and his mouth felt dry. "What happened? What did they do?"

"I don't know," Kallista said, sounding out of breath. "But whatever it was, I don't think we're supposed to know about it."

Trenton noticed a discolored spot on the floor. At first it looked like more soot, but it was more brown than black. Dropping to the ground, he reached for the spot and froze, his fingers only inches from the floor.

"Kallista," he said, his voice shaking. "What does this look like to you?"

She knelt on the floor beside him, and suddenly the two of them were holding hands, their fingers ice cold. "Dried blood. So much of it."

Trenton met her dark eyes. She looked drained and much too pale. He wanted to go straight down the shaft and never return, but he couldn't do that until they investigated the rest of the level. Gripping each other's hands tightly, they wandered through the large, empty space.

The level below them had been abandoned at some point, either because the people had outgrown it or because they'd simply moved on.

But that wasn't what had happened here. Something had *driven* these people out, forcing them to burrow deeper into the mountain. Scattered about were the signs of a terrible struggle: blasted metal and stone, shattered glass, bits of rusted machinery they didn't recognize that crumbled when they touched it.

They passed foundations where buildings had once stood, and occasionally they found something recognizable—a bent spoon, a broken gauge, the head of a hammer. But more often than not, everything was so melted and misshapen that it was impossible to determine what anything used to be.

At one point, Trenton thought he saw a tree branch, bleached nearly white. He reached for it, but Kallista yanked him back. He looked closer and realized it wasn't a branch at all, but a bone. A human leg bone.

"Let's get out of here," he said.

The air was so cold that his breath plumed in front of his face, and the only sound came from the whirring of the air exhaust system in the center of the cavern.

"Hold on," Kallista said. "I see something this way."

Thirty or forty feet ahead, the wall of the cavern appeared to bulge inward. As they drew closer, they discovered a pile of rocks forty feet high and equally wide reaching from floor to ceiling. The rocks were held together with mortar, forming a complete seal.

"This has to be the original entrance," Kallista said. Moving to the right of the rocks, her light reflected off a section of wall that had been polished to a smooth, black surface. Carved into the rock and painted in gold letters now dimmed with age and smoke was the word COVE. She ran her fingers across the letters. "The founders carved this."

The rumbling sound came again, much closer this time. It seemed to come from outside the entrance, a deep roaring that raised goose bumps all over Trenton's body. He put his ear to the pile of rocks and felt a vibration.

"It's the wind," Kallista said. "Maybe the weather got messed up from all the pollution, making huge storms outside." She pulled his hand. "Let's go. I don't want to stay up here anymore."

Trenton didn't want to either, but he thought he saw something else carved into the wall on the other side of the entrance, and he had to read it. Moving closer, he discovered names cut into the rock, one below the other in tightly engraved letters. There were three tall columns, each stretching from over his head down to the ground. Hundreds of names.

"Are these the founders?"

"I don't think so." Kallista's voice was barely audible. She ran her fingers over something carved next to the lists of names.

Trenton looked closer. Engraved beside each name were two numbers. "What are those?"

Kallista chewed her lower lip. "I think they're years."

Cove years counted from 01 to the current year, 150. The number beside the first three names was 01, the year Cove was founded. The next two names had 02. Slowly, the numbers increased, until, about a third of the way down the first column, the number reached 29. The rest of the names had that number—the rest of the first column, the second, and the third. Trenton stared at the list, trying to understand what it meant.

Why did most of the list have the year 29 beside them? All at once, it came to him, and his chest tightened until he could barely breathe.

He turned to Kallista, his heart pounding. "Are they . . . ? Does it mean . . . ?"

"It's a list of the dead." Kallista clasped her arms across her chest. "Those are the years they died."

Trenton looked back at the list. Three people dead the first year. Two the second. Some years had a few deaths, some none at all. Until year 29, when . . . He turned away and faced the destruction. The fire, the blasted rock, the destroyed buildings, the stains on the ground. All those names, hundreds of them, all dead the same year.

Something terrible had happened here. Something so awful he didn't want to think about it. His throat felt the size of a straw.

"We have to leave," he gasped. "We have to get out of here now!"

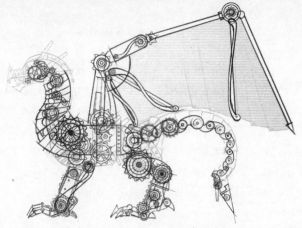

 34

As they walked toward the chute to climb back down, Kallista pulled Trenton to the left. "Stay away from the exhaust fans."

He looked around and realized they'd strayed toward the center of the cavern. Frigid air blew in his face, sucked past by the fans. He rubbed his arms. "You were right. It feels like we're walking through a city of the dead."

"We are," Kallista said. "And whatever happened here, the city has created lie after lie to cover it up."

They reached the opening, and Trenton was all too glad to leave the level behind him. He climbed out of the chute, back to the old mine shaft below. Immediately he stopped shaking. The air on this level wasn't as cold as the air above, but that wasn't the only reason.

"What did you mean back there about lies?" Trenton asked, moving away from the chute.

Kallista held up a finger. "First of all, I don't remember ever hearing about a war in the city."

"A *war*?"

"You know, where people fight each other? Kill each other?"

"I know what the word means." He'd read about wars in school. According to the history texts, they were the result of change. When people stopped doing things the way they'd always been done, fighting was inevitable. "But what makes you think that what happened up there was a war?"

Kallista snorted, the sound echoing in the eerie darkness of the mine shaft. "You think those people died from illness or pollution? That was from violence—*inside* the city. Weapons, fire, explosions. What else could have done any of that?"

She was right. Whatever had happened there had been violent.

"The *Book of Chancellors* is a lie," she said.

Trenton gasped. The *Book of Chancellors* was the most sacred document in the city. To call it false was practically criminal.

"We read the beginning," Kallista said, the night we broke into the museum. "Did you read anything that could explain what we saw up there?"

"No," he admitted.

According to the lessons they'd learned in school, the first years of the city were spent starting farms and mining coal, the people working together to create a magnificent machine. If the *Book of Chancellors* wasn't true, what else might be a lie?

"Of course we didn't see anything about it," Kallista said, breathing hard now. "They took it out or changed it because they didn't want anyone to know what really happened." Her face flushed. She snapped a piece of coal from the wall. "Have you ever wondered why we have to climb through coal chutes to get to both of these levels? There must have been openings to them at one time, but they were sealed off. The shafts, too. My guess is that my father is the one who cleared them."

"They were sealed to keep people from coming up here."

"And to keep people from knowing the truth." Kallista pointed toward the dark opening of the chute they'd climbed through. "Whatever happened up there was so horrible that the leaders must have sealed the upper levels, changed the *Book of Chancellors*, and have been lying about it ever since." Her helmet light bobbed as she spoke, casting unsettling shadows around them. "I think my father found out about the upper levels, and he was killed to keep him quiet."

Trenton nodded slowly. "And now we know the truth too. If anyone finds out—"

Kallista glared at him. "We tell no one."

"Let's get back to the foundry," Trenton said, walking toward the mine entrance. "I want to turn on a whole bunch of lights."

"And I want to start Ladon's furnace so we can get warm." Kallista headed for the entrance too, but then stopped, turned around, and looked deeper into the mine shaft. "Did you see that?"

Trenton turned too. "See what?" He stepped beside her, and his light glinted off something metallic on the wall.

Together they walked deeper into the tunnel. The walls and ceiling were covered with a gold mesh-like material connected to the beams in the walls and the ceiling, Some of it had pulled loose. He knelt down to touch it.

"It feels like metal."

"But it's flexible, like cloth," Kallista said, twisting it between her fingers. "I've never seen anything like it in the mines."

Trenton yanked at the fabric as hard as he could. He might as well have tried to tear a piece of steel. "It's strong."

Kallista pulled a knife from her tool belt and ran the blade across the surface of the gold material. It didn't leave a mark. She pushed harder and harder until the blade snapped.

Suddenly all thoughts of the destruction above them had disappeared. They looked at each other—eyes wide—and, at the same time, said, "Wings."

• • •

The metal was exactly what they needed—light, flexible, and so strong that they had to use a blowtorch to cut it. The mesh bent almost like cloth, but it was fine enough that the air would flow over the surface instead of going through.

Over the next few days, they collected as much of the fabric as they could carry, then carefully welded it onto Ladon's wing struts. Kallista was the better welder, so while she worked on the wings, Trenton installed a pair of leather harnesses to hold them in their seats in case they had any more accidents. It was exhausting, but Trenton was almost sure it would work. Still, something bothered him.

"Isn't this amazing?" Kallista asked as she welded the last piece in place. Trenton grunted, and she looked up from what she was doing. "What's wrong? Aren't you excited to test the new wings?"

He tried to smile. "I guess."

Kallista put down her tools and swung under the wing to sit beside him on the scaffolding they'd made. "You've been quiet all day. Are you worried about crashing again?"

"It's not that." He twirled a screwdriver in his hand. "You always say that your father had a reason for everything he did. Well, what if his reason for having us build this wasn't to actually make the dragon?"

"I don't understand," Kallista said. "Why else would he have left the plans and all of the clues we've found?"

Trenton ran his hand over the surface of the wing. "This material could have saved my mother. If it had been installed on the walls of the mines she was working in, the collapse might never have happened, and she wouldn't be crippled. She was lucky. A lot of people haven't been—they've died down there."

"It's strange that they stopped using it," Kallista agreed.

"No." Trenton slapped the handle of the screwdriver against

his palm. "*Strange* would be if there were only *one* thing that's off. But it's more than the gold fabric. Yes, they stopped using the material in their mines. But they also stopped using the coal crusher and the turbines. I've noticed at least a dozen other little things used on this level that aren't around anymore. Things that would make our equipment safer, faster, and more efficient. I'm sure I've missed a lot of other things too."

He got up and stared at the buildings around them. "Doesn't it seem like a coincidence that we've discovered a better metal, safer mining equipment, and a way to generate power that would let us create twice as much electricity with half the coal, all while building this dragon?"

Kallista chewed her lower lip. "I've been so caught up in finishing the dragon that I didn't think about any of that until now. But you're right. My father wanted us to see all of this. That has to be why he left those things out of the plans."

"I'll bet there are a lot more improvements, too," Trenton said. "The question is, why? Why would the city intentionally leave behind better technology and replace it with equipment that's less efficient and less safe?"

"Do you think it has something to do with what we found up there?" Kallista asked, pointing toward the level above them.

He nodded. "I've been thinking about what you said. About the *Book of Chancellors* and how it could have been changed or faked to rewrite history. But what if the record wasn't changed?"

She snorted. "You're saying that they somehow forgot to mention hundreds of deaths when they wrote up the yearly reviews?"

Trenton held up a hand. "Of course not. But what if the city wasn't founded in 1939, like we've been taught? What if it was founded almost thirty years earlier? Maybe the war on the first level was so terrible that they decided to start over. They dug out a new level, sealed off the first two, and pretended that none of the other stuff ever happened. They could have even started over numbering the years."

"That would explain why the deaths aren't mentioned in the book," Kallista said.

"It would also explain things like how the fish tanks down below are stamped with the years 01 and 02, when the level they're on couldn't have existed then. And why no one ever comes up here. But I still can't figure out why they'd start over with worse equipment."

"Maybe . . ." Kallista tugged at a strand of hair, clearly working the idea over in her mind. "Maybe they blamed the equipment for the war. They could have decided that they'd be better off going back to older technology. What I can't understand is how they could convince everyone to go along with that idea."

Trenton knew how she'd react to what he was going to say, but he pushed forward anyway. "We have to bring people up here, show them what we've found."

"Are you crazy?" Kallista jumped to her feet. "No one would ever believe us. They'd lock us up."

He turned around and faced the dragon. "They'd believe us if they saw Ladon."

"No!" Kallista shouted. "Absolutely not. He's a gift from my father to me. The people in the city would see it as an invention. They'd say, 'Look what terrible, crazy thing Leo Babbage has done now.' I'm not letting them have this. I won't."

Trenton tried to take her hand, but she pulled away. He exhaled. "Miss Huber said your father understood people's thoughts as well as he understood machines. He probably knew you'd react this way."

"So what?" Kallista demanded, once again the girl who'd fought Trenton in the street to get what her father had left.

"Your father made sure the dragon required two operators so you'd find a friend," Trenton said, his voice soft. "Maybe he wanted you to have a friend so that person would tell you the things you didn't want to hear but needed to know. It's been great up here—working with you, talking to you, getting to know the real Kallista who hides inside her angry shell—but we can't keep this a secret anymore. I think that's what your father has been trying to tell us. Maybe that's why he died. Maybe that's why we're in extreme danger." He reached for her hand again, and this time she didn't stop him.

She looked at the dragon, her eyes glistening. "They won't let us keep him."

"Probably not," he admitted. "And they could do to us whatever they did to your father."

She tilted her head, chin trembling. "Why would they tell so many lies? Why would they make things worse for everyone?"

Trenton shook his head. "Your father might have known why, but I don't."

"Give me some time," Kallista said. "I know that showing Ladon is probably the right thing to do, but it has to be my choice. You can't show anyone the dragon unless I agree first."

Guilt welled in his chest. He shouldn't have brought Simoni here without telling Kallista. But if Simoni was okay with it, maybe everyone else would be too. They had to find a way to explain how much better things could be if they used Leo Babbage's discoveries.

"It's your decision," he said.

"Thank you." Kallista squeezed his hand. "But first I want to take Ladon out for a real flight."

"I think he deserves it," Trenton said.

She smiled. "I think *we* do."

• • •

Trenton snugged his new leather helmet onto his head. It was amazing, with padding all around and built-in goggles. "Where did you get these?" he shouted over the roar of the turbines.

"I made them," Kallista said, tightening her own helmet.

"Since when can you sew?"

She glared at him. "I can do a lot of things you don't know about." She grabbed the leg controls. "Ready to go?"

He raised the tail. "Let's do this, big Don."

Kallista walked the dragon out of the gate so smoothly that Trenton barely had to use the tail to balance the dragon. She worked the front and back legs so it hardly felt like they were moving at all.

"You've been practicing without me," he said.

She looked back at him and arched an eyebrow inside her goggles. "Maybe."

After they'd cleared the gate, she opened the wings. The mesh crackled a little, but it looked amazing.

"Give the wings a slight angle," she said. "That will keep us from running too fast, and I think it'll help us take off, too."

He pulled back on the stick ever so slightly.

"Strapped in?" she asked.

Trenton patted the leather harness he'd designed, showing that it was tightly buckled across his chest. "Go for it."

Kallista increased their speed, moving the legs faster. "Pressure okay?"

Trenton checked the gauge. "Holding steady at eighty percent."

"Here we go." She pushed the throttle all the way up.

The sudden acceleration threw Trenton back against his

seat. With each step, they moved fifteen feet, then twenty, thirty, thirty-five.

"Take him up!" she yelled.

Trenton pulled back on the flight controller. The wings tilted and began to flap. Forty feet, fifty. The mesh-clad wings clawed at the air, and, just like that, they were flying. The first time they'd taken off, it had felt like rolling down a hill in a barrel—thrilling but completely out of control. This time, it was like watching a dancer leap gracefully into the air.

"Higher," Kallista called.

Trenton tugged on the stick, and the great metal wings strained toward the ceiling. He pushed the stick forward slightly, and soon they were gliding like a bird.

Kallista pointed the dragon's head downward, and the eyes lit up the ground below as they raced over buildings and equipment. She banked to the left, and Trenton held his breath, watching the wings. There wasn't so much as a ripple across their glittering surface.

She turned left so sharply that Trenton's stomach rolled.

"Don't forget the tail," she called.

He whipped the tail around to even them out. "Let's dive-bomb something," he suggested.

Kallista nodded and pointed the dragon's head toward a tall metal tower. Trenton pushed the stick until they were diving toward it. Fifty feet from the tower, he pushed the flame button. A ball of fire blasted the tower into a heap of slag.

"Bull's-eye!" he yelled.

"Ladon says it had a suspicious mustache," Kallista called back, and the two of them howled with laughter. "Let's take him all the way up," she said.

Trenton pulled the stick back again, letting the dragon climb.

They got so close to the top of the cavern he felt as if he could touch the ceiling by standing up. He quickly leveled the wings.

It really is like being a bird, he thought as Kallista maneuvered, flying them from one end of the level to the other.

As he was about to take them back down, she pointed to their left. Trenton turned in time to see something red flash past.

She circled around and edged closer to the wall, where he could make out some painted words. But how could they have gotten there so high up on the wall? Whoever left the text must have scaled the wall itself. The letters were ten feet from the top of the cavern—impossible to see unless you were this high up and had bright lights to read by.

He slowed as they flew past, but even so, he made out only part of the message.

To learn the

Then they were beyond it.

"Did you get it all?" he called.

Kallista shook her head and flew back around. On their second pass, he got more of text.

To learn the truth, go to

"I didn't catch the end," Kallista called.

"Me, either," Trenton said. "One more time."

She circled for a third pass, and Trenton slowed their speed as much as he could without losing altitude.

To learn the truth, go to the beginning. L. B.

The letters at the end were crooked and paint had dripped onto the wall, but there was no question who had painted them.

Leo Babbage had intentionally written a message somewhere they'd never find it until the dragon was complete.

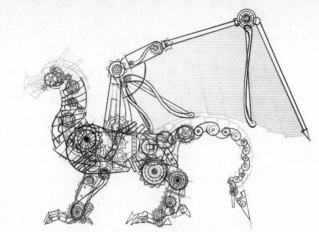

35

"G oing back up there is a really bad idea," Trenton said as they headed into the mine shaft.

Kallista glared back, hands on her hips. "He told us to go back to the beginning. That's what I'm doing."

"How do you know he was talking about up there?" Trenton asked. He tried not to look at the coal chute they'd climbed up a few days earlier, but the dark hole seemed to watch him like an empty eye socket. The idea of returning to the top level terrified him far more than he wanted to admit. "For all we know, he meant for us to go down to the feeder belt where I found the first tube. That's where this whole thing began for us."

"He *didn't* mean that," Kallista said. "I played hundreds of these games with him, maybe thousands. I always thought he wanted me to improve my reasoning skills, and that might have been part of it. But now I wonder if he was planning something like this all along. He knew that someday the only way he'd be able to communicate with me would be by leaving messages." She checked the fuel level in her mining helmet and tightened it on her forehead.

Trenton rubbed his arms, trying not to think about the growling they'd heard outside the sealed entrance. "So what? You two played a lot of games. Why does that mean the next clue is upstairs?"

Kallista looked back at him, and the glare of her lamp forced him to shade his eyes. "My father could come up with more bizarre clues than you can imagine. Sometimes I got so frustrated, I cried. But eventually, by thinking through the puzzles logically, I figured them out. He always stuck to two rules: First, just when you thought the game was done, there was always one last clue. Right when you thought you knew where the game was headed, he'd throw in a twist. Second, no two clues were ever in the same place. There won't be another clue where you found the first one." She pointed to the ceiling. "Whatever he wants me to find is up there on the first level."

She turned around and marched toward the mine shaft as though an invisible spotlight led the way.

Trenton tried to force down the dread building up inside him. Something terrible had happened up there. It felt cursed. Never mind the fact that they'd already searched it. But it didn't matter what he thought. When Kallista had her mind set on something, it was impossible to talk her out of it. Forcing aside his doubts, he followed her into the mine shaft.

When they reached the chute, she climbed in without hesitation. As Trenton climbed in after her, he thought he heard something behind him. He looked back. "What was that?"

Kallista barely paused. "Wind again?"

"No, it . . ." He listened, but whatever it was had gone. He turned back to the shaft, only to find Kallista already out of sight. "Wait up," he called.

By the time he reached the top level, she was already walking across the cavern. "Why are you in such a rush?" he said, trying to ignore the shattered rock and smoke stains.

"This is what he's been leading us to all along," Kallista said. "It's the final piece of the puzzle. I can feel it."

"How can you be so sure?"

"I just am," she said, puffing from the climb. "He's been

teasing us along—a little bit here, a little bit there. Remember how upset you were when you found out that my father was the one who left that tube?"

Trenton didn't like to think about how close he'd come to throwing the tube away. If he had, none of this would have happened. "I didn't understand."

Kallista stopped to catch her breath. "If someone had told you back then that the city was intentionally denying us paper, that we were using old equipment, and that the two of us could build a mechanical dragon that actually flies, would you have believed them?"

He shook his head. "I would have thought they were crazy."

"I might have, too," Kallista said. "And that's coming from the daughter of Mad Leo Babbage. He had to feed the information to us slowly, like a baby learning to eat solid food. The dragon kept us going. It helped us know that my father wasn't crazy. But you believe all of those things now, don't you? The paper, the equipment, the dragon?"

She clenched her fists, hands shaking with fear and excitement. "My father has been leading us to something important—even bigger than the dragon. Whatever it is, we're about to find out. She spun around and headed off.

"Where are we going?" Trenton asked.

"To the entrance," Kallista said. "Where Cove began."

When they arrived at the rock wall, Trenton cocked his head and listened for the growling. Nothing. Maybe it had been the wind after all.

"Check for loose rocks," Kallista said. "Or false fronts. Anything. My father was a master at hiding things in plain sight."

Trenton wasn't too excited about the idea of pulling at rocks that were the only things protecting them from the poisonous air outside, but the wall was solidly mortared and he figured one rock wouldn't make a difference. Taking off his gloves to get a better grip, he pulled, prodded, and twisted every rock he could find.

Kallista worked with a manic energy, moving from one stone to another as if the next one might hide a vast treasure. The longer they searched, the more frantic she became. After two hours, they hadn't found so much as wiggly piece of mortar.

"Maybe we should come back tomorrow," Trenton said. "It's getting late."

"Go if you want to," Kallista said. "I'm not giving up."

Trenton sighed. "I'm not giving up either. But I have to leave soon, or I'll miss curfew. For all we know, the clue might be a rock we can't reach. We can bring a ladder with us tomorrow."

Kallista silently continued checking rocks, ones that Trenton was almost certain she'd checked earlier. Exasperated, he walked away and found himself beside the gold letters on the wall. COVE. Early on in school, they'd all learned the definition of the word *cove*: a recessed place, a protected bay or inlet. That's what the city had been for the people who founded it—a place of protection, shelter, safety.

The founders had come here to lock themselves away from the dangers of technology that had destroyed the rest of the world. But had they gone too far? Had they abandoned technologies that were actually helpful?

As he started to turn away, his headlamp shined at an angle that illuminated something he hadn't noticed before. "Look at this," he said, running his fingers over the wall to the left of the C in Cove. "Does this part look less shiny than the rest of the rock to you?"

Kallista hurried to his side. She touched the wall. "That's not rock. It's some kind of plaster. Like they filled something in or covered it over." She pulled out a chisel, placed it on the right spot, and tapped it with her hammer. A chunk of black fell away. She cleared off more of the black substance, uncovering a few specks of gold.

Trenton looked from the word on the right to the gold on the left. "It's the same color," he said. "It looks like someone covered up another letter."

Together they cleared away the rest of the filler, revealing the letter *S*.

"*Scove?*" Trenton said. "What's that supposed to mean?"

"There's more," Kallista said, chipping to the left of the *S*. Tapping away at the letters, they uncovered an *I* and a *D*.

When they were sure there was nothing more on the left side, they moved to the wall on the right side of the *E*, but by then Trenton already knew what they would find. His heart raced as he tried to comprehend it. They chipped the last of the black away from an *R* and a *Y*, and then stepped back to examine their work.

DISCOVERY

"They didn't name the city Cove," Kallista said. "They named it Discovery."

"Even the name of our home is a lie," he whispered, feeling slightly dead inside. *Discovery*. Not a place of hiding, but a place of learning, of exploration.

What did this mean? Why would the government change the city's name?

Kallista knelt and tapped a lower section of the wall. "There's something here." She continued working her hammer and chisel. On the first strike, a small section of the wall gave way, revealing an opening. She worked at the rest of the covering until she'd revealed a hole roughly twelve inches high, twelve inches wide, and two feet deep. A metal box lay inside, taking up the full width of the compartment. An envelope rested on top.

"Your father dug this out?" Trenton asked.

Kallista nodded. With trembling hands, she reached for the envelope but pulled back. "I don't think I can do it. I want to, but . . ."

He put an arm around her shoulder. "Do you want me to?"

Her chin quivered. "Would you? Please?"

"Of course."

Trenton slid the box out of the opening. The box was maybe six inches tall. He handed the envelope to Kallista, but she shook her head. "Could you read it to me? Please."

"Are you sure?"

She nodded.

Setting the box to one side, Trenton carefully slid his finger under the flap of the envelope and took out a piece of paper made of the same rough, slightly brownish stock the dragon plans had been drawn on. The handwriting was clearly the same person's. He wet his lips.

"*My Dearest Daughter,*

"*If you are reading this, it means you were able to follow my clues. Congratulations. You always were good at my games. It also means that you built and flew the dragon. I wish I had been there to see it. Unless you modified my plans—something I wouldn't put past you—you have also made a friend. Please offer him or her my thanks.*"

Kallista laughed shakily. "Thanks," she said, her voice husky with emotion.

"You're welcome." He checked to make sure she was okay, then continued reading.

"*Unfortunately, it also means that I am no longer here. I've considered several ways such an event could occur, but I want you to know that however it happened, I always had your safety foremost in my mind.*

"At this time, you have a decision to make. You may destroy this box and go on with your life. Cove—or Discovery, as you probably know it is really called—is far from perfect. But at the time of this writing, it is safe, at least. The information inside this box will likely change your life in ways that make going forward as before impossible. I know it changed mine."

Trenton heard Kallista sniffle. "We can take it down below and finish it later, when you're more . . ." He didn't know what the word was. He couldn't imagine how she was feeling at that moment.

"No," she whispered, wiping her eyes with her sleeve. "Finish reading."

He turned the letter over and continued.

"I collected the enclosed documents over a period of years. At first I didn't understand what I was seeing. As the pieces came together, I realized that our history as we know it is a badly twisted version of what really happened. It was my hope that the leaders of our city would, if not embrace, at least accept my discoveries. (Pardon the pun, but at the moment, puns are about all the humor I can muster.)"

Despite the urgency of the message, Trenton couldn't help smiling. Maybe Kallista's father had a sense of humor after all.

"Instead, they have branded me deluded at best, and quite possibly a traitor. They see my continued presence in the city as a threat. That makes me a danger to you and all those close to me. I left you clues to what I found in the hopes that you would learn about the deceptions we have been taught and decide for yourself how you would respond."

Trenton scanned the last few paragraphs, then read them out loud.

"If you choose to open the box, do it knowing that you will

remain in extreme danger as long as you live here. What you will find inside is hard for me to believe even now.

"If you choose not to open the box, I will not think less of you, but please destroy it so that its contents do not put innocent people in jeopardy.

"When I realized that my presence put your life in danger, I descended into a pit of darkness so black I could see no light. If everything crumbles around you, and you should find yourself plunged into such darkness, know that I have always, and will always will love you, and that hope continues to shine even in the dark.

"Love, your father, L. B."

Kallista snatched the letter out of Trenton's hand and read it silently. Tears rolled down her cheeks, splattering the dusty floor. "He loves me!"

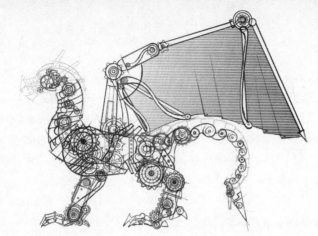

36

From the other side of the blocked entrance, the wind had picked up, roaring like a great beast. Trenton thought he heard rocks tumbling down the side of the mountain. He stared at the metal box. "Do we open it?"

"I have to," Kallista said. "Not opening it would feel like a betrayal."

Trenton chewed on his thumbnail. He felt as if a poisonous snake was coiled in front of them, and they were about to set it free. "He said he wouldn't think any less of you if you didn't."

"The betrayal wouldn't be to him," she said, straightening her shoulders. "It would be to myself. Ignoring the truth would be like sticking my head in the ground. I'd be accepting the lies. I can't do that. You don't have to stay, though. You can go back down and I'll read it myself."

"And live the rest of my life with the knowledge that you know something I don't?" Trenton shook his head and grinned. "I don't think so."

Kallista smirked. "Don't let that stop you. In the ocean of things I know that you don't, this would barely make a ripple."

"Keep telling yourself that." Trenton nodded at the box. "Let's open it."

The box had no lock. The very fact of where and how it was

hidden was lock enough. Kallista slid the box across the floor until it was right in front of them, then lifted the lid.

The first thing they saw was a series of black-and-white pictures that looked more real than anything Trenton had ever seen. He touched the glossy surface of the first one. "It doesn't look painted."

"It isn't," Kallista said. "They're called photographs. My father told me about them. They're images captured with something called a camera."

She took the photographs out of the box, and they studied them one by one. Most showed people carrying equipment into a mountain cave.

"The founders," Trenton said. "That must be the entrance."

Kallista flipped to the front of the stack again and worked her way through them. "Look at all of the food and supplies they brought. They look scared, but none of them look sick or starving."

She was right. The paintings in the museum showed men and women with gaunt faces and barely any flesh on their bones. But here, he saw only a few people with slings or bandages, and even they looked well fed and otherwise healthy.

Outside, the sound of the wind grew stronger, but Trenton and Kallista hardly noticed it.

Trenton took several large pages out of the box. They were printed on rough paper, yellowed with age, and folded in quarters. Newspapers. He'd learned about them in school. He carefully unfolded the fragile pages.

The first pages were from 1906—thirty-three years before Cove had supposedly been founded. The stories described earthquakes in cities called Columbia, San Francisco, and somewhere called Chile. Something called Mount Vesuvius had also erupted.

He turned to the next page, dated 1908, looking for stories about sickness and pollution. Instead, everything was about finances, sports, and various political events.

The only unusual thing at all was a small story at the bottom of the page saying that a new animal had been spotted in a place called China. The story seemed to be a joke, with the writer suggesting that the report was a hoax or a prank.

Where were the stories about technology and poisoned air?

"Let me see those pictures again," he said. Kallista handed him the stack, and he thumbed quickly through it. "Look at the sky. Does it look polluted to you?"

"It's hard to tell for sure," Kallista said, holding up the black-and-white pictures. "But it does look clear. That's supposed to be good, right? The museum paintings have dark skies filled with smoke."

She pulled other another newspaper out of the box, and they both spotted the same story at the top of the front page: *Giant Winged Reptiles Appearing Across Asia and Europe.*

Giant winged reptiles? Trenton looked at Kallista. "Please don't tell me this is another one of your father's made-up stories."

Kallista stared at the page. "No. He was obsessed with fantasy creatures, but he wouldn't have gone to all this trouble for a story."

Trenton slammed his fist against the stone floor. "The paper talks about *dragons*. It's another one of his fairy tales."

The next thing in the box was no fairy tale, though. It was a large color ink drawing of a great, green creature with broad wings, a scaled body, and a ferocious-looking snout. A jet of flames was shooting out of its fang-filled mouth. Except for the fact that it was alive instead of mechanical, it could almost have been Ladon's twin.

Handwriting on the back of the photograph said *Miami, Florida.*

"No," Trenton shook his head. "That can't be real."

But the more they saw, the harder it was to believe all the pictures and articles could be fakes. Dozens of pages documented a story that became impossible not to take seriously. The accounts were horrifying.

All over the world, dragons had appeared in vast numbers. No one knew where they'd come from, only that they were multiplying faster than anyone could believe. Their numbers and strength overpowered any defenses the humans attempted.

The last article showed entire cities destroyed and residents fleeing homes that were in flames.

The truth stared them in the face. The earth hadn't been destroyed by technology. Pollution and disease hadn't driven the founders into the mountain.

Impossible as it seemed, actual dragons were responsible for it all.

Trenton stared at the pictures. "These can't be real. It has to be some sort of joke."

"My father wouldn't joke about something like this," Kallista said, her face pale.

The box was nearly empty now. Trenton pulled out several sheets of paper covered with handwriting. The heading at the top of the first page read *City of Discovery Articles of Incorporation.* Reading the page, he found nothing about wheels and cogs, nothing about a magnificent machine. No bans against inventions, creativity, or technology.

"They didn't build the city to hide," Kallista said, clenching her hands until her fingers turned white. "They built it to protect themselves from the dragons until they could figure out a way to fight back. They weren't *against* technology. They were trying to come up with *better* technology."

"But why did that change?" Trenton asked. "Why did they give up trying to fight the dragons? And why haven't we heard anything about the dragons until now?"

The next set of papers explained everything. They looked like pages from a journal. Trenton recognized the handwriting immediately; it was the same as in the first pages of the *Book of Chancellors*. The writer had been the first leader of Discovery. The story was told so bluntly and clearly that it made Trenton's stomach churn.

The people of Discovery hadn't given up. For nearly thirty years, they'd developed a plan of attack and built weapons inside the mountain. Then, twenty-nine years after sealing the doors, they were opened, and the citizens fought for their freedom.

What followed could only be described as a slaughter. Badly underestimating the strength and number of the creatures, the people quickly found that their weapons were no match. Again, the dragons forced the people to retreat, but this time the monsters followed them into the mountain, killing hundreds of people and destroying nearly everything on the first level. Homes were razed, machinery melted. Over half of the people who went into battle never returned.

Hiding on the second level, the survivors waited until the dragons left, then sealed the city for good. That's when they made a pact to remove all mention of dragons, along with every other mention of fantastical creatures of any kind.

Paranoid and afraid, they devised a new plan to ensure that no one ever went outside again. After swearing an oath of secrecy, they sealed off the upper levels and told their children that the outside air would kill them. They even changed the name of the city from Discovery to Cove. Instead of a place of learning, it would be a place of hiding.

"That's why they returned to old technologies," Trenton said, laying the last few sheets on the cave floor. "They did it to make sure that no one would ever again try to fight the dragons. The books and paintings we saw aren't from someone's imagination. They're *history*."

Kallista nodded. "Everything was changed, from machinery to clothing, to an earlier time. They started the city all over again. Banned stories and pictures so no one could create an account of what had happened. Banned changes to equipment to keep us from ever repeating history."

She rubbed a hand across her face. "The chancellor must have realized that my father knew it all. That's why he was in danger. If the city finds out *we* know too, they'll lock us up—or worse."

"There's one more thing in the box," Trenton said. He reached inside and pulled out another letter written on the same paper and with the same handwriting as the one in the envelope.

"It is now the eleventh hour. You have seen what I have gathered and know what I know. Understand that I am sure everything in these documents is true. I have been traveling outside secretly. The air is clean and fresh. But on three occasions I have seen real dragons for myself.

"More than thirty years ago, when Discovery was built by our founders, no one expected it to last this long or grow to such degrees. Huge piles of dirt and rock have built up outside to the point they are impossible to miss. Smoke plumes like a beacon. No doubt they both draw the dragons to our location. I have seen the beasts circling our mountain as though called here. I do not know whether they smell our scent, see our debris, and hunt us, or if killing is simply a part of their nature.

"Whichever is the case, I can tell you that they will discover us

*shortly. The great beasts come closer with every passing month. They
will discover our city soon, and they will not stop until they get inside."*

Trenton looked up. "*Real* dragons. What should we do?"

"We could leave," Kallista said. "Find somewhere to hide.
You know enough about farming for us to survive on our own."

"How would we get out?" Trenton said.

"My father found a way." She pointed at the box. "He must
have squeezed through the vents or found a way through the
air-exchange pipe."

Trenton shook his head. "He went out, but he came back."

"And look what happened to him." Kallista put everything
back in the box and slammed the lid closed. "You think we
should warn everyone, don't you? Offer to protect them. Don't
you understand? They wouldn't listen to my father, and they
won't listen to us. They'd kill us, too. They'll fight change until
it's too late. Our only chance is to leave."

Outside, the growling sound rose to a fever pitch, and the
walled-over entrance shook. They both spun and stared at it.
The wall shook again, and this time, several rocks broke loose,
leaving a small opening. Immediately, icy wind blasted through
the hole, carrying small, white flakes inside.

Kallista snatched the box, and the two of them stared at the
hole, waiting for something more. When nothing else happened
after several minutes, they crept to the hole. Shielding their eyes
against the frigid wind, they peered through the opening. At
first their lights revealed nothing but a swirling world of white.

"I think it's snow," Kallista said.

Something rumbled outside again, and before they could
pull away, a huge shape appeared. It was so large they couldn't
tell exactly what it was, but their lights clearly revealed rows of
shimmering green scales.

They stumbled backward.

"A d-d-dragon," Trenton stuttered.

"Run!" Kallista shouted, pulling him from the wall.

"Did it see us?" Trenton called, racing to the coal chute.

"It doesn't matter. It's going to realize we're here and break down the wall."

He stopped. "We have to warn the city!"

"So they can do what? Send it to retraining?"

Kallista shoved him into the chute opening. "Once the dragon gets in the city it will start killing. We have to get Ladon into the air. He's our only chance of fighting that thing."

Falling and sliding, they scrambled down the chute. The growling sound faded with distance, but Trenton had no doubt it would be back.

Hand in hand, they ran toward the lights of the foundry. A hundred feet from the building, they stopped. People were all around the mechanical dragon, shining lights on it and talking.

One of them spotted Trenton and Kallista. "There they are!"

"What are you doing here?" Kallista shouted.

A girl broke from the group and raced toward them. Long, red hair flowed behind her as she ran up to them.

"Simoni," Trenton said. "What are you doing here?"

Kallista turned to gape at him, betrayal written across her face. "You promised you wouldn't show anyone."

"I'm so sorry," Simoni clutched her hands to her chest. "I had to tell them. It was for your own good."

A pair of security officers led by Marshal Darrow stepped forward, roughly grabbing Trenton and Kallista and yanking their hands behind their backs. "You are under arrest," the marshal said, "by order of the chancellor."

As the men dragged the two of them toward the foundry, Trenton—sick with guilt and shock—looked back at Simoni and whispered, "I trusted you."

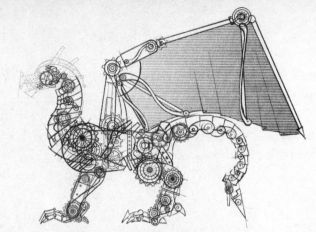

37

Bring them forward," Chancellor Lusk said. He stood at the base of the dragon, which was covered by men busy undoing bolts and removing parts.

Marshal Darrow and his security team pushed Kallista and Trenton through the entrance of the foundry.

"You're all in danger!" Trenton shouted. "You—"

An officer rammed an elbow into Trenton's stomach, sending a burst of pain through his broken ribs. "Speak when you're told to," the officer grunted.

"Leave him alone!" Kallista said, struggling to get free, but the marshal had her arms pinned behind her back.

"You promised you wouldn't hurt them," Simoni sobbed.

"So I did," the chancellor said. "And I intend to keep that promise, so long as they do what they're told. This will be a civilized proceeding, and shouting is most definitely *not* civilized." He turned to Kallista and Trenton. "You will speak when I tell you to, or you will be imprisoned immediately."

Kallista glared but held her tongue. Trenton clutched his stomach, gasping for air.

"Much better." The chancellor looked up at Ladon. Holding out his walking stick, he tapped a wing, which had already been removed. "This is . . . *something*."

"It's the city's only hope of survival," Kallista spat. A

security officer stepped in front of her, his fist pulled back, but the chancellor raised a hand.

"In deference to the fact that you are a girl, I will allow this one mistake." He adjusted his monocle. "You *are* a girl, aren't you? It's hard to tell with your spiky hair and those boyish clothes."

"Looks like a boy to me," an officer shouted, and the others laughed.

"Be that as it may," the chancellor said, "I will not accept any further outbursts from either of you. For the moment, you are guaranteed safety as citizens of Cove. Should you disobey again, I will be forced to remove that citizenship, and with it, any guarantee of your physical well-being. Understand?"

After they both nodded, he continued. "I have several questions for you. If you answer completely and honestly, you will have the opportunity to speak further. Is that clear?"

"Yes, sir," Kallista said, her eyes smoldering.

Trenton glanced at the ceiling. How long would it take for the dragon to break through the entrance and find a way to this level? They should be preparing to fight it instead of standing around, accusing and judging.

"Let us begin," the chancellor said. "Do you admit to building this *invention?*"

Trenton nodded.

"Yes," Kallista said.

The chancellor snapped his fingers, and the woman who had denied Trenton's transfer unrolled Leo Babbage's plans. The chancellor gestured toward them. "Are these the instructions you used to build it?"

Trenton glanced at Kallista, regretting that he'd ever shown Simoni the dragon. What had he been thinking? How could he have possibly believed she would keep it secret?

Kallista refused to look at Trenton. "They're *my* plans."

The chancellor slid a hand into his vest pocket. "I see. And I also see that these plans were drawn up by your father, Leo Babbage the lunatic."

"Leo Babbage the genius," Trenton said.

Chancellor Lusk leered. "Genius and insanity are not mutually exclusive." He looked up at the workers climbing over the dragon. "Have you inspected this piece of equipment?"

"We have," a man called down.

"Would you consider it a danger to the citizens of Cove?"

"No doubt about it," the worker shouted down. "The method of power generation is unapproved and could cause a powerful explosion. The flame thrower attached to the head is a city fire waiting to happen. And, although the contraption could never get airborne, it could do serious damage to people and property in the attempt."

Trenton fought to keep from telling the worker he was a fool.

"Thank you," the chancellor said. "So, in your professional opinion, would you then say that this would qualify as unapproved equipment? Perhaps even an . . . *invention?*"

"There's not a piece of approved machinery anywhere on it," the man said. "It's a bent gear from top to bottom."

The chancellor walked back and forth in front of Trenton and Kallista, as if performing on stage. "We have two citizens who have admitted to building what is not only unapproved equipment, but machinery that is a danger to themselves, other citizens, and the city as a whole."

With tears in her eyes, Simoni looked at Trenton. He couldn't be mad at her. She still thought she was doing this for his good. He should never have put her in this position.

"Well," the chancellor said. "What do you have to say for yourselves? The girl first."

Kallista glared over her shoulder at the marshal, who was

still restraining her, then back at the chancellor. "Are you going to let this oaf break my arms?"

The chancellor smiled indulgently "Darrow, release her. If she attempts to escape, you have my permission to do more than *try* to break her arms."

The marshal let go of her, and she rubbed her elbows.

"We have all been lied to by our government," she said, looking at everyone in the room except Trenton. "Our city wasn't founded because technology had ruined the world. It was built because fire-breathing creatures called dragons attacked the people on the outside."

Several security officers, including Angus, burst into laughter.

"It's true," Trenton said. "Leo Babbage knew it." He glared at the chancellor. "That's why you killed him."

"The only person to kill anyone was crazy Leo," Marshal Darrow growled.

"We have proof," Kallista said. "It's in the box you took from me."

The chancellor's eyes narrowed. "What *box*?"

An officer trainee carried the box forward.

With obvious distaste, the chancellor took it from him. "Have you looked inside?"

The trainee shook his head. "No, sir."

"Very good," the chancellor said. "I'll deal with it." He looked from Kallista to Trenton. "Is there anything else either of you wish to say?"

Trenton spoke up. "I know it's hard to believe, but there *are* dragons. They are huge creatures with wings and scales. That box has pictures of them." He pointed to the ceiling. "A dragon is trying to break into the city right now. We saw it outside, ripping down the seal over the entrance. Once it gets in, it *will* find a way down to the city."

Angus, Simoni, and a few of the others looked up.

"A dragon?" the chancellor mocked. "Up there? Right now? Tearing down seals and coming to take our lives?" He climbed the steps of the foundry and put a hand to his mouth, his lips twitching. "Oh my, that does sound serious."

"It's true," Kallista said. "If you don't do something about it now, it'll kill everyone in the city."

The chancellor held a finger to his lips. "Everyone be silent. Let's listen for this terrifying beast that is about to destroy our beloved home."

They all grew silent. Trenton strained to hear, praying that the dragon would let out a roar.

"I don't hear anything," the chancellor whispered after a moment. "Perhaps it's a very quiet dragon. A stealthy beast."

Marshall Darrow burst into laughter, and almost everyone else joined him. The only people besides Trenton and Kallista not laughing were Simoni, who only looked sad, and Angus, who was looking at the ceiling with a thoughtful expression.

"You say you saw this make-believe beast from the outside," the chancellor said, "which is clearly a lie. If you had access to the outside, the air would have killed you instantly." He raised his walking stick, and Trenton recognized that the creature on the top of the staff was a dragon—how had he never noticed? The chancellor said, "I am ready to pass judgment."

"What about the city council?" Trenton quickly asked.

The chancellor pulled out his pocket watch. "It's too late to bother them, and I'm afraid we must finish this business now."

"Don't you people understand?" Trenton yelled. "He's lying to you. Kallista and I have been exploring up here, and you know what we found? A metal alloy that's stronger and lighter than steel, a mesh fabric that can prevent mine cave-ins, and a new way of burning coal that produces twice as much energy as what we have now. It's all been here for years, but the government doesn't want us to know about it." He looked from one person to another, hoping someone would believe him. "They'll do anything to keep you from knowing the truth. City Hall has a room full of books and paintings, but it's locked up so no one will find out what really happened. Go there. Look for yourself."

"That's *enough!*" the chancellor shouted, spittle flying from his lips. "The safety of the citizens of Cove is my responsibility. If technology exists that we're not using, that's because it's dangerous. Yes, we locked up books written by people like yourself who were intent on spreading fear and lies. Leo Babbage spouted the same lies a year ago—right before he killed himself and others with unapproved equipment. He made up these nonsensical stories about these so-called *dragons* to hide the fact that he intended to endanger everyone in the city with *inventions!* He wanted to bring back the exact things that destroyed the outside world."

"Kallista said she isn't the kind of person who can bury her head in the ground," Trenton said, "but that's exactly what *you're* doing. You think you're digging your way to safety. But you're actually digging your own graves."

The chancellor pointed an accusing finger at Trenton. "I find you both guilty of stealing, lying, trespassing, making false accusations, building unapproved equipment, and endangering the citizens of Cove. By your own admission, you broke into the city offices and damaged valuable documents. I sentence you to twelve months of retraining and a lifetime of imprisonment."

"No!" Simoni cried.

Trenton looked at Kallista, but she was staring at the ground between her feet.

"What do you want us to do with this *invention?*" one of the workers asked.

"Take it apart and bury it in the mines!" the chancellor

shouted. His eyes glistened, and a slow smile spread across his face. "Better yet, send the pieces up the feeder belts to the smelters. Melt them to slag." He held up the box with every piece of proof Kallista's father had gathered. "Burn the machine the same way I will burn this abomination."

"No!" Kallista tried to run forward, but the marshal yanked her by the arm. She stomped on the inside of his foot, and he howled in pain.

As several officers ran toward her, she picked up a pipe and swung it around and around, knocking them away from her. Trenton pulled off his mining helmet and shoved the flaming lamp against the uniform of the man behind him. Screaming, the man batted at the flames burning his shirt. Several of the others ran to help him.

Using the confusion as a distraction, Trenton pulled Kallista's hand. "Come on," he yelled. "We have to run."

"I have to save Ladon!" Kallista screamed. "And my father's letters."

"There's no time," Trenton said, pulling her away.

She looked at the dragon, her face contorted in misery, then turned and ran.

Seeing his prisoners escaping, the chancellor shouted, "Arrest them!"

The officers chased after them, but Kallista and Trenton had the benefit of knowing the level. Ducking between buildings and hiding behind machines, they made their way to the air vent, where security wouldn't be able to follow.

Gasping for breath, Trenton pulled off the cover.

Just before they climbed into the duct, they looked back in time to see the dragon tilt, and then fall. Ladon crashed to the ground with a clang of metal on stone, and a cheer erupted.

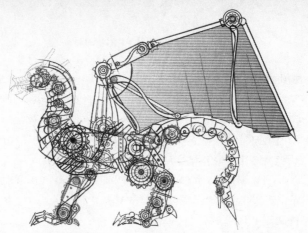

38

Sorry was something you said when you accidentally bumped into someone or dropped a tool on their foot. It couldn't begin to make up for the pain Trenton had caused, the betrayal.

So he said nothing as they slipped through the dark streets and alleys of the city, avoiding the security officers who seemed to be everywhere.

Clearly they couldn't go back to either of their apartments. Only one place might be safe—her father's repair shop. But when they reached the soaped windows, the lights were already on and a line of uniformed men and women were carrying crates of tools out the front door.

Tears dripped down Kallista's face as she watched everything her father had left behind now being carted off. Trenton touched his cheek and realized he was crying too.

"If there's anything I can do . . ."

Kallista smeared her tears away with both hands. "I don't want to talk about it. Where else can we go?"

Trenton tried to think. His family had to have been alerted by now, and for all he knew, his mother would turn him in the moment she saw him. His teachers would know too, so the food-production level was out. No place to hide in the mines or manufacturing levels, either.

"I know a place we can hide for a while," he said.

Sticking to the shadows, he led her back to the power-distribution station where it had all begun. They passed under the giant turning gear where he'd once built a swing. Looking up at it, he tried to remember how innocent he'd been, not thinking beyond trying to make a girl smile. That boy seemed like a completely different person.

The lock on the door to the power station was broken. One of the reasons he'd chosen to build the swing here was so he could hide the parts inside. They entered a small maintenance room, where they collapsed against the wall and slid to the ground.

Trenton closed his eyes. It was over. Really over. Without the dragon, tools, or a home, they had nothing left. Even escaping the city was out now. For once in his life, he couldn't talk, lie, or sneak his way out of the consequences of what he'd done. He had no one to blame but himself. His chin sank to his chest, and his body shook as he quietly sobbed.

An arm slid around his shoulders. He looked up to find Kallista sitting beside him. They wrapped their arms around each other and cried in the darkness.

When at last their tears had dried, they disentangled themselves.

Trenton swallowed. "You can hate me forever."

"I don't hate you." Kallista took a deep breath. "And I don't blame you, either."

"How can you not?" Trenton asked. "This is all my fault. I lied to you. I betrayed your trust."

Kallista faced him, only her silhouette visible. "You might have lied to me, but only because you were trying to tell the truth to everyone else. You were trying to warn them. My father did the same thing, and he's the smartest man I've ever known."

Trenton wished that was all he'd been trying to do, but he couldn't even take credit for that. "I wasn't trying to warn anyone," he said. "I was trying to impress Simoni."

Kallista said nothing for several seconds. Then, "Okay, maybe I *do* hate you." She made a noise, and in the darkness he thought she must be crying again. But tears weren't making the sound. She was . . .

He squinted at her. "Are you laughing?"

She pressed her hand to her mouth and snorted between her fingers. "*Trying to impress a girl.* Seriously, what do you see in her?"

Trenton didn't know how to answer. He'd never given the idea a lot of thought. Simoni was easy to talk to. She was fun to be around. Until today, she'd been a great friend. Was that it? Was that all he saw in her?

"She's nice," he finally said.

Kallista laughed even harder, and he wondered if she'd completely lost it. "Compared to me, anyone would seem *nice.*"

"How can you laugh about any of this?" Trenton asked, honestly bewildered. "Because of me, the dragon is destroyed. Scream at me. Hit me."

She laughed, tried to stop, hiccupped, laughed again, and finally managed to get her giggles under control. "Without you, there wouldn't have been any dragon. I would never have figured it out on my own."

"But your father's tools, his letters—"

Kallista shook her head. "All this time, I've been thinking that I needed things—objects—to remember him by. Now that they're gone, I realize I don't need his books or tools. I have my memories of him. And he gave me the gift of flight and knowledge. No one can take those things from me. Thank you for helping me realize that."

Of all the things she could have done, Trenton never would have expected her to thank him. "So you forgive me for telling Simoni about the dragon?"

"No." She hiccupped. "*That* I will never forgive you for."

Kallista began giggling again, and, although they'd been crying together only moments before, now they couldn't seem to stop laughing.

When at last they got themselves under control, Kallista looked at Trenton, her eyes serious. "You need to talk to your mother."

Trenton stared at her, trying to understand the sudden change in the conversation. "About the dragon?"

"No, about her visit to the chancellor. About how you feel."

Why did she have to bring that up now? Trenton got up and paced the small room. "We're probably all going to get killed, and you want me to start an argument with my mom?"

"Of course not." Kallista stood. "You've already been arguing for months without saying a word. I want you to make peace with her. I have so many things I wish I'd told my father before he died. I never got that chance, but you do. Tell her how you feel while you still can. Who knows where we'll be tomorrow?"

Footsteps sounded from outside, and they both froze. Trenton pulled a wrench from his tool belt, and Kallista took out her hammer.

The door swung inward slowly, and a figure stepped into the doorway. Trenton raised the wrench over his head, squinting at the dark silhouette. "Stay back. We won't let you take us."

"Trenton," a female voice said with relief. "Thank goodness. When I heard you hadn't gone home, I thought you might be here." It was Simoni.

Trenton lowered the wrench. After everything she'd done, he couldn't believe she'd dared to come looking for them. He folded his arms across his chest. "What do you want?"

Simoni tugged at a strand of hair. She opened her mouth and then closed it.

"Really, Red," Kallista muttered, "haven't you done enough today?" She glared at Simoni.

Simoni's chin trembled, and Trenton realized she was crying. "I'm s-sorry," she stammered. "I swear I had no idea they they'd treat you that way. I was trying to protect you."

"*Protect* me?" Trenton shook his head. "You betrayed me. You lied to me." As he spoke, he realized that he'd just accused Simoni of exactly what he'd confessed to doing to Kallista. The idea made his head pound and his stomach churn.

"I didn't mean to," Simoni said, wiping her eyes. She stepped into the room toward Trenton. "I *know* you. You're a good person. You made a mistake. But you never would have done something like that on your own." She glanced at Kallista and quickly looked away. "If you go back to the chancellor and explain . . ."

"Explain what?" Trenton said, his hand tightening around the wrench. "You think Kallista talked me into building the dragon? That she tricked me? That maybe I thought I was building a bicycle or a really big roller skate?"

"I didn't—" Simoni began.

"You're right." Kallista cut her off. "That's exactly what happened. Trenton had no idea what he was doing. I made him help me in the beginning, and when he realized what he was building, I threatened to turn him in. The two of you should go back to the marshal to explain. I'll take the blame."

"I knew it." Simoni nodded. "That's what I was trying to tell them."

"I can't believe this!" Trenton yelled. He slammed the wrench against the wall. The sound of metal on metal echoed in the small room and Simoni flinched. "No one talked me into anything. You once told me that I think different from other people. For most of my life, I thought that was bad. I thought something was wrong with me."

He turned to Kallista, his heart pounding. "You taught me that I wasn't some kind of freak. You showed me that it's okay to be creative. Better than okay. It's *good*. Because of you and your father, now I know that the founders of our city invented things. They had ideas. They made up stories and painted pictures. Maybe their ideas didn't work the way they wanted them to, but that's not a reason to stop thinking, to stop hoping." He held out his hands to Simoni, trying to make her understand. "Our city, it's . . . it's dying. Not because of the dragon, but because we let ourselves become stagnant."

"Oh, you're a freak all right," said a voice from outside the door. Angus stepped into the room, holding a thick metal rod. He stared at Trenton. "I heard everything you said. You're sick. Retraining was invented for people with crazy ideas like yours."

Trenton raised his wrench, but Simoni stepped between the boys and faced Angus. "You followed me."

He nodded. "And you led me straight to them." He cocked his head at Trenton's wrench. "What are you going to do, *tighten* me to death?"

"Try me." Trenton cocked his arm, ready to swing.

"Don't bother." Kallista slumped against the wall. It's only a matter of time before the dragon breaks into the city. With nothing to stop it, it will kill us all."

Simoni's eyes widened. "There isn't really a *dragon*, is there? You only said that to get away, right?"

"Of course there isn't," Angus said. "They're both liars. I'm surprised it's taken you this long to figure that out. There's no such thing as dragons. They're make-believe."

At that moment, a horrible, grinding sound came from the center of the city, followed by an echoing roar that brought goose bumps to Trenton's scalp.

"What was that?" Simoni asked.

The four of them hurried outside the building to look. The creature roared again.

"There's your 'make-believe' dragon," Kallista said. "It's inside."

Angus opened his mouth, but no words came out.

"It *is* real," Simoni whispered. "It can't get down here, can it?"

Another metallic screech filled the air, and Trenton realized what must have happened. "It's made it into the air-exchange pipe. It's heading for the city."

Angus shook his head. "Whatever it is, it can't get past the fans and grates."

Kallista grimaced. "It will rip those apart or melt them with its flames. I'm guessing it'll follow the smell of humans until it reaches this level."

All of the blood drained from Angus's face. It was the first time Trenton had seen him look scared of anything.

"How do we stop it?" Simoni asked.

"We don't," Trenton said with a shake of his head. "If we still had the mechanical dragon, we might have had a small chance. Now's there nothing we can do."

Simoni clutched the front of his shirt. "You can't give up. You're always thinking. You always have ideas."

"Don't you get it?" Kallista yelled, pulling Simoni's hand away from Trenton. "We *had* ideas. We *had* a chance. We *had* a way to defend ourselves. But because of people like you, all of that is gone. My father tried to warn people. When they wouldn't listen, even *he* ended up so depressed that he quit."

The roar sounded again, and Trenton was positive that he also heard screams. He turned to Kallista. "No, he didn't."

"What do you mean?"

"He never gave up. When no one listened, he started leaving clues for you. He didn't quit; he made a plan."

"A plan," Kallista whispered. Her eyes widened. Without any warning, she pulled Trenton to her and planted a smacking kiss on his lips. "You're a genius."

Simoni's mouth dropped open.

Trenton was so shocked, he could barely speak. "Um, thanks. But what did I say?"

"That my father didn't give up," Kallista said. "His plan was to leave me clues. Ours is to get to the mines before they melt Ladon. Then we put him back together and fight the dragon."

For a moment Trenton thought that Kallista had come up with a real plan, but what she was suggesting was impossible. "How are we supposed to stop them from melting Ladon?"

"I don't know," she said, all of her energy back. "We'll figure that part out when we get there."

Trenton shook his head. "They'll have people watching all the vents."

Kallista shrugged. "Then we'll find another way down."

"There are security officers looking for us everywhere. We'd never make it."

"We can help with that," Simoni said. She turned to Angus. "Can you get them security uniforms?"

He grunted. "Why would I do that?"

Trenton couldn't believe Angus was being so stubborn. "Maybe because you don't want to get eaten by a huge flying reptile." As if to emphasize his point, the dragon screeched again.

Angus looked toward the center of the city and nodded slowly. "Okay. I'll do it. But if this is some kind of trick . . ."

"It's no trick," Trenton said. He wished it was. Even with uniforms, their chances of getting to the mines in time were small. Still, a weak plan was better than none at all. "If we make it down to the mines, we'll need someone to help us find our way. And I know just the person."

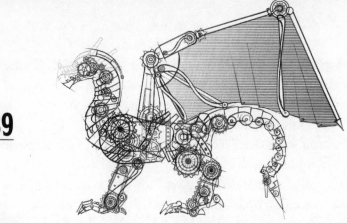

39

Halfway back to Trenton's apartment, they heard the elevator rumble to life. A few minutes later, a group of people ran out, screaming.

One of the men clutched a security guard by the front of his uniform. "Something's up there!"

"It's eating the animals and burning everything," a woman cried. Her cheek was swollen, and part of her hair was burned away.

"Come on," Trenton said. "We have to hurry."

They ran to Trenton's apartment building, passing more people who'd obviously come from working night shifts on the food-production level. Several of them had charred clothing and burned skin. Lights were coming on all over the city, and people rushed outside to see what was happening.

Trenton wondered what the chancellor thought now, then realized he didn't really care. If they came out of this alive somehow, things would undoubtedly change in major ways. But for now, they had to find a way to survive, and chances were good that a lot of people would get hurt or killed tonight.

The lights of his apartment were on when he arrived, and when he opened the door, his mother and father were sitting in the living room.

"Trenton!" his mother cried when she saw him. She tried to get off the couch and hobble across the floor to him, but

Trenton's father reached over and urged her to sit. She settled back down, then said, "We heard you were arrested."

"We heard screams, but I didn't want to leave your mother alone," his father said. "What's happening out there?"

"It's a long story," Trenton said. "I'll tell you everything later, but right now, we need your help." The others came into the apartment and crowded behind him.

"Who's *that?*" his mother asked.

Trenton stepped aside to let them in. "You know Simoni. This is Angus Darrow, and she's Kallista Babbage."

His mother's face hardened, and her lips turned white. "I will not have that—that *inventor's* daughter in my house."

Kallista turned and started toward the door.

"No," Trenton told Kallista. "Don't leave." He turned to his mother. "You don't understand. She's my friend. She's helping me—"

His mother pointed a shaking finger at Kallista, her eyes wide and glittering. "Don't you dare call her a *friend*. Her father was a murderer and an *inventor*." She spat the second accusation as though it were worse than the first. "I won't have her in my house."

"I'll go," Kallista said. But Trenton's father crossed to the door and shut it.

"You're not going anywhere," he said. "Leo Babbage was one of the finest men I've ever known. His daughter is welcome under my roof anytime, day or night."

Trenton's mother opened her mouth, but her husband stepped in front of her. "I haven't said a word about the way you've badgered our son. I let you say things I didn't agree with because I love you and know how much pain you're in every day. But I won't let you send this girl away. I won't."

Trenton's mother stared up at her husband, her mouth

working but not saying a word. This was the first time Trenton had ever heard his father raise his voice to her. She put a hand over her eyes, but she didn't say another word.

His father turned to face Trenton and the others. "What's happening out there?"

"A creature is attacking the city," Trenton said. "You wouldn't believe me if I told you what it is, but it's on the first level, and it'll be here soon. Kallista and I built something to fight it, but the chancellor had it disassembled, and he's ordered the mechanics to send the parts into the smelter. We have to stop them, but we don't know our way through the mines."

"I can get you there, but . . ." Trenton's father looked at his wife and back to his son. Then he looked to Simoni. "Would you stay with her?"

Simoni stepped forward. "Of course. You go."

He kissed his wife and whispered, "I'll be back soon. I love you." He hurriedly grabbed his coat and helmet. "Take care of her," he told Simoni. "She means the world to me."

As Angus opened the door and the others began filing out, Kallista looked at Trenton and tilted her head toward his mother. Trenton paused.

His father stopped at the door. "What's wrong?"

"I just need a minute," Trenton said. He walked over to his mother and knelt at her side. He looked back, and Kallista nodded her encouragement before walking out the door. Trenton took his mother's hand. "Mom, I know that you told the chancellor to keep me out of mechanic training."

She stared at him, her face tired but firm. "It was the right thing to do. I'd do it for you again."

"I know you would," Trenton said. "And I want to tell you that if something happens to me, well . . . thank you."

His mother blinked. She opened her mouth to speak, but

Trenton hurried on. He didn't have time to say everything he wanted to, but he'd do the best he could. Kallista was right; no matter what his mother had done, his relationship with her was too important to lose. "Thank you for caring enough to try to protect me. I'm still a mechanic at heart. I always will be. And because I am, there's a chance we can save the city. But you were right too, about the food-production level. It is beautiful. I learned a lot. If I don't come back, know that I love you."

He had a lot more to say, to explain, but no time. So instead, he kissed her cheek, turned, and hurried out the door.

"Thank you," his father said, patting him on the back.

They'd barely left the building when a ball of fire exploded in the center of the city. Metal screeched, and a huge, green creature clawed its way out of the air-exchange pipe, crushing the metal like sticks of chalk with its teeth.

A ball of ice swelled in his chest. Even with Ladon, he didn't think they could stop a monster that powerful.

His father stared up at the beast as it spread its wings and roared. "What is that thing?"

"A dragon," Trenton said.

The creature launched itself into the air and blew a stream of flame, lighting an apartment building on fire. Sirens went off, and suddenly lights came on all over the city, making it look like midday.

Angus stared up at the beast, eyes wide. "I didn't . . ."

"No time to worry about that now," Kallista said. "Let's go."

They raced for the elevator, but security had it closed off as hundreds of people tried to escape to lower levels.

"Why aren't they letting them on? Trenton said. "They'll get cooked here."

His father shook his head. "We'll never get through."

"Leave it to me," Angus said. He raised his badge in the

air and bulled his way through the crowd, shouting, "Security! Move aside! Security! Out of the way!"

Even in their panicked state, the people responded to the law as they'd been trained to. Trenton, his father, and Kallista followed in his wake.

"Elevator's off-limits," an officer said as they approached. "Official orders."

"The orders have changed," Angus said. "I have direct word from my father, Marshal Darrow. I've been ordered to escort these people to the mines. Take as many others as we can safely fit into the elevator. After that, get as many below as fast as you can. Send word to the elevators in the other quadrants to do the same."

The officer looked suspicious.

"Do you want to be sent to retraining?" Angus bellowed.

The officer turned to the others. "Get these people to line up. Women and children first."

Angus turned to Trenton and shrugged. "Looks like I learned something from my father."

The elevator filled quickly. Trenton tried to block out the screams coming from above as the car descended. He gripped Kallista's hand. "If only I hadn't shown Simoni."

"Don't blame yourself," she said, squeezing his hand until it hurt. "If we find a way out of this, it'll be because you didn't give up. And if we don't . . ." She ran her fingers through her hair, making it looking even spikier than usual.

"Let's not think about that," Trenton said.

When the elevator stopped and people swarmed out, a couple of miners hurried over. "What's going on up there?"

"The city is under attack," Trenton's dad said. "A lot more people will be coming down. Take them to the steam pipes where there's less dust and it's warmer." As the workers turned to guide the other people to safety, Trenton's father pulled one of the workers aside. "We've got a problem," he said under his breath. "We've got to stop some people from making a serious mistake. Round up every man and woman that you trust and meet me at the feeder to smelting plant three. It's the only one running at this hour."

"Right away," the man said, dashing into a nearby tunnel.

Trenton's father found helmets for the four of them, shouldered a pickaxe, and led them down a tunnel to the right. Trenton would have been lost in minutes in the maze, but his father led them unerringly to where a group of about a dozen miners stood around a pile of shimmering gold parts. One of them was about to place a wing strut onto the feeder belt when Trenton's dad stepped forward.

"Put that back," he ordered. "This belongs to these kids."

Two security officers stepped out of the group and blocked his way. "They're unauthorized, and they're supposed to be destroyed. Chancellor's orders."

"You don't understand," Angus said. "A dragon is attacking the city. Go look for yourselves if you want proof."

"Sorry. We have orders." The man holding the strut put it on the belt and reached for the lever to start the feeder.

Trenton's father lifted the pickaxe from his shoulder. "I can't let you do that. The machine those pieces are from may be our only chance to stop the attack."

The security officer in charge glanced at the men behind him and smirked. "You and the kids are going to stop us from carrying out orders?"

Footsteps sounded from a nearby shaft, and at least two dozen men and women strode out of the darkness, each of them carrying a pickaxe or shovel. Their arms bulged from regular physical exertion, and their eyes gleamed white against their coal-darkened faces.

"What's happening?" one miner asked.

"We're carrying out direct orders from the chancellor," the senior officer said. "If you don't want to be arrested, you'll stand back and let us do our job."

The workers looked at Trenton's father.

"Is that true?" a female miner asked.

Trenton's father took off his helmet and stepped up to the group of miners. "Two levels above us, men, women, and children are dying," he said. "Your husbands, wives, and children are all in danger. The only chance to stop the danger is the machine these men are trying to destroy."

"What kind of danger?" a man asked. The miners began edging back toward the elevator.

"My kids are up there," another said. They all seemed to be on the verge of running back to the elevator.

"Stop! Listen to me!" Trenton's father shouted. "We don't have time for that. My wife is up there too. If you want to see your families again, then help these kids."

The miners whispered to one another.

"Ray Coleman has never lied to us before," the woman said. "I don't see why he'd start now."

The men behind her nodded. One of them, a man with shoulders twice as broad as Trenton's, raised his pickaxe. "I think you folks better let the kids through."

Trenton's father reached forward and grabbed the strut from the astonished worker by the feeder. He turned to Trenton and Kallista. "How we can help you?"

• • •

Kallista slammed her hand against a piece of Ladon's leg. "It's no use."

They'd assembled as much of the dragon as they could with the tools the miners had rounded up, but they couldn't figure out how to put several of them together without Leo Babbage's tools. And even if they could make it up to where they'd built the dragon, they had no guarantee the tools were still there.

Trenton wiped sweat from his face. Despite the cold, his shirt was soaked with perspiration. The miners had been a great help in putting Ladon back together, especially his father, who was surprisingly good with tools. But now they were at a standstill.

"If only Leo were here," Trenton's father said with a shake of his head. "I've never seen a man better with machines."

"How did you know Kallista's father?" Trenton asked.

"He came down here to work all the time. Said the quiet helped him think. A few of the men complained at first, but after he repaired their equipment so well that it ran better than new, that stopped.

"He was there when the wall collapsed on your mother and the beam fell on her legs. I knew if we didn't get her out of there quickly, she'd die, but we didn't have the right equipment. Leo rigged up a couple of pulleys, a chain, and a drilling machine. Several workers tried to stop him because what he was making wasn't approved. They threatened to have him arrested, but he didn't care. He did it anyway to save your mother's life."

Suddenly Trenton understood his father's actions back in the apartment. Did his mother know that Leo Babbage—the man she despised—had saved her life?

Kallista's mouth dropped open. "He never told me that."

"Your father did a lot of things he never told anyone about. Things that would have had him in retraining for the rest of his life. People kept his secrets because they knew that if they ever had a problem, he'd be there for them. If he were here now, he'd be the first person working to fight the dragon."

Kallista dropped the wrench she was holding. "The final clue."

Everyone turned to look at her.

"What clue?" Trenton asked.

Kallista shook Trenton by the shoulders. "Remember how I told you that one of the rules of my father's game was that he always left a final clue? Whenever I thought the game was over, there was always a last clue I didn't expect. I thought the box was his final clue. But it wasn't. In the letter, he said he *descended into a pit of darkness*, and that we might, too, if everything else fell apart. And you were the one who reminded me that he didn't give up. That he wasn't suggesting that we quit. He was telling us where to go for the last piece of the puzzle."

"*A pit of darkness so black I could see no light*," Trenton said. "*Hope continues to shine even in the dark*. He was talking about the mines."

Kallista turned to Trenton's father. "You said my dad worked down here. Maybe he left some tools in case his were seized. He always had a backup plan."

Trenton felt the faintest flicker of hope. Maybe they weren't done yet. He turned to his father. "Do you know where Leo Babbage worked down here?"

"Of course," his father said. "He spent all his time in an abandoned coal shaft near mine number three. It's not far."

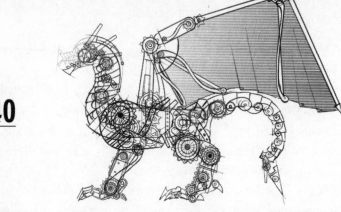

40

Trenton tightened the last bolt, and he and Kallista looked down at their work. Ladon was back together, but even with his neck down and his legs bent, his head still scraped the top of the mine.

"You can really fly that thing?" Angus asked.

"If we can't, feel free to arrest us," Trenton said. "The problem is getting up to the city."

His father blinked and scratched his jaw. "How *are* you going to get it up?"

Trenton glanced at Kallista. "We've been talking about that. We're going to have to go up the same way the dragon came down."

"The air-exchange pipe?" his father asked. "It's not big enough to fly through, is it?"

"We'll worry about that when we get there," Kallista said. "How far away is it?"

"Not far," Trenton's father said. He jumped on a nearby loading car. "Follow me."

Kallista lit the dragon's furnace and called, "Everybody stand back!"

Angus and the miners backed up as the turbines kicked in. Trenton brushed dirt from the gauges and checked the fuel level. "We have barely enough coal to keep us in the air for half an hour. We need more."

"We can't afford the extra weight," Kallista said. "It'll be tough enough to get up the pipe as it is." After lowering the dragon's head until it almost touched the ground, she walked the dragon forward, following Trenton's father as he led the way in the loader. Rocks fell from the ceiling and walls as the dragon banged and scraped them.

A few minutes later, the exchange pipe came into view. Air blasted past their faces, and the noise was nearly deafening.

Trenton's father shut down the loader. "I can't get any closer." He hopped out, climbed one of the legs, and took Trenton's hand. "I know we haven't talked as much as we should have over the last few months, but whatever happens, I want to say I'm proud of you."

Trenton felt a lump in his throat. "If anything happens to us, tell Mom . . ." He couldn't finish. Instead, he hugged his father and nodded.

As they started toward the air-exchange pipe, he glanced over his shoulder for one more glimpse of his father, who watched them with obvious awe and pride. Trenton hoped it wouldn't be the last time they saw each other. The closer they got to the pipe, the more the wind pulled at them.

They strapped themselves into the harnesses, and he shouted, "Good thing I added these."

Kallista stopped the dragon just outside the pipe and yelled back, her voice barely audible above the roar of the fans. "Once we get inside, I'll point the head up and extend the wings. We won't be able to actually fly. We'll have to rely on the suction to pull us up. Burn away the exhaust fans and grate before we hit them, okay?"

"Got it. By the time we reach the city level, there will only be one fan above us," Trenton called back. "The dragon destroyed the rest coming down."

"That's what worries me." Kallista reached back and squeezed Trenton's arm. "Don't fall out."

Trenton was so scared, his entire body shook, but he forced a smile. "Do a good job of steering, and I won't."

Kallista positioned Ladon's head toward the pipe, and Trenton hit the fire button. A burst of flame blasted the pipe open. As Kallista walked the dragon through the opening, the wind increased so much that Trenton could barely breathe. His eyes felt as if they were being sucked from their sockets. He stuck the dragon's tail out to create extra lift.

Kallista yelled something he couldn't make out over the roar of the wind. She aimed the dragon's head straight up and pushed the lever to extend the wings. The dragon began to shake. The metal wings shuddered, and the struts made a deep groaning that vibrated throughout the entire body.

The dragon wasn't built for this. It banged against the floor, clanging its metal feet as if complaining about the rough treatment. The left wing shuddered, and wind pulled the right side up more than the left. They tilted to one side. Trenton swung the tail to counterbalance, and Kallista desperately worked the legs.

The left wing jerked out, and for a moment they fell in the other direction. Before Trenton could swing the tail back, the fans pulled them upward. He'd imagined a steady rise, but instead, they bounced around like a feather. The wings shook and strained but continued to open.

Kallista turned and screamed something. Trenton looked up; they were almost to the first fan. The nearly invisible blades whirred just above their heads. He pounded the fire button, but the flame missed, hitting part of the pipe instead. Kallista jerked the head around, but Ladon shook so hard that aiming accurately was impossible. The blade was right above them. He slammed down the fire button again. This time he hit the fan.

Burning hot metal exploded around them, and they were sucked higher. Something hot landed on Trenton's arm, and before he could knock it away, it melted through his sweater. The wings were fully extended now. The fans sucked them up more quickly, and the dragon slammed against the sides of the pipe. Trenton tried using the wings and tail for balance, but he felt like an insect trying to steer a twig down the middle of a rushing river.

They sped toward the next fan, and he hit the fire button again. This time, he blasted it on the first try. He caught a quick glimpse of the manufacturing level as they blew past it. Lit by the dragon's eyes, the edges of the pipe raced past.

Another fan. He fired again. A splinter of metal stabbed his leg. Another fan, he fired. Missed. Fired again. The dragon was completely out of control, spinning and shaking, bouncing off the edges of the pipe like a marble in a tin can.

Trenton blasted the next fan, and their upward climb slowed, then stalled, as the current pulling them up weakened. He could see the city level twenty feet above them. With only one more exhaust fan between them and the highest level, there wasn't enough suction to lift the dragon any higher. Trenton reached for the flight lever, but the space was too small to fly. If he tried to work the wings now, he'd lose what little lift they had and they'd plummet back down to the mines.

Slowly, the dragon began to drop.

"We're aren't going to make it!" He looked around, searching for some way to slow their fall. Fire, tail, wings—none of those would help.

"Tilt the wings up," Kallista called.

What was she thinking? If he tilted the wings up, they'd drop.

She tried to turn in her seat to reach the wing controls herself, but her harness had twisted, locking her in place. "Do it!" Kallista screamed.

Praying Kallista knew what she was doing, Trenton pulled the wings backward until they pointed straight up and down. The dragon's head came up, throwing Trenton into his seat. They began to fall.

At that moment, Kallista pistoned the legs out. The dragon's talons tore into the sides of the metal pipe. She clamped down hard, making the claws dig into the metal. Soon they'd stopped sliding down and were clinging to the side of the pipe.

Trenton couldn't believe she'd taken the risk. He looked over his shoulder at the mine floor hundreds of feet below. If the claws had missed their grip, they'd both be dead.

Carefully, Kallista released the front left talons. Gripping the wall with the other three feet, she moved the leg up and forward before slamming it back into the pipe wall. Doing the same thing with the back right, she began crawling them up the side of the pipe.

"You're nuts!" Trenton yelled, his heard racing.

"What do you expect?" Kallista yelled back. "I'm Leo Babbage's daughter."

Trenton checked the pressure gauge; it was dropping. He yanked the hatch open. At this angle, the dragon's feeder was no longer pulling coal into the crusher. No more powder was being blown into the furnace.

"Go!" he screamed. "We're losing power."

Kallista looked back, and her eyes widened. With no time to be careful, she maneuvered the legs so they climbed up the pipe in lurching strides. Trenton watched the temperature gauge slide lower and lower. The pressure was dropping too fast. The dragon's legs began to move sluggishly.

Realizing they'd never make it, he pulled off his harness and crawled through the hatch. Metal hot enough to scald his skin glowed all around him. From this angle, everything looked wrong. But he didn't have time to think. Leaping from one piece of equipment to another, he made his way to the fuel bin. The coal was all piled at the far end. To reach any, he had to hang from his feet.

Dangling upside down into the bin, he thought about the day Simoni had called him a monkey on the swing.

"She should see me now," he muttered.

He scooped coal into the front of his sweater until it bulged and couldn't hold anymore, then pulled himself back up with his legs. The turbines were about to stop completely. He yanked open the cover of the crusher, shoved handfuls of coal inside, and waited. The grinder churned. His pulse thudded as he waited to see if there was still enough power to run the blowers.

The turbines stalled, started up, stalled, and then roared back to life. "Yes!" he shouted, pumping his fist. Quickly he dumped the rest of the coal from his sweater inside.

The dragon began moving again, making it hard to climb back up. By the time he pulled himself out of the hatch, they'd reached the city level. Kallista swiveled the dragon's head around, and Trenton climbed into his seat and slammed the fire button, blasting the side of the pipe away with a burst of flame.

"I can't believe you did that," Kallista said.

Trenton shrugged and grinned. "What do you expect? I've been spending a lot of time around Leo Babbage's daughter."

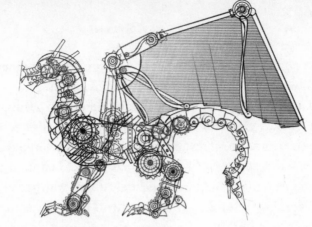

41

Let's get in the air," Kallista said.

Trenton checked their fuel. "We've probably got twenty minutes of flying time, tops. Do you have any ideas for how we stop the dragon once we find it?"

"No clue." Kallista raised Ladon to his full height, turned down Main Street, and made the dragon run.

"Everybody out of the way!" Trenton yelled.

His words didn't do much, but the sight of the golden dragon racing by—giant feet clanging against the street with every step—scattered the people in front of them.

But one boy waved his arms wildly. "Trenton! What are you doing up there?" Clyde yelled.

Trenton waved as they thundered past. He pulled back on the flight stick, and the wings began to flap.

Clyde yelled something that sounded like "Girls are going to love that thing!" as they rose into the air.

The damage to the city was worse than Trenton expected. Buildings were in flames. The fire department was trying to extinguish them, but they couldn't keep up as new fires sprang up all over the city. In the distance, a long line of people waited for the elevators—at least they still worked. But several bodies lay motionless on the ground; not everyone had escaped.

"Over there," Trenton said. He pointed to a huge, green

shape circling City Hall. The dragon belched flames and occasionally dove in an attack with its talons and fangs.

Kallista turned them toward the creature. "Save your fire until we're close. It uses fuel faster than anything else."

The nearer they flew, the more Trenton doubted their plan. The real dragon was at least twice the size of Ladon and moved with a grace they couldn't come close to matching. When they were several hundred yards away, the dragon spotted them, swung its head in their direction, and screamed.

"Here we go," Kallista said.

The two dragons flew straight at each other. Trenton kept his hand poised over the fire button, but before they could get within range, the creature opened its mouth and launched a stream of flame at them.

Trenton slammed the flight stick forward, and they barely dropped in time to avoid getting roasted. The flames passed so close over their heads that they singed Trenton's hair.

Screeching at missing its prey, the dragon whirled around.

Kallista circled too. She turned Ladon's head, and Trenton slammed the fire button. The flames made a direct hit on the green monster's scaled chest.

"Take that!" Trenton screamed. "How do *you* like the heat?"

The dragon howled, but it didn't look damaged. It dove toward them, fangs bared.

Kallista tried to dodge it, but the dragon's talons scraped their left wing, gouging a strut. The attack knocked them off balance, sending them plummeting downward. They fell within fifty feet of the ground before recovering.

"It's faster than we are. Stronger, too," Kallista yelled as they flew back up.

"We have to outthink it," Trenton called. "Get us close, and I'll use our tail to hit it."

Kallista turned and once again set them on a collision course with the monster. As before, the dragon attacked them with flames. Trenton tucked them below the fire, but this time, instead of diving, he pulled back up. As they passed under the beast, he pulled the tail control violently toward him.

The metal tail slammed against the dragon's foot, and something snapped. The dragon howled and turned away. Its leg hung at a bent angle.

"We hurt it!" Kallista yelled.

Trenton pumped his fist. "Maybe we can find a way to outmaneuver it. Let's get closer to the ground."

As they headed toward the city square, a figure with a top hat and walking stick came running out the front door— Chancellor Lusk. Incredibly, he shook his walking stick up at them and shouted, "Get that invention of yours out of the air! It is not approved."

Trenton glanced over his shoulder. The dragon was right behind them. "Look out!"

Kallista banked to the right, but instead of following them, the green dragon swooped toward the square and opened its jaws.

"No!" the chancellor cried just before the creature snatched him off the ground. His legs kicked between its teeth, then disappeared down the dragon's throat.

For the next ten minutes, they dueled the green dragon. Occasionally, they made a hit using their tail or flames. Once, Kallista even managed to strike its belly with a talon. They took plenty of damage too. Kallista's right arm was burned, and blood streamed from a gash across her forehead. Trenton's pant leg was soaked with blood, and somehow he'd injured his left wrist.

Of the two dragons, Ladon was the most injured. Both wings were damaged, and the front right leg had broken almost completely off. Even worse, the real dragon had figured out most of their tricks. It kept its distance, striking only when it had a clear advantage. Staying low no longer helped; the creature could outmaneuver them in between the buildings.

As the dragon chased them, Trenton checked the fuel meter. "We're almost out of coal. We have to land."

"I'm not sure we can." Kallista pointed to the broken leg. "I don't think we could get back in the air, either."

Behind them, the dragon peeled off. Trenton spun around to see where it was going. On the street below, several adults were trying to sneak a group of children toward an elevator. The dragon was heading straight for the group.

"It's going for the kids!" he yelled.

Kallista saw it too. She pulled the dragon into a turn at the same time Trenton changed the angle of the wings, sending them into a dive. "Run!" she cried to them.

But the dragon would reach the kids before they could. Trenton shoved the flight control all the way forward. Wind blew his hair back from his forehead.

The adults looked up and saw the danger. They tried to rush the children to safety, but they were only halfway across the street, and the children were panicking. Hoping to create a distraction, Trenton blasted a stream of fire toward the dragon.

The green beast hurtled toward the children, who screamed. Trenton squinted his eyes, knowing what was about to happen.

At the last second, the dragon pulled up, wheeled around, and charged at Trenton and Kallista, his mouth open. Attacking the children had been a trick.

Kallista tried to turn, but it was too late. The dragon caught their wing in its huge jaw and yanked them around, then released them, sending them into a tailspin. The mesh cloth ripped as they spun out of control.

Swinging the tail hard right, Trenton fought to regain their balance. Kallista managed to pull them out of the spin, but the dragon was close behind. Trenton pulled the flight stick back, hard, and Ladon clawed at the air. The dragon closed in.

The fuel gauge dropped to empty. The turbines shuddered.

"There's no more coal," he yelled.

Kallista pounded at her controls, but there was nothing either of them could do.

The dragon was coming fast. It was so close now, Trenton could count its teeth. But they were out of both power and time. With no way to escape, he tilted the wings all the way forward. The dragon smashed into them from underneath, and Trenton yelled, "Kallista! Talons!"

She nodded with understanding and rammed all four feet forward—closing the talons like she had done to grab the wall in the exhaust shaft. Only this time, instead of closing on metal pipe, the metal talons drove through dragon scales.

The dragon screeched and tried to pull away, but Ladon's talons were locked tight on its back and wings. Kallista shut the oxygen valve to the furnace. As the turbines wound down, the wings stopped beating, and the weight of the mechanical dragon forced the real one down.

With the last of their power, Trenton smashed the monster with Ladon's tail. Then they were falling. The ceiling of the cavern faded quickly away as the ground raced toward them. Trenton got one quick glimpse of people staring up in horror before both dragons slammed to the earth.

His head banged against the seat, and the world began to spin. Before he passed out completely, though, he leaned over the side of the mechanical dragon and looked down. On the ground beneath them, the green beast lay deathly still. Its wings were crushed, and its neck was broken.

They had done it. They had saved the city.

Epilogue

The next few weeks in Discovery—as the city had been renamed—were filled with work and confusion. While recovering in the hospital, Trenton and Kallista got most of their news from Clyde and Simoni, who visited often, and Angus, who showed up now and then.

At first, many people tried to blame Trenton and Kallista for the appearance of the dragon. One group refused to come up from the mines for fear that they'd die of poisoned air coming through the smashed seal. Others swore that the dragon was a mutant caused by outside technology.

Fortunately, cooler heads managed to calm the protests. With the death of the chancellor, Miss Huber stepped up to take temporary control of the city, which surprised many people. She turned out to have a base of people in powerful positions backing her.

Mr. Sheets suspended the people who had dismantled Ladon and led another group of workers to rebuild the exhaust fans and secure a gate over the original city entrance, which the dragon had torn down. They all agreed it was only a matter of time before more dragons arrived, but before they could do anything about that, they had a lot of work to finish inside the city.

Trenton was amazed to discover that one of the people making repairs was his father. Apparently, his father was not only good with machines, but he had once been in mechanic training. He'd been reassigned to the mines after disagreeing with the city over the size of coal feeder chutes.

His mother had good days and bad days. One morning Trenton looked up from a book he'd been reading in his hospital bed—one of the many books recovered from City Hall—to find his father wheeling his mother into the room.

"Leave us alone for a few minutes?" his mother said.

His father looked uncomfortable with the idea, but Trenton nodded. "It's okay."

Kallista, whose room was across the hall, shut her door to give them some privacy. His father walked out and closed the door behind him.

For a few minutes, they simply looked at each other. She appeared weaker than the last time he'd seen her. Then again, he didn't imagine he looked too good himself. He still had a cast on his wrist and stiches all over his body.

"Do you still think it's wrong for me to build things?" he asked at last.

If he had expected his mother to admit she was wrong, he was disappointed. "My opinion doesn't appear to have stopped you," she said, stubborn as ever.

Trenton sighed. "Our invention saved the city."

"And you nearly killed yourself," she said without so much as a blink.

"If we hadn't built Ladon, the dragon would have destroyed everyone in Discovery," he snapped.

"A lot of people believe it was our technology which led the creatures to us in the first place," she replied. "They smelled our machines and came to punish us."

So this was it—a standoff. Just like it had always been. She wouldn't accept that machines were his life. And he wasn't about give up what he loved.

"Why did you come to see me?" he asked.

She folded her hands in her lap. "I went to the chancellor because I wanted to protect you. I'd do it again." She set her jaw in the same way he did when he was determined. "But that's not why I came." She looked up at the ceiling for a moment, as if searching for the right words. "I came to tell you that I know what you're planning to do, and I don't approve."

Before he could respond, she added, "But I still love you."

She couldn't possibly know about the plans he and Kallista had been discussing. They hadn't told anyone. Yet somehow, he felt sure she did. He reached out and squeezed her hand. "I love you too, Mom."

Later that afternoon, Simoni, Angus, and Clyde showed up, and they all gathered in Kallista's room with good news: the green dragon hadn't completely destroyed food production, but it would take a while to get everything back to normal. In the meantime, strict rationing had been put into effect.

"The best part," Simoni said, "is that Miss Huber has stopped forcing everyone to eat the same thing every day."

"And the ban on creativity has been lifted," Clyde said. "Although most people still think it's a bad idea."

Trenton could believe that all too easily. Ideas that had been taught for generations wouldn't change overnight. He looked at Angus. "What happened to your dad?"

Angus shrugged. "He was just following orders—doing his job."

Trenton had his doubts about that, but he figured that the truth would come out sooner or later.

When Simoni and Angus left, Clyde lingered behind. "I've got some bad news for you," he said, glancing into the hallway to make sure the three of them were alone. "Those two have been spending a lot of time together lately."

That didn't surprise Trenton at all. He still liked Simoni, and maybe under different circumstances they could have ended up together. But lately he'd been thinking about how little they had in common.

"At least," Clyde said, brightening, "almost every other girl in the city wants to meet the guy who rode the dragon."

Kallista rolled her eyes. "What about me? Do all of the guys want to meet the *girl* who rode the dragon?"

Clyde shifted his feet. "I, um, don't really know. But I could ask around."

Trenton grinned. Kallista was still as feisty as she'd always been, but he was coming to appreciate that. "Better tell them not to wait around," he said. "We dragon riders are pretty picky about who we choose for our friends."

• • •

A week before they were to be released, Miss Huber visited them. "I guess I have a pretty good idea what Leo was working on," she said with a mischievous smile.

Kallista laughed. "It wasn't oatmeal cookies."

Miss Huber examined their bruises and cuts. "Are you both healing well?"

Trenton nodded. "I should get my cast off in a week, and the doctors say Kallista's burns will heal almost completely."

"We'll both have a few scars," Kallista said. "But we earned them."

Miss Huber, who still wore her work uniform, nodded. "I've spoken with the council, and we all agree that the two of you are heroes. There would no longer be a city without you. I've come to let you know that whatever you want—within our power to give you—is yours."

Trenton and Kallista looked at each other before speaking. They told Miss Huber that there were only two things they wanted.

She smiled and nodded at the first request, but she seemed surprised by the second. "Are you sure?"

They nodded. "We've been discussing what we want to do next," Kallista said.

"And we both feel like it's the right thing," Trenton added.

"Very well," Miss Huber said. "I'll see that it's arranged."

• • •

Three weeks later, a small group gathered on the top level. Everyone was bundled up against the frigid air pouring in from the entrance. Trenton's father was there, along with Miss Huber, Mr. Sheets, and Mr. Blanchard. Angus, Simoni, and Clyde were also there.

"Even if the air isn't poisonous, it's still dangerous out there," Trenton's father said, glancing at the new gate, which was made of Leo Babbage's alloy. Beyond the new gate was the outside world. "You're sure you want to do this?"

"I'm sure," Trenton said. He hugged his father. "Tell Mom I love her."

"I will," his father said, hugging him back. "She doesn't always show it very well, but she loves you too."

Miss Huber handed Kallista Leo Babbage's metal box. "As I promised, I've done all the research I could."

Kallista froze. "What did you find out?"

"From what I can tell, your father *did* cause the explosion in the apartment building."

Kallista's shoulders sagged.

"However," Miss Huber said, "at the time of the explosion, no one was living there. No bodies were found in the wreckage. Not your father's, either."

"I knew it!" Kallista shouted. "He set up the explosion to make everyone think he was dead." She peered through the gate. "He's somewhere out there."

As the others carried supplies to the dragon, Simoni pulled Trenton aside. She twisted her hands together and seemed nervous to meet his eyes. "I don't want you to take this the wrong way, but . . ."

Trenton smiled. "You want to break up?"

Simoni exhaled, clearly relieved that he had said it first. "It's just that you're going out there, and I'm going to be busy in here." She glanced at Kallista with an expression that looked almost like jealousy. "I think the two of you are a better couple anyway."

Kallista? Trenton raised his eyebrows. "We're *not* a couple." He didn't know how anyone could have gotten that idea. Half the time they were fighting, and the other half they were—well, close to fighting.

Besides, it wasn't as if Kallista liked him or anything. Did she?

He rubbed his hands through his hair, wishing Simoni hadn't brought the subject up. "So, you and Angus?"

Simoni sniffed. "I don't think so. He's okay. But honestly, I think I'm going to take a break from boyfriends for a while. I'm only thirteen." She gave him a quick hug. "I'm sorry about turning you in."

"It's okay." He laughed. "Let's call it even for me not taking you to the dance."

As he walked back, Kallista was packing her father's books

and maps into a bag. "Did she say she'll wait for you? So you can go on more picnics?"

He grinned as he shrugged and said, "Who wouldn't?"

She punched him the stomach, briefly knocking the air out of him.

Angus stepped forward and shook their hands. "Try to survive."

Kallista rolled her eyes. "You do the same."

Clyde enclosed them both in a huge bear hug. "Now that art isn't against the law anymore, I left you a gift."

"What kind of gift?" Kallista asked suspiciously.

Clyde pointed up at the dragon's controls.

Trenton and Kallista climbed up and discovered that Clyde had painted a large portrait of his grinning face on the back of Ladon's neck in front of the first seat where it would stare back at them whenever they flew.

"Just to keep you company!" Clyde yelled up.

Mr. Blanchard handed up boxes and bags of food until they said they couldn't carry any more weight. "If you don't mind my asking," he said, "what will you do when you run out of coal?"

Trenton patted the dragon. "We made a modification to Mr. Babbage's plans. The furnace can operate on wood now, too. Sawdust burns more quickly, but there are plenty of trees outside."

Mr. Sheets unlocked the gate and swung it open as Kallista started the furnace.

Trenton's father climbed up the dragon's leg and hugged his son, swallowed hard, and said, "I know this dragon is made for two, and I probably weigh too much to fly it anyway. But I want you to know that if I could, I'd go with you in a heartbeat."

"Thanks, Dad." Trenton hugged his father back.

"Be careful," Simoni called over the whine of the turbines.

"We will," Trenton yelled. "And we'll come back as soon as we know what's happening outside." He pulled on his helmet, slid his goggles down, and turned to Kallista. "What do you think, is Don ready to fly?"

"*Ladon*," Kallista said. "He hates nicknames."

Trenton shook his head and patted Ladon's scaled back. "Okay, big guy. Let's go."

Kallista turned the dragon toward the gate. Taking the leg controls in hand, she started walking, then running. They raced out the gate and to the brink of a cliff. At the edge, she coiled the dragon's legs and they leaped into thin air.

For a heart-stopping moment, they plunged over the cliff toward the jagged, ice-crusted rocks below. Then Kallista spread Ladon's wings, and they pulled out of the dive.

Trenton shoved the flight controller forward, and they soared off into a cloudless blue sky. Squinting his eyes against the biting cold, he looked at the shining yellow orb called the *sun* for the first time. He looked down at a carpet of trees thicker and greener than anything he'd ever imagined.

"Let's go find my father!" Kallista yelled.

Trenton grinned, threw back his head, and whooped with joy. He had no idea where Leo Babbage was or what new clues he might have left for them. He didn't know where they were going or what dangers they might find when they got there. But whatever lay ahead of them, he knew one thing for sure.

It would be new, and definitely unapproved.

ACKNOWLEDGMENTS

Thanks so much to my agent, Michael Bourret, who believed.

To Chris Schoebinger, Lisa Mangum, Heidi Taylor, Karen Zelnick, Richard Erickson, Michelle Moore, and the rest of the Shadow Mountain staff who took a chance on this book and worked so hard to support it.

To my critique group, the Women (and Men) of Wednesday Night: Michele, Sarah, Annette, Heather, Rob, and LuAnn, who tightened every sentence. We miss you, LuAnn. A special thanks to Annette Lyon, who polished the prose.

To my early readers, Jennifer Moore and her sons, Joey and Andrew, and James and Rebecca Blevins, who encouraged me.

To my incredible wife, Jennifer, who makes the impossible possible every day; my children and children-in-law—Nick, Erica, Scott, Natalie, Jake, and Nick—who give me the gift of laughter; to my grandchildren—Gray, Lizzie, and Jack—who are walking (and crawling) bundles of joy; to my parents, Dick and Vicki Savage, who taught me I could do anything; and to my wonderful brothers and sisters, who pushed me to do it.

And as always to the readers young and old who take the words in my head and turn them into worlds more vivid than any movie.

Thanks to you all.